The Game of Rochambeau

The Game of Rochambeau

Nancy K. Chadha

PETALS
PUBLISHERS

PETALS PUBLISHERS & DISTRIBUTORS
KIDWAI NAGAR MARKET,
LUDHIANA – 141008
E-mail: mail@petalspublishers.com
www.petalspublishers.com

First Edition: December 2023

The Game of Rochambeau

Printed in India

For my kids and my grandkids:
I wish to let you know that you are loved beyond words

For my sister, my soulmate, my joie de vivre, Pansy:
What an ordinary life I would've had if it wasn't for you.

In the world of words, some books ignite the imagination, while some unearth life's harsh truths. With this book, my fervor wish is to weave a tale with both worlds.

'You're only young once, but you can be immature forever.'

~ Germaine Greer

There must a precise moment of a precise day
when we are expected to cross-over, to where maturity lies.
One that transmutes us, never to return to the other side.
Why else do we not dwell in the realm of perpetual immaturity all through our lives?

AN OPEN LETTER

From:

Papier

To:

Mr Razza Umana

CEO of Mondano Terreno

Respected Sir,

I hope the turn of this year has you well and in pleasant form. It is my understanding that the past few years have been quite trying on you. Considering the circumstances, a reach out from you would have been much appreciated, but, as inconspicuous and insignificant as I am to you, it is not surprising none came my way. Be as it may, I felt the need to come forward to apprise you of certain things.

Before I get to the purpose of this letter, I would request to be pardoned for addressing you as Mr Umana. In all probability, you could be Mrs/ Ms Umana. Since I am not privy to the correct information, I find it only appropriate to generalize the title. Please do not think I am sexist. I assure you I am not; I use 'Mr' to address you, as, with ambiguity in gender, Mr/ he has been used for generalization only out of convenience and not because of any gender dominance.

I may have also made a slip in assuming you to be the CEO of the aforementioned organization. I presume that could be because I have, over the years, been watching you work the system with complete command and control. The reins, as much as I have been able to assess, seem to be in your hands. I do, once again, ask for your pardon if my assumptions are inaccurate.

Now, coming to the reason for my missive to you, which I assure you I would never have sent had it not been of the utmost importance. I am well aware of how busy your life is and I know what losing even a single second means to you monetary-wise. Wasting no more precious moments of yours, I shall present forth the purpose of this missive.

Tell me, sir, have you stopped undoubting the unbelievable? Have you stopped unquestioning the impossible that you cannot see? The existence of magic, maybe. Are you grabbing every moment that comes your way and making it yours? Exploiting it to the fullest, skinning it to the bone. Or are you letting life pass you by with busy nothings? Maybe, halting your whimsical thoughts midway in their stride; coaxing them, even going to the extent of bribing them, to turn back to where they came from.

What I would like to know is, have you ever detached yourself from your core-self and, from a veritable distance, looked at yourself more closely? To see what others see?

Am I getting you flushed? Are you shifting in your seat? Loosening your collar? I wouldn't want to get you worked up. Allow me to redirect our attention to lighter matters, sir.

Let's talk about the motto splashed all over your social media platforms: *YOLO*. Even *carpe diem*. In bold. Are they there all over your pages just to make you look sprightly, or do you plan on being sprightly too?

Just the other day I was watching you as you watched a kid climb up a tree; as you watched another kid laugh with glee, and another as he went on a tumbling spree. I watched you pull away. But there was a bit of you left behind, a bit in all the three. Do you often leave behind bits and pieces of yourself at places such as those? Do you even know you leave behind pieces of yourself in such places?

You must think this is a ridiculous joke. Or that I've flipped my lid. I assure you neither of these premises is true. It is, in fact, most crucial for you to give due attention to these facts. You may not acknowledge this, not yet, but believe you me, you will by the time I have said all that I have to. So, I request you to stay with me with a little forbearance.

For a better perspective, here's an observation I'd like you to make:

There's a very important meeting you're headed for. You're almost there, but then, you see a rain puddle in your way. Will you side-step it? Or will you jump into it like you did as a child?

Will you risk getting messed up?

I would like to make it known to you that there are two perspectives of 'messed up' here:

Perspective # 1: You don't want to get your suit all *messed up.* There's that very important meeting you're headed for, right?

Perspective # 2: How *messed up* would you feel if you had to put in a sizable effort to fight the urge to roll up your pants, taking your shoes and socks in your hands, splash in the puddle—*splash, splash, splash*—just the way you did as a child? And because you didn't splash in the puddle, you didn't get to smile the I-did-it-because-I-felt-like-it smile?

So, tell me, which *messed up* would you prefer to be?

Messing with you? No, I'm not messing with you. Trust me; I have a justifiable reason for my need to learn this about you. I need some clarity, something to understand you better. I haven't been able to understand you for some time, sir, and it is of utmost importance that I do.

Before you begin to question the obscurity and absurdity of it all, I shall make my reason for this missive known to you: I am bearing the consequences of your life in exchange for mine. I am, quite literally, paying the penalty for your life with my own. So, yes, I would appreciate some clarity. A clearer picture to know whether you are worthy of my life. In fact, I would say, I'm entitled to the information.

You must wonder why I, a total stranger according to you, am amenably giving up my life for you. The thing is that I am no stranger to you. You know me pretty well. We go back a long way, from the time you began to think up thoughts on your own; from the time you were brimming with imagination, brimming with magical whims; from when you had an insatiable appetite for fictional ingenuity. I can, irrefutably, claim that I gave you the best of your times. I was your so-called soulmate. Now, I am nothing but a stranger to you. That's because, with time, you stopped paying attention to me. You started ignoring me. Ignoring *me*! Imagine that!

In all honesty, I'm not too sure whether I should blame you entirely for crossing me out of your life. After all, I did vanish from the scene, all of a sudden. In my defense, all I can say is that I wanted you to tread troubled waters all by yourself for a while, for you to get a feel of what it was like to not have me around. So you wouldn't think of ignoring me ever again. *And what did you do, in retaliation?* You erased me completely from your thoughts. You erased every iota of my being from your life. You, brazenly, omitted me from your memory folder; a memory no longer needed. Synaptic pruning, it's called—the natural process that eliminates connections in the brain that are no longer needed.

You may try to pass it off as a misstep. Hmm, I wonder!

Let's revisit that day of many, many years ago, when something—a deliberate premeditated move or just an impulsive thought—took away *a* thing that came to be *everything,* and disturbed the holistic outlook of your entire lifetime. To the day your youthfulness succumbed to its fate at your hands.

It was not a pleasant day for me. I remember being immensely displeased. I had protested; gone against your wishes and commiserated with your youthfulness. I had lain next to it, with its head on my shoulder, my hand on its heart; the pace of the rise and fall of my hand slowing down steadily, slowing down … until it became almost non-existent. I remember dust and grime being poured over us; we were covered in it completely. Even today, the smell remains preserved and ready to be reconstituted in my mind; the smell of a freshly dug grave. Alas, your youngness had little fight left in it. It just lay there: *Earth to earth, ashes to ashes, dust to dust …*

As for me, I remember calling out for help. Barn-owl screeches. I'm sure you heard my cries. I heard you leave with a shuffle. With unsure steps. But no help came.

Well, today, I'm making sure I'm heard loud and clear. Like a church bell. I'm making sure you pay attention. I'm making sure you do not ignore me. You tend to do that a lot even now. But believe you me, after getting to know my more resilient avatar, and my well-intended motives (which, I confess, are carried out in diabolic ways at times but are, nonetheless, well-intended) you, sir, will eat your heart out for ever letting me go.

Tell me, have you ever observed the pattern of your breath—how you take breaths at alternate intervals while evading beats that race too fast for you? Have you realised that you've been crushing your heart's desires for the desires of those around you? Perpetually, in the desperate urge to please them. Been taming your urges, shushing the adrenaline rush … *Hush now!* Like one would hush a child that is throwing tantrums in public. Sir, have you given profound thought to the fact that you haven't accorded life the reverence that you should have? Yes, I understand, you have things to look into. You get so tied up un-mangling yourself from mangled-up issues and struggles that you snuff out the zing within you—that delirious thing that brings verve into you. And then, over time, with your proclaimed maturity standing tall by your side, you callously watch your youthfulness, still in its ripe, die a premature death.

Think about it, sir, isn't your youthfulness the very feisty thing that adds gusto and drive to the mundane-ness of everyday life? That adds true meaning to all the *YOLOs* and the *carpe diems* and every related remark you glorify on your pages? That makes 'an everyday life' into a story?

Is *your* story worth telling? Or is it one of those that are better off left unread? That are glad to be left unnoticed, like back-benchers in a class.

We could've worked out a fabulous story for you, together you and me. One you would have wanted to showcase in gold. Proud moments of your life exhibited like rare crystal collectibles, or worn on your shoulders like medals won in war. You could have had all of that, had you not turned to look the other way; had you not discounted my existential significance in your life. But it's rather late in the day now. Elvis has left the building.

Yes, I have finally given up on you. And, it is through this letter that I wish you to know what you missed out on.

Let me tell you a story.

There was this man who wished to be happy. No matter what he did, he was not happy.

He had a fabulous job, but he was not happy. He bought a beautiful home, still not happy. He then got the perfect life-partner … and yet unhappy.

I couldn't see him troubled. I moved in with him; watched every move he made. Can't say I approved of many, so I nudged him to make life-changing shifts. He wouldn't listen to me, wouldn't budge. I nudged him some more. Still nothing. What choice was I left with but to hound him? So, I hounded him and hounded him. Like a nagging cough. I could have used the analogy: *Like a nagging wife* here, but I didn't do so for two reasons. First, I don't think wives nag. Second, I've never had a wife, so I don't know what a nagging wife sounds like.

Anyhow, the man had no choice but to give in.

He shifted his job, yet he found no change; he was still not happy. He then shifted his home. Again, nothing. He even threw his life-partner out. Still nothing. He was perplexed.

At last, I sat him down, to introspect, to reflect. To listen more carefully, more intently, *to me*. Like one should listen to the wife, to begin with. Then she won't need to nag.

At last, he brought a shift in his attitude. And lo! He found the happiness he was looking for.

What did you think about the story? It's a true one, you know.

I wonder if you'll ever achieve the happiness you're looking for. Yes, you too, are looking for it. Everyone I know is looking for it. In all the wrong places.

Happiness is not something that can be found—you move from place to place, from person to person, in search of it; you climb social ladders keeping your eyes at the top, in all hopes to find it there. Happiness is not a child playing hide-and-seek with you; teasing, waiting to be found. No!

Happiness … has to be created. Conscientiously. It is a decision, a state of mind to be attained. It is the choice of a way of life, a life that feels good on the inside. A choice that has to be made by you. Only you.

Would you like to hear another story? One closer home. One that is nearing its end really soon. Really soon as in today. Yes, today. It is underway as I write to you. A story about wanting and geniality; about a love that wrapped up before it could begin, and a friendship that smelled of a freshly dug grave. A story about misgivings. About inhumaneness. About second chances too.

A story that has yet to come upon a finale. A finale that is conditional on you.

Yes, you, sir.

Have I piqued your curiosity enough for you to know which story's finale, and more importantly, *how* that story's finale is conditional on you?

So, let's get to it. You never know, it may help you see the real you. The *you* that others can see. That would definitely scratch my itch.

By the way, do you know the meaning of your name, Razza Umana? Have you ever looked it up?

In the realm of self-understanding, I reside
For I know what I am about
And what the world's journey is about
And the bonds of friendship … strong and true
Oh, how I long for this bond to stay
And to never un-know it, come what may

~ Nancy Chadha

THE YEAR 2026

I. AM. NOT. GOING. TO. JUMP.

This is the story of Papier.

As narrated by Papier.

My name is Papier, and I won't be jumping off this balcony. Not because I'm afraid I'd die, but because I'm afraid I won't.

Given my physique, I would just be gliding in the air at an agonizingly leisurely pace and, at the most, wind up with a fractured limb or two, which would be painful. Or perhaps a cracked head, which would be extremely painful. That end is the total opposite of what I am aiming for. I'd rather die in one single moment. Boom! Like a balloon. Yes, I know a balloon goes *Pop!* But pop doesn't sound as dramatic as boom. So, Boom! With distorted fragments strewn all over, impossible to put back together. The air confined within, dissipating into formlessness, into nothingness. I'd rather go in a flash: one moment I'm there, and the next I'm not.

Come to think of it, I should have relinquished my life long back, ceased to exist even theoretically, with a name like Papier. This is the name my parents gave me. I figure they liked the sound of it when said with flair, the way the French say it: *Papier!* Their upper lip and lower lip touching each other, at first with curiosity like in a first kiss; the second touch, with a sudden appetite for a more pronounced amorousness—long-drawn, sensual, not letting go. Once satiated, their lips let the last bit trail in the air: *Pa-pi-er!* To be honest, it does sound sexy. And I guess

I must have been shockingly skinny at birth. Skinny à la paper-thin. Well, my parents sure are lucky I didn't get fat along the way, or they would have never heard the end of it. I can never imagine paper to be anything but thin. So, I guess I shouldn»t be complaining. Also, my name shouldn»t be the reason for me to end my life.

It isn't. But I'm still going to.

For the moment, an utter state of unrest has muddled my sane judgment. Even so, there are things that don't go unnoticed by me. The wind, which at present is not at all gentle up here, has been threatening me, just because I am this thin. With a single huff it can blow me away. Far away. And the eighteen-foot drop, from where I stand to all the way down, has been daring me.

Jump!

It knows: I. Am. Not. Going. To. Jump.

And yet.

A Revelation:

I am going to take my life.

You know this already. What you do not know is why.

The Why. A disturbing one. A worrisome one.

It's not easy you know, to set your mind to it. Takes days, even months, of cajoling and convincing and gathering up of nerves. Me, it took but one night. One night—from the incipient drooping of the sun's eyes to the cock-a-doodle-doo of the rooster this morning—was all I needed to assure myself that I was doing the right thing. One night. Not even an entire day.

My urgency, you ask, sir? It was due to the extreme extent of my agony. The cause of that extreme agony?

You. Yes, you, sir.

A Confession. And an Attempt *(not to take my life but, rather, to prevent it from happening).*

I have to confess, this is not the first time that I've thought of taking my life. It was exactly six years and seven months ago that I was standing in the same spot, right here on this very balcony. I remember, clearly, the year 2020 had just begun. Back then, it had taken nearly an entire month for the realization to kick in, to be certain that I wanted to do away with myself. No, not *wanted* to. I *had* to. *Had to.* Who would *want* to take their own life? To be honest, I had tried every which way to get out of it. An earnest, strong-willed effort, as strong as a Rock, was made to defer my decision. But that effort had been curtailed; stopped in its tracks. In fact, it was clipped out of my mind, as though, snipped from my line of thought by a pair of Scissors and discarded. Any further thoughts to defer my decision were made ineffective, banned, as though written on Paper. (Did you catch what I did here, sir? With the analogies? I just dropped you hints about the three main characters of my story.)

There was absolutely nothing to hold me back. But, luck—or Magic as I would like to think of it—worked its number on me. As you can very well see, sir, I'm still here.

Some Informational Talk on 'Ants'. *Yes, ants.*

And on Balance. *On why it is important. Without which you are, let's say, out of balance.*

And a Warning: Do not fall in love with me.

Today, too, as I stand on my balcony, I'm dilly-dallying. I know I have to do it; I'm most certain I do not want to carry on living with the way things are. And, unlike the last time when I was not certain I had the gumption to take the plunge, this time, I have my nerves by the throat: *Not a whimper out of you guys.* But I'm still playing for time. Watching ants, of all things. Yes, ants. There's an army of them I've been eyeing with displeasure for the last half hour. They're playing 'Follow the leader'. If the leader zigzags its way to its destination, the ones following also zigzag in perfect synchronicity. If the leader bobs its head to sniffle prospective nibbles en route, they, too, bob their heads at the already-rejected fare. The ants are not the problem, sir. The real thing bothering me is that I had scattered red chillies all around the crack in the left corner of the balcony so that the pervasive invaders could not get out and take charge of my fort. Yet, they're out. The entire colony of them. And they're daring me.

Or are they just daring?

In the city below me, the disillusioned 'ants'—that's what they look like from my balcony; disarrayed, disillusioned ants trotting about in high heels—don't play 'Follow the leader'. They play nothing, for that matter. They think the saying, 'All work and no play will make Jack a dull boy' is only for Jack … the Jack from 'Jack of all trades, master of none'. Besides, they think 'playing' is for kids; that it will make them seem immature.

Immature, a word terribly misconstrued. Terribly misconceived.

Finer nuances of the word 'Immature'.

More often than not, we lean towards the brusque cognizance of the word 'immature' while measuring up others, and at times, while assessing our own selves. *How immature is that!*

If one were to capture the finer nuances of the word, it would bear semblance to I'm-mature: I'm mature enough to balance work and play; I'm mature enough to juggle the highs and lows of life; I'm mature enough to know the right balance between aging and youthfulness. Balance, without letting the child within dissipate or lose its individuality in the face of adulthood.

Let me tell you though, those 'ants' down below don't know crap about balancing. They are the sorry ones who clearly breathe life out of their souls at no one's doing but their own. The lesser souls. Nondescript. Unimaginative. Without character. Without colour, just mostly grey. Even black in some places. Like a photograph that was last seen in a burning pile of old memories, charred on the edges. Mechanical beings that have dried up, with no laughter in their veins to resuscitate their hearts. The ones that make their bucket list only when on the deathbed. The ones that begin their sentences with: *I wish I had …*

Had they been doing a great balancing act, they would have been pros at it by now—at the game.

The game, you ask? The magnificent, dazzling, intellectually written game: Life.

However, there are a few that stand apart from the rest. The spunky 'ants' I call them. These wonder-people could be fifty-nine or ninety-five years old. The expression: 'As they age, they become like kids again' is true of them in more ways than one. They dream with their eyes open, all over again. They make bucket lists of things others have long given up on, and strike out items on that list like striking off numbers on a winning Bingo ticket.

Which of these 'ants' are you, sir?

To be honest, I know which one you are. I just want to know if you know.

Am I sounding too offensive? I hope I haven't given you reason to stop reading my story.

The thing is, once you hear me out and my heart-wrenching predicament: 'To be or not to be'—as Hamlet had said on how death, specifically suicide, would be preferable to the wretchedness of human life, would it not be for the fearful uncertainty of what comes after death—I know for a fact you'll understand my temperament and my sentiments much better. You may even feel for me. Just give me your unsolicited promise that you won't fall in love with me. I'm not planning on being here long. Thanks to you.

As my story unfolds, you may for a moment think that the reason behind my decision to take my life the first time around was feeble as compared to the present one. You may think I was too quick to jump the gun, giving up my life over something so trifle. But sometimes, when emotions are brimming over, just a tiny trigger is enough to spark a fire and burn the house down.

A Deadline.

Twenty Minutes.

This time around, I set a close deadline, leaving no time for me to chicken out. Right at this moment, that deadline, the promissory note for my death, is ticking in my ears: *tick, tock … tick, tock … tick, tock,* at the same speed as time ticks after one is bitten by a Black Mamba snake. Do you wonder what must be the first thought that crosses one's mind when bitten by a Black Mamba? *This is it! Twenty minutes till the venom gets to my heart. Twenty minutes and I'm dead. Nothing can save me now.* It is in those twenty minutes that a kaleidoscope of fragmented images of one's life story races by. It is in those very twenty minutes of my life that I am telling you my story. A story that begins not from the beginning of my story, but from the fag-end. A story in which the beginning, and everything that transpired in-between, is yet to be told. The story without an ending. Yet.

That said, from where I am standing right now, on my balcony, a make-shift balcony actually, I can see the end of my story sneak up on me earlier than I had prepared myself for. It feels so close, so close I can almost smell it. The smell similar to that of flesh that is beginning to rot. The beginning of an end. My end.

Or, if I have my way, the end of many things unwanted.

But before that …

A Déjà vu moment. *(I wonder, will it still be called a déjà vu moment if you, yourself, recreate an already experienced moment in a later time frame?)*

Have you ever had a déjà vu moment? Where you feel you have already experienced a moment you are presently experiencing, or have been at a place before. You stand there, zoned out, wracking your brain, trying to figure out how it is even possible. That cognitive dissonance has you feeling out of sorts.

I am experiencing that zoned out feeling, at this very moment. I am having a déjà vu moment, and I am feeling out of sorts. Out of sorts, not because I feel I've not experienced this moment before, but because I have. It was on this very balcony where I had stood; where I had tried to convince myself, and gather up the nerves to take my life; same place, same time of day, six years and seven-odd months earlier.

REMINISCING THE YEAR 2020

THE BEGINNING OF AN END

Pills.

My story without an end, my deadline, my twenty minutes, and my déjà vu moment, all began with pills.

A tiny description of the Pills:

Unfriendly. Round. Tiny. White wonders, as tiny as they appeared to be, but having the true-blue promise to take one's life.

Pills, mingled with the perspired dampness flowing through the major creases of my hand, had begun to tickle my palm. The white mess running through my lifeline, obscuring it; whitewashing everything the line represented—a lifetime that had been lived, a lifetime yet to be lived. Every progressing second ticked off a second from my life, as I stood on my balcony that day, in the year 2020. Perturbed. Nervy. A total wreck.

I remember taking a moment there; a moment to breathe in the promises of a new morning; a moment to give the joyous sounds of a buzzing day a chance to swarm their way up and talk sound sense into me; to let the early morning breeze hit me across my face like a cold splash of water and snuff out my foggy thoughts. Anything to clean-slate my mind so I could start afresh with better thoughts to configure the perfect first line to begin a new story with.

I dropped my ears in a swift movement, like that of a yoyo, to swing down and bring back up with them, every minute detail of the chirpy sounds from down below. The sound of early morning-walkers pleased with themselves for having started their day well. (Were they, inadvertently, mocking the start of my day?) The cute babbling of toddlers while crossing paths as their mothers pulled their prams along. And the clinking of mugs of coffee lovers under the black and white awning that lends a beguiling character to the Biscuiteers Boutique. Coffee lovers, not for their love for coffee, but lovers who use coffee meets as an excuse to spend time together.

Camaraderie and sociability ran riot in varied flavours and colours; adoration hung in the air like balmy mist on a sultry day. Yet, here I was, standing alone on my balcony, enduring impassioned whispers not meant for me. Here I was, standing on edge, not wanting to be blown away by the insistent breeze, but ardently waiting to be blown away by persistent love. Here I was, standing deranged with the deadly white weapons fisted in my hand, fighting a war with me, myself and I.

A whiff of wet mud tickled my nostrils just then. Petrichor, the harbinger of rain. Ah! I love the smell of wet earth. Raw. Unclad. Nature in the buff. The undomesticated smell never fails to endow a calm serenity in my mind. Had it been a typical day, I would've taken in deep breaths of it, letting it trip my endorphins and make them brim over. That day I didn't as much as sniff at it. I didn't want the earthy scent to manoeuver my rational senses; didn't want it to make me mush and knuckle under, so it could carry me into my room and cozy me up in bed; snuggle me in for safe-keeping. The pretensions of this world were fooling me no more.

At that rattled moment, convincing me to get back into the game of life was like convincing a college drop-out to go back to college.

All night I had been playing dodge with life: *Yes. No. Yes. No.*

I had been playing hard to get:

Be mine forever.

I can't.

At least stay with me, for time to come.

I can't.

Not even for the night?

Umm … maybe just tonight.

Coaxing, cajoling, pulling me into its arms, life led me back into my room, into familiar terrains, in the hope to get me back into its game.

On the bedside table my reading glasses stood atop the book I had been reading. The book, a light romance, had been left upside down and not closed with a bookmark; I had intended getting back to it. But I hadn't. I couldn't. No matter how hard I had tried the psychedelic composition of the letters couldn't titillate me; couldn't hold my attention. That once, I couldn't be the protagonist of the book, couldn't do phantasmal things, or go to exotic places. I couldn't fall in love in the book. Or with the book. That once, my book was just that—a book with black somethings spilled all over its insides, depriving the whites of delightful lyrical utterances, and not endowing me with the splendor of wisdom or versed wonder.

All night I had tried to talk sense into my mind, had tried to tame it down, but it seemed to be on a trip of its own; flustered and highly strung, as it ricocheted from one idea to another.

At first, it suggested I stab myself.

I don't have the friggin' balls for that!

Then hang yourself.

Doesn't that require me to be heavier than the rope?

Okay then, get run over by a train.

Hell, a bicycle will be good enough to run me over! But keeping me pinned down with the way the wind is blowing …

On that note, something shivered. My eye fell on an artistic amalgamation of crisscross lineages, worked with intricate precision, hidden behind the clock. A spider must've worked on it for days. I had been too busy working on the cobwebs inside my head to notice it before.

I looked at the clock, gave it the hard look, accusing it of not affording me enough time.

Have you ever felt the need to do that, sir? Have you ever doubted time's reliability? Or its intentions? Do you, too, think time is inconsiderate? It keeps moving ahead, unrelentingly, leaving us with no time to pause and think. Leaving us with no opportunities to look back and grab a second chance to retrace our steps and undo what we did. Or to do what we didn't do. It just keeps marching on. So inconsiderate!

It was half a minute shy of 6 am. *Already?*

It was still dark. *Everyone is still sleeping.* It would've only been right to give them a chance to stop me.

Half a minute later, the clock, well into its grandfather days, yet standing tall on the wall left to the balcony door, chimed. Was it mannerly for the clock to be ticking on time, at a time like this, when my time was so questionable? And a pigeon cooed. That damn bird, most likely with its inconceivably emerald-and-amethyst-bejeweled neck, sounded so soothing and in love. And the din of the air-conditioning, not unlike a child's smooth and almost-silent snore, was making me drowsy with sleep when, of all times, I needed to think straight.

Were they, too, mocking me?

That day, I could say I was a mockery of sorts. Vivid strategies had been dramatizing their most convincing performances in my mind all night. I'd grab an idea, go over it, weigh the pros and cons, and if it seemed to be the one for me, I'd finalize it. But when I'd scrutinize it, detail by detail, one last time, I'd find a flaw. If even a tiny flaw, I'd scrap the entire plan; discard it like a flawed peach. Then I'd go for another idea, scrutinize it, turning it round and round, and then scrap it for some reason or the other. Or for no reason at all. *Jitters, you think?*

I had been jotting down every procedure, diligently, on the blank backside of a previously used sheet of paper. I must tell you, sir, I hate throwing away paper unless I have used every corner of it. That paper I had been writing on was once a tree. That one tree had given us a lot many sheets of paper. Many sheets from one tree. What a thrill! Much like the thrill we used to get as kids when we'd give a $10 note for a $1 bill payment and get lots of change in return. *Look Mommy, I got so many notes in exchange of one note. I'm rich!* Fool's gold, sir. Fool's gold.

Just as the new morning came to be, I hit upon the right technique to do the job; one that would be the most convenient; one which would go easy on me. No jumping off the balcony, no getting run over. That day, I can grievously say, I realised that I was not cut out for that kind of stuff. Less dramatic is what I am about, and less dramatic is pills.

But before I kicked the bucket, there were things I needed to look into. I jotted down my To-Do list on the blank backside of another one of my already used sheets of paper:

» Sort out all my possessions in my will: Donate everything I own to charity. (The thing is, sir, I don't have anyone besides two friends, Snippy and Rock, and they deserve nothing of mine. You shall soon understand why. There is Mom, Roo-mom as I like to call her, but of what use are my things to her? The grandfather clock in the hallway is already hers. My watch was gifted to me by her. My laptop, which is in shambles with a partially shattered screen and a missing key, will be a bane for her rather than an asset. The Elvis and Bob Marley wax figurines sitting handsomely on the chest bang-opposite my bed so that they're the first things I see on waking up every morning, are not invaluable to her.)

» Leave a hand-written apology letter for Roo-mom, citing my reasons, and my undying love for her.

» Leave a note on my bedside table stating that I want an electric cremation. (I can't add more pollution to this world.)

» Put the sleeping pills into my empty vitamin bottle. (To deceive my mind into believing they are my vitamins, just in case I chicken out at the last minute.)

- Keep two bottles of water at the place of action. (That many pills would require that much water.)
- Wear my new nightwear. And my good underpants. (Didn't want to be seen dead in my tattered wear. And to think I was saving those new clothes *for a better day.)*
- Send emails to both my friends, saying my last goodbyes. (I needed them to know they were the reasons behind the extreme step I was taking.)
- Breathe. Do not panic.
- There is no Plan-B.

WHAT ARE FRIENDS FOR!

A nefarious feature of Friendship:

Did you know that an ulterior intent, even only one, can twist the entire essence of a friendship around and set everything that the friendship stands for, aflame? So much so that every amicable gesture and every well-intended move of years gets singed like a charred photograph off which you have to scrape the ash to see what lies beneath? Only the ulterior motive stands out, like a victory flag hoisted right in the centre of a battleground. Its triumph flickering sprightly for all eyes to see, far and wide.

Sir, if I have given you the impression that a single wrong act by a loved one can fog out years of love and bonding, then you have not been wrong in understanding what it is I wish to say. And, if from this, you presumed that the reason I considered ending my life the first time around could have been because of my two friends, then you may, again, not be in the wrong. To some extent.

My friends, my so-called friends, had wronged me.

What are friends for! I had lost all bearings on that phraseology.

We had a great friendship going, the three of us. I can't say we were the best of friends, but we were great enough friends. You must wonder what 'great enough' friends are. Together, twenty-four hours of the day, seven days a week, totally inseparable, but even so, just 'great enough' friends. Well, that's because it wasn't a friendship of choice. We were thrust upon each other although we were worlds apart in behavior and idiosyncrasies. Like a peanut butter and banana sandwich—outrageous syncrasy, yet delectable. It just so happened that we three were at the right place at the right time to be of help to a group of people. Our impromptu mode of action, the spontaneity with which we, in unison, resolved the situation was baffling even to us. Brilliant synchronization of acumen and wit and timing from our end; we were exceptional together. We received huge accolades for our feat. Thereon, whenever anyone was in distress or couldn't come to an agreeable conclusion, we were called upon for help. We were, inevitably, teamed together. It was all three of us, or none at all. Just as it was with the Three Musketeers.

Come to think of it, we share many a similarity with the Three Musketeers. There were three of them, there are three of us. Just like the three of them go by the name The Musketeers, we too, go by an exotic name: Rochambeau. Although our names, Papier, Rock and Snippy, are not as exotic as theirs: Athos, Parthos and Aramis. But how enigmatically, mystifyingly royal the name of our squad sounds: *Rochambeau*. Don't you think so too, sir? That's the name we were known by, aeons ago. And that's the name I want to be known by even now, till the end of time. It may be a myth, but there is word that a French general, by the name of Rochambeau, introduced us to the Americans.

As for more similarities with the Musketeers, just as their strength was in them being banded together: 'One for all, and all for one', so was ours. Just as they had a fourth one join in later, so did we. Just as they had a fall-out, so did we. Even the reason for the fall-out was the same: breach of loyalty.

The breach of loyalty in our case, one amongst many, but the one that was the tipping point, making me consider self-death was because … because Rock circulated certain photographs of me. Photographs that I had begged him—and trusted him—to rip off. Photographs that even I was ashamed to see. Photographs that he had taken when we had gone skinny-dipping, one odd afternoon. Just so you know, I was skinny-dipping not out of choice but because Rock ripped off the last piece of my modesty as I jumped into the lake. I was ripped and stripped that day. And every day after, by every gaze in my direction. Snippy only added to my misery by smirk-*ing* her perfect lips in mockery at the very mention of my … my *Li'l one,* which unfortunately looked even littler in the photographs.

Li'l one, that's what they were calling it now: *Li'l one.* Ridiculous! Just so you know, it's not *that* little. It's … it's … about average. But you know how bullies are, right? They'll go to any length!

Every single night, on retiring to my room, I would wipe tears from my ever-moist eyes, only to make way for more stormy and overwhelming ones. I'd howl and howl. I'd muffle my howls with the duvet so Roo-mom wouldn't hear them, but the howls would sneak out from under the covers. They would make a bold appearance; every single one of them. They didn't like being constrained. *They are howls; they are designed to be heard. Out in the open, loud and clear.* Unruly and unstoppable, as they were, it needs be outlined that they were not happy with the way things were for me. If anything, they didn't want me to go on living the way I was, anymore. Simply said, they didn't want me to go on living. They had a point: I couldn't live on their support all my life. That realization made me howl all the more.

How many deaths I died at the thought that Roo-mom will not be able to bear the loss of another child! Wasn't the loss of one, too many already, for a mom?

They say, time heals. They say, as time moves on, it helps us to move on; helps us forget, as we make newer moments. But memories, sir! Memories hold on to every moment as though they would die if they didn't. And they take us back in time, as though they exist solely to make us relive our erstwhile moments; the good moments, the sad moments; the crazy and frenzied moments.

Some memories we do not want to relive. But then, there are some that we do. Let me take you to one such memory of Roo-mom. Roo-mom—that's the name I gave her the day I met her.

Not my real mom, but a mom with a warm home, and a warmer heart.

Rock, Snippy and I had been living with the Tysons for some years. At this point in my story, I guess I could say we were like nannies to their children, Pete and Lara.

One time during our stay there, things had gotten pretty rough between Rock, Snippy, and me. It was one of those times when I couldn't deal with their victimization any longer. They would not treat me right at times, yet I had carried on being friends with them because they had kind of adopted me; I was homeless before I met them. I had only recently run away from my home, away from my biological mom and dad. It was on our second *Musketeer-ing* encounter that Rock and Snippy realised I had been running helter-skelter, looking for shelter. They took me under their wings, and from then on, were there for me in my moments of anguish, which I must admit, I had an abundance of. Whenever I needed a shoulder to cry on, Snippy was only too ready to offer one. Whenever I needed a boulder to hide behind, as sure as fire, Rock was there, standing firm.

It's funny how Rock would let no one kick my butt, but would never let go of the chance to do so himself. The two of them, Snippy and Rock, were great at times and shmucks the rest of the time. If I tried to leave them, they would cajole me into staying back with the promise of never being a-holes again. Then, there was my duty always holding me back. The three of us, together in unison, were the phenomenal god-sent marvel of making magic happen for those in need of help. If I left, or anyone of us left, the other two were rendered useless. We had to stick together, no matter what. But that one time, their atrocities outweighed the purpose of our unison. Oblivious to the repercussions, I had run away from Rock's continual condescension and Snippy's snide remarks to find my way back to my biological mom and dad, knowing they would take me in even after all these years. I had slipped out in the middle of the night with a small trolley bag; I had a long, wobbly journey ahead of me; the lighter I was the faster I would be. Besides, I knew once I got to my parents, they would spoil me rotten with all that I needed, or wanted.

After days of misplaced orientation, I finally came upon the street where, back in the day, loneliness had never found its way. On seeing me, chiseled memories came venturing out. Descriptive words that I had graffiti-ed back then, peeped out in bits and pieces through layers of dust on an aged wall that had hid behind it neighbours I used to find grumpy and snappish. Initials of friends' names etched within hearts whispered from the barks of trees; wary, uncertain if they still had the right to call out to me. Some memories just stayed put, gaping with wonder, and disbelief.

When I neared the main entrance to our house, I knew something was amiss. The aroma emanating from within didn't have the warm-honeyed whiff as it did back then. The grey and white pebbles, outlining both sides of the paver stones that walked one to the house, were scattered here and there; not in place as Mom always had them.

I was right. My parents hadn't been living there for more years than I was ready to believe. I sat over coffee with the present occupants of my childhood home, at the dining table from my younger years, probing for some clue or sign as to my parents' whereabouts, mindfully running my fingertips on a smudgy carving on the right-hand edge of the table. That, there, was cue enough for the glistening pearls, contained thus far at the brim of my eyes, to come rolling down. Half a zillion memories affiliated with the pocket-knife-carving I had done on the table came pouring out with the tears. Memories of being grounded, memories of apologies for ruining the table, memories of taking peeks under the tablecloth to see if the reason for me being grounded—etching my name on our dining table—was still there or had been sanded off before it was covered with the tablecloth.

Memories! That's all I seemed to have been left with, to relive those moments. If those memories were not just things in my head, I would pull them out and case them in gold. I'd listen to the things they had to say, all day, in the voices of Mom and Dad. If they could spread out their arms, I'd let myself be nestled. I'd lie in their laps and let them tousle my hair, till I lulled into a reposeful sleep. Memories!

I soon came to realise that the only place to find my parents was basically nowhere. I knew Mom or Dad wouldn't be on Facebook, or on Insta. They didn't know how to use either; I never taught them. Who would have taught them after I left? Who would have been the son I wasn't?

I used to fight with them, often, over trivial issues. Over senseless issues. Trivial and senseless now, but then, they were reasons enough for their only child to walk away and leave them in lonesomeness. I couldn't deal with their fault-finding, their fussing. But I want to, unabashedly, admit that I can deal with all of that now. I want to grow with all of that now. I have, over the years, learned the value of my parents. I, now, understand it was their protective instincts and love for me that made them rebuff my dogged demands. But, back then, all I could see was them standing in the way of my aspirations.

Why could I not understand their concern for me then, sir? Why was their love not visible then? It was right there like a big wide bowl of whipped cream heaped to the top, with some brimming over, sitting assuredly, endearingly, in the center of the table, waiting to be lapped up and cherished. Was that why I hadn't seen it? Because it was always there, easily available? It's the things one has to put up a fight for, those are craved. Things that are within reach, or in abundance, are not valued enough. Isn't that how it works? You would know very well, sir.

Sitting in my childhood home, I felt homeless. I *was* homeless. I returned to Rock and Snippy more disheartened than when I had started out. On arriving, I was startled to see the two in the midst of moving house. Apparently, the Tysons had no use for our services anymore. How could they, with one of us missing from action? Well, I was back, and things would have fallen back in place, but both Snippy and Rock were adamant about moving out on the pretext that I was too disoriented. *Still not myself,* was what they had implied. That a new place would be a pleasant change; would cheer me up. Would help get my mojo back.

I smelled a rat, yet I said nothing. I dared not. Not when I needed them more than ever. So, I went along, no questions asked.

Rock, Snippy and I moved in with the Rais when their daughter, Samara, was just four. Their son, Samar, their firstborn, was around eight. He's thirteen now. Amidst those years, there was another addition to the family: a cute, curly-haired tiny-tot, with eyes like those of a frog that was forever hopping in and out of muddy puddles. The Rais had wanted to name him Samid. (Samar, Samara, Samid… jeez.) Well, it didn't have a great sound to it: Samid Rai. Sounded much like Semi-dry. So, they named him Robin instead. One goof up was good enough a lesson to not go down that lane again—Samar's friends can never get enough of doing virtual actions of sword-warring on seeing him. Samar Rai, the Samurai!

It was there that I came into contact with my 'not real' but warm-hearted mom. There was me, with shoulders that made me look like a semi-deflated Hit-Me toy; with eyes that, for the last eight-odd days, had seen nothing but a pair of shoes dragging the feet they belonged to; with a sturdy and upright trolley-bag by my side, coercing me to stay equally sturdy and upright.

And there she was, Roo-mom, standing tall, but not in her entirety. Elegant, but a tad less. Her head lifted in acknowledgment, but her eyes kept reflecting the chevron pattern of the wooden floor. There was a stillness in her pupils. A deadness, as in the boundless hollowness of a black hole. An expression that could come about only when one had, for a significant period of time, been suppressing the most crushing and the most devastating of emotions.

I faltered, shuffled; made to move back a step. But then, our eyes met. I blinked. She blinked. And we both smiled. She was my assuagement, my hope for cheer. And I believe I was hers.

She opened the doors to her home with a glint in her eyes; tears of joy or sorrow, I guess I will never know. At that moment, I was simply grateful to have a new home. It was mushy and moist, fuzzy all over, and there were two wrinkled black dots in place of nipples that had dried a long time ago. But it was home. As warm and cozy as a kanga*roo*'s pouch could be.

And that is how the name 'Roo-mom' came to be.

I learned later that evening that Roo-mom had lost her baby about a year and a half ago. A poacher was out hunting for some kangaroo. Kangaroo leather is much in demand for making sports boots and gloves. That day, the poacher had gone back with cold feet and stiff hands; his aim had gone wrong by a few inches.

The moment she felt the jolt of a gunshot at her midriff, Roo-mom sensed what had happened. Once she was in a safe place, she pulled out her little one from her pouch and put him to her chest; for her to feel his heartbeat, for him to be stimulated by hers. But there was only one fast, very disquieted one. She all but gave up, holding on to him for thirteen long hours in her arms in the hope to hear his breath. Thirteen long hours she waited; she didn't let go, although thirteen hours back she had known. When she did finally let him go, *she* let go. She became soulless, with colourless blood in her veins; her eyes like glass, much like a plush toy's.

She was brought to the Rais' soon after, on a Christmas morning. In her bluish-grey velvety coat, wrapped in red and green festive adornment, she looked stunning; as stunning as she could sans the smile. It was the Rais' first Christmas in their new house after they had migrated from their home country. Having to sleep all alone in her new room had been keeping Samara up on most nights; she was only too happy to let Roo-mom snuggle her to sleep. When Robin turned one, Roo-mom was shifted from Samara's pillow to Robin's arms. Just as well, because Samara had begun to out-grow her. Robin thoroughly enjoyed his hand-me-down companion; he took her wherever he went. No one could tell if he was clinging on to her, or, she that was clinging on to him.

Till today, I find Roo-mom crying when she's all by herself. She misses her joey. I try my best to fill his shoes. It's been five years, I'm still trying. I guess, I never will, although, she has never let me feel any less. That's the thing about a mother's heart. It's like an infinite sky, vast and expansive, with the capacity to embrace new constellations of stars without diminishing the radiance of those that have shown brightly before. It is akin to an ocean, boundless and over-flowing, with the capacity to embrace new streams of love, merging them seamlessly with the currents that have flowed before. It is a testament to the extensive nature of a mother's love, ever-growing and resilient in its ability to hold many heavens within.

Roo-mom pampers me to the core. Maybe that's why I'm such a gullible softie. And if anything ever happens to me … *Roo- mom will not be able to bear the loss of another child.*

Yet that day, with the white devils in my hand, I was giving the why and wherefore to my death.

WAS GOD CRYING? FOR ME?

I could hear rumbling outside, which sounded more like grumbling. The skies didn't sound happy; they were spitting out spears, bounteous sleek, silver tubes splattering on the hard stone of the balcony. Raindrops! *Or was that God crying? For me?* Because I had called off my friendship with Rock and Snippy? The thing is, our friendship didn't feel real anymore; it lacked the warmth it had promised. Calling it off set me free; I felt absolved, released. But it left me feeling friendless. Alone. They were the only friends I ever had.

Could such friendships end? A friendship that had been flourishing through generations and generations, gone just like that?

I felt a shiver, then. There was a sudden nip in the air. But I had a spine-chilling task at hand, and the pills had begun to tickle my palm all the more. "Okay, I can do this," I thought to myself. Convincing. Fighting. *Losing?*

I had sent an e-mail to Rock and Snippy. They were both party to the crime. Here is my email to them, for your perusal:

Hi,

These past few days I have been going over the many disagreements and clashes we have had over the years. Clashes to win an argument, to prove a point, to be one-up on each other; petty and superfluous stuff. Things that were, subliminally, forming a dent in our friendship.

The photograph episode was the last nail in the coffin. It has hurt me no end and has taken away the essence of our friendship. Our so-called friendship! Ha!

I'm done with you guys. I gave it my best. Through the years I kept trying to assure myself that things will change for the better, but you guys just won't stop making me the butt of your jo_es and pran_s.

I don't have a home to go back to, I have no idea where my parents are. Therefore, I have no choice but to NOT continue living anymore. You will carry not just the guilt of having led me to my death, but also the guilt of ending the only chance of happiness for all those gentle souls that need us. I pray you find a way to live with that.

Au revoir

Papier

P.S. In case you are wondering what I mean to say by 'jo_es' and 'pran_s', the letter of the alphabet that falls between J and L is missing in my keyboard. Fill in the blanks and figure it out.

A final GOODBYE.

Was it okay, sir? Was my agony visible enough? Then why hadn't they replied immediately? Maybe I should have stressed my angst more. Why the hell did conventional letter-writing become obsolete? I could have written on paper and let a few tears roll onto the ink, letting it bleed, so they could know that I had been crying. That would have surely pulled at their heartstrings. For a moment there, I considered sending them another email, a more melancholic one. Would that have seemed too silly? Too desperate?

Rock, I could have given a pass to, but there was not a word from Snippy.

An under-wraps revelation, only for you, sir: I had the *hots* for Snippy. Who wouldn't? Her Brit accent only added to the lure. But I kept it to myself. I was so terrified of her, of the burlesque aura she had painted around herself, that I was sure if my romanticizing didn't agree with her, she would have chopped me into smithereens in an instant.

Exactly twelve minutes had gone by with no reply from either of the two. My hurt deepened. I pulled out a few flimsier-than-me sheets from the tissue box to wipe the down-pours streaming from my eyes, and the ones from my nose. I crumbled up the sheets and dunked them into the waste-bin. One tissue-paper fell out; it must have been weighed down with the snot. I picked it and, with an added effort, put it into the bin. I didn't want anyone to find snot-y tissue-paper scattered around in my house and think I was a messy person. I have lived an immaculately clean and disciplined life, and in my last moments, I would not be any different.

I straightened myself, creased down my saved-for-a-better-day nightshirt and pulled up the shirt collar. I faraway-*ly* sized up myself in the mirror inside my dresser, all the way from where I was standing in my room. Death likes to look pretty too, sir. I feel it has a personality of its own. Aristocratic. Distinguished. Unparalleled. *Deadly* personality, I must say! I wanted to match it.

My hands had barely eased off the collar when I felt a near-enormous lump; a suffocating vacuum rising in my throat, reaching up to my ears, engulfing them. It had made its way up to where my thinking power-house is. It was mumbling words, broken words, in a language my brain refused to comprehend. And its tone didn't sound happy. I swallowed it down; bitter saliva pressing it in further; bile drowning it. It was time! I lifted my fisted hand to my mouth. I wanted it to be short and quick, but time was taking its own sweet time. Or was I giving time a tough time? Putting up a struggle? It was a task convincing my fingers to loosen their hold on the pills, but the titanic task was keeping my head still. Every time I took my pill-filled hand towards my mouth, I pulled my head back by four inches. *Maybe if I stood with my head against the wall …*

Before my brain could register what hit it, in a split-second move, I popped the pills in; a few of them. Well, obviously, I popped-in only a few at a time, else I would have choked to death. Isn't that so, sir?

Duh! I should've choked to death! The task would've been faster done with! I could have immediately popped the remaining pills in, but I let the moment pass. I still need to figure why, though.

I lifted the bottle of water, took it to my mouth, and …

Ting! A chime, a not-too-distant sound, made its way towards me; persistent, fighting its way to where my alert electrons lay. Every cell in my body wanted to register it. But I didn't. I couldn't. I gulped down water, letting it gush down my throat like a rain-induced landslide that takes with it rocks and debris with frenzied force. Takes down even round, white pills that threaten to take one's life. I put all the remaining no-longer-perfectly rounded monsters into my mouth; I choked, I coughed, but I forced them down, too. A sigh of relief bubbled up and rang out from somewhere within me. And then, a throaty, low-tone one of resignation eased out. *I did it! It's finally done!* I felt myself slump to the floor.

Within seconds, an involuntary, up-scaled sound escaped the back of my throat, of a different genus from the previous ones. High-pitched but weak in the knees, its ending note quivered. *I was over the hump. Why was I losing the gall now?*

I made a dash for the washroom.

You know what the worst part was, sir? I didn't know which one was the clincher: finally proceeding with my plans, or stopping myself in time.

Would I have wasted precious time if I stopped to figure that out?

I hurled myself over the crapper and started convulsing in a desperate attempt to spew the trouble-makers out. A pill dribbled out. One slimy pill of the twenty or more that I had swallowed. Can you believe that? One measly pill.

I shoved my fingers down my throat, tickling my uvula, but nothing came out. *Why didn't the reality-check creep in before I took the pills?* I tried self-inducing again, with two fingers this time. *Tickle.* Nothing. *Tickle. Tickle. Tickle.* A gag, but nothing. I gave one last tickle, but all that came out was drool and some bitter tears. I slumped; doubled on the floor. Those tiny white-wonders had grown larger than life.

Ting!

Again? What is this damn sound? It was really bothering me. *Wait!* That was the sound I'd been waiting to hear. Scrambling off the floor, I headed for my laptop, grabbing it from the clutches of my bed like a mother snatching her baby from the clutches of its kidnapper.

Yes! Yes! Yes! There were replies from those heartless creatures. A reply from each.

I hadn't sent them my message on WhatsApp or on Facebook.

With a zillion forwarded messages flooding their phones all day long, I didn't want my 'cry for attention' to get lost amongst those. Standing there, while the cursor on my laptop did circles like a ballerina who had only recently learned to pirouette, I wondered if I should have just WhatsApp-ed. In the idling wait, my heart was doing a drum-roll, the beats rising to a deafening crescendo. The taste in my mouth had gone utterly bitterly *eww*; it felt as though my heart had wrangled its way up my throat, and into my mouth. The taste of anxiety! Or …? *Did I pop the pills out? Christ!* I made a dash for the washroom, and induced puking, and went on inducing till I retched and retched, and had coughed out every one of those murderous pills. And lots more. Scrambled half-digested bits of the previous night's pizza—pepperoni and cheese—and many other exotic undigested left-overs came gushing out at full steam. Wasn't a pretty sight, and it smelled like the guts of a pig who had chewed on left-overs and rotted garbage. I didn't stop till I had turned my insides out; till I felt empty. Hollow. A dilapidated abode with an eerie emptiness. Vacant. But it felt good. I stayed bent over till I had drooled and spat all I could. Soothed, I fell to the bathroom floor.

What wonders even a brief show of concern can do, sir. When earlier I tried to throw up, all I had gotten out was one measly pill, that too, because it had lodged itself in the spot where I was missing a tooth. Perhaps it was an unwilling accomplice to my murder. But on receiving Rock's and Snippy's replies, and although their replies were still unread, I puked out every crappy pill with not much effort.

Once the mind has the conviction, it can overcome any hurdle, no matter how big. That's something to take cognizance of, sir.

I dragged myself back to my bedside, to find my laptop dangling at the foot-end of the bed. In the desperate attempt to hold on for dear life, I must've thrown it there. I scooped it up. *Have my walloping efforts to spew out the weapons of my destruction been worth the while?*

Rock's mail had me teary-eyed even before I could read all of it, but it was the *not-there-yet-there* words, the words between-the-lines, that had my lips curving upwards. Two paradoxical emotions, tears and a smile, walking hand in hand; a testimony to triumphant joy.

I've pasted Rock's reply for your perusal here, sir. Let me forewarn you, you will not find his reply to be a very enterprising one. As for it being emotional, that's totally out of the question. And yet it had me misty-eyed.

Here it is:

"Yo man! U friggin crazy?! Wat u wanna do dat for?

And who d hell would wanna play with just d two of us, anymore? It wudn't be the same, wud be senseless. It wud be the Beatles without Paul McCartney. How crazy is dat?!

Mate, get out of dat wacky mode and get some beers chillin'. We'll b der in a bit!"

Oh, my dear, dear lord! Thank you! Thank you! And he called me their Paul McCartney. Aww! I was all smiles; teary smiles. Of relief, of jubilation, of longing. Of hope. I do admit I was being presumptuous; I may have read more into it than actually stated in his reply, but I was reveling in the euphoria of feeling wanted, of feeling loved. Oh! The high it was giving me. And there was Snippy's mail to be read, still. *She must be in tears after reading my mail. Poor babe!*

I couldn't open it fast enough:

"Idiot!"

I scrolled down …

… and further down, but …

That was it! Just one word! Not even a line, leave alone two for the in-between-the-lines stuff! *She must've been in a mad rush to get here. Yeah! That must be it, for sure!*

A sense of profound elation swamped me. Laptop discarded on the floor, soaring to the entirety of my height, arms in the Titanic pose, I let myself fall backwards, onto my bed. Rolling into the covers, muffling my face in them, smiling my widest smile, I let out a long, almost involuntary *hmm* sound somewhere from the back of my throat. And then a loud outburst: *I love you guys! You are the bestest! Ever!*

I suddenly had the urge to step out into the rain. The petrichor was calling out to me again, wafting towards me like a genie sailing through air. It carried me out on its Persian carpet, past the sheers, into the boundless tears of joy the clouds were chivalrous enough to shed for me. I let their wetness tickle my feet, I let them tap-dance on my outstretched arm. I would've let them seep into my body, consume me whole, saturate the unsaturated sponge, but there was beer to be chilled for my darling friends. I scooted back in, shutting the doors behind me.

***

Loud banging on the door, with a tailgate of expletives, announced Rock and Snippy back into my life. I would rather not elaborate on the expletives that spilled out of their mouths. They are, in no way, going to add to your vocabulary, sir.

I had the door open barely an inch before they barged in with frenzied force, letting the door slam against the wall with a deafening thud; the glass rattling hard, just short of getting shattered.

Rock bulldozed into me head-on, throwing me onto the floor. He then deposited his drenched self on top of me. I tried hard to topple him, but Snippy made a grab for my neck with her sharp-edged legs, pinning me down further. Without warning, in a flick of a second, the two were all over me, tickling me and doing crazy things between bursts of laughter; doing whatever it would take to get me relenting.

"Get away from me you … you …" It was an uber-easy task to control myself from calling them everything between ass-face and morons, twits and shit-heads, because those cuss-words wouldn't cut the mark. "I want nothing to do with you … you …" I did, sir. I wanted everything to do with them. I was so damn thrilled they were there, so damn thrilled they cared. But I couldn't let them know. I did not want to give in so easily, either. I was hurt and angry, sickened with disgust. I could see them dusting remnants of remorse under the carpet already. Making it history already. But conscience clearing has a price to pay, there are debts to be dealt with, so that it doesn't come barging its way in, another time. I was not going to forgive them, just then. In fact, I was in no mood to forgive them, at all. Just less than an hour ago, it would have been very nearly over for me.

And I, like a fool, had chilled beers for them!

A MAGICAL SOLUTION TO ALL YOUR PROBLEMS?

BUT, OH, IF ONLY YOU BELIEVED IN MAGIC!

So, that's a tiny glimpse of my friends. Frenemies, rather. To be quite honest, they're not all bad, there's some good in them too. You just have to go deeper in to see it, like rifling through layers and layers of bleached-white wool in search of a white pearl.

On the outside, Rock is bold and has a tough demeanor. He is smart-alecky; a bully, always throwing his weight around. He is kind of bulky too, has a bit of a slouch; his weight pulling along behind him. As big and bulky as he may look, he has a cuteness to him which he doesn't let others see too often. I think he likes to impersonate a toughie, but he's not all bad. Soft on the edges, rather. That's our Rock, all right! The cutest thing I find about him is, when laughter gets the better of him, and in his fits of laughter he rolls over; rolls over, and over. 360-degree rolls. And if he happens to come across a sloped pathway or a hill, he loses control of his gigantic self and goes rolling down the hill. Yelping and hollering, we go scampering behind him in the desperate attempt to bring him to a stop; which is no easy task, mind you, for we get dragged along with him a couple of feet, till we screech him to a halt.

Then, there's Snippy: quick-witted, eloquent, and very snappy. Always ready to snip off one's head. If you so happen to come in her way when she is in a not-very-great mood, which is more often than not, be assured you won't get out unscathed, without a snip here, and a sliver shaved off there. That's because she is Scissors. Fearless as she may be, there is one thing, though, that will have her sweating bullets: the fear of not being able to fit into her hot pants lest she puts on a few pounds. She has nightmares about that. You will always find her sexy, athletic legs in booty-shorts, walking them tall. She has a waist that may have, for endless years, been cast in an age-old corset, the strings of which have been pulled to their extremes. And her bust, so robust and …

Finally, there's me. Well, what can I say about myself? I'm a mellow ole' fellow, not as brash and audacious as them. I don't react as impulsively as them, either. I'm the calm and composed kinds; the one wrapping up situations when they get out of hand. I'm Paper, after all. I'm usually the one cleaning up the mess at the end. Not the rear-end, just to be clear. I'm not *that* paper!

I used to be quite proud of my physique and my personality, crisp with debonair confidence. Oozing gravitas. But recently, since I seem to have lost the élan to hold on to our friendship, to my dreams, to my life, I've lost that crunch. I'm much thinner and paler now, too.

So, that's us: Rock, Paper, and Scissors, the most sought-after hand-game at your service. Just for kicks, we fine-tuned our names to Papier and Snippy. Rock remained Rock; nothing imaginative could be done with his name.

Over the years we've taken on so many names and forms it's not funny. We weren't Rock, Paper, and Scissors to begin with, you know. To be honest, we don't even know our actual birth names, or even our birth dates, for that matter. All I know is that we were given our very first identity back in the era between 206 BC - 220 AD.

Yes, all the way back then! At the time, our hand game was called Shoushiling. Well, that's what a book called Wuzazu, by a Chinese Ming-dynasty writer, Xie Zhaozhi, claims. Apparently, one of us was a frog, another one a slug, and the third a snake. Don't ask me which was which, I ain't telling. Gives me the creeps even now, but back then, I guess frogs and slugs and snakes must've been the in-thing. We were only too thrilled when the Japanese cloned us and took us home, modifying us into a supernatural fox, a hunter, and a village head. We weren't complaining! Come the 17th century, we were graciously upgraded to the Jan-ken forms, which, when kidnapped by the West, were translated to the names we are known by today: Rock, Paper, and Scissors.

And why are we the most sought-after game, you ask? Isn't it obvious? We are the perfect choice for a fairly unbiased method of resolving issues. We propose a very amiable and effective way to sort indecisiveness between individuals. Even the silly stuff, like when kids debate endlessly over who will have the first go at a sport activity or a game, or who gets to sit in the front passenger seat of the car—decisions that even the parents can't take without being biased. Amongst the older lot: who goes out to get the beer, or who gets to pay the bill. Silly stuff, yes, but try resolving these issues without us. See how long it takes? How embarrassing it gets?

Ever since we were teamed together, we, the 'great enough' friends, have made decision making a fun thing for you; a tough decision for you, suddenly, becomes a thing of fun. When we're with you, to play with or to make decisions with, there's no dearth of joy and youngness in your hearts. That's our stratagem: to make it fun for you; to give you delirious glimpses of your long-lost youthfulness; to keep you young at heart. Always.

A youthful attitude keeps your cardiovascular health in better shape, hence, rendering a healthier, longer life. But you know that already, don't you, sir? What you do not know is that I would have gone the extra mile to make sure you stay in the pink of health till the end of your days. What you do not know is that I would have slowed down time for you, for it to walk in-step with you, and not try to run ahead of you.

Hell, I would have taken you back in time so you could have done all of those free-spirited things you so nostalgically miss doing. I would have helped you do the things you've been missing out on doing—burning passions that burn the insides of you because your I'll-do-it-once-I'm-done-with-work moment never came; things your friends reminisce cheerily, but get you feeling left out on; life experiences that would have made happy memories for you and grand stories to share with your friends and your kids, and your grandkids.

If I had my way, I would have taken you back in time so you could relive the simpler and fun times all over again. Childish and frivolous moments, like when you rang your neighbours' doorbells and hid behind bushes, then giggled over their puzzled faces when they came to the door; when you ate a chocolate and threw the wrapper behind the bed the minute the rightful owner of the chocolate walked in; when you opened a 1-Liter container of your favorite ice-cream and licked all over the top surface in front of your family or friends so no one else would go for it.

Yes sir, I would have definitely done all of that for you. For you to hold on to your childhood palates and crazes until the end of time.

Point to note: I said *I would have.*

Meaning: Not going to happen now. Not anymore. It's too late for that now.

Don't try to throw it on me. I'm not the villain here. Nothing to do with me. Uh-huh! It's all you.

Yes, you, sir.

How so? —you ask.

I could summarize *it* in one word: Man.

Sir, have you ever realized that the word 'man' is holed-up in your name? U*man*a.

***A thumbnail view of Man's life—his Naked Truth*:**

Man is mostly joyless and woeful over reasons that are very nearly obnoxious and, entirely, self-created. He has never felt complete; never has everything he wishes for, is never content with what he does have. As a result of which he is almost always miserable. He has led himself to a high-efficacy existentialism which he glorifies with modern-age technology that keeps breaking boundaries, yes, but in the process, one that has become the path to his self-destruction. Wrong choices, wrong decisions that have taken the life out of him. He knew where that path was leading him, yet turned a blind eye to it.

Let's move on to you, sir. Do not fret; I need to know you better before I can speak so blatantly of you. So, let's get down to knowing you better, right away.

Tell me, do you remember when was it that you lost your young-*ness*? Was it at a precise second of a precise age when you told it to shoo away? *Shoo!*—and to not bother you ever again, because you wanted to be mature and wise. Or were you just jumping the band-wagon, going with the flow? *They* were looking smart so you, too, wanted to look smart. Or was there some turning point in your life, a juncture, when things didn't seem to be going too well, that made you take the extreme step of shutting it out completely, and you matured overnight?

Was it that, as a kid, you were told to *Behave!* And just to please your elders, you may have behaved more maturely than your age warranted? For which you were duly praised and applauded, but while you were basking in the praise, you were, on the sly, sweet-talked into brushing off your youthfulness well before it's time.

Hormones! Was it those? The overactive ones? Damn them!

Or, were you the adult who was reprimanded, solicited to do away with the youngish-*ness* so as to not look like a fool? *You're seventy-five, for cryin' out loud. Act your age!*

Which one of these were you, Mr Umana? How old were you then, or erroneously-aged-before-time, I would say, when you coughed up a very odd stifled laughter instead of your characteristic belly laugh because you feared it would get you stares?

Did you know back then, and have you even come to realise now, that while you were washing your hands off your youthfulness, you were shutting your doors to all the Magic, as well?

You don't remember anything, do you, sir? Even the memory of the Magic zapped? Gone?

A short lived Memory of Magic:

The incident when a chandelier in your lounge fell a quarter of a second after you passed under it. The incident that you passed off as a fluke, because you didn't believe enough.

A not-so-short-lived Memory of The Magic:

The Jamie Ogg incident of the year 2010 that you may have heard of, or read about, where Jamie, cradled in his mother's arms even after being pronounced dead by the doctors, gasped and opened his eyes more than two hours after being declared dead.

In my world we call such Magical moments *miracles*. In yours, they're called 'chance happenings.' In my world, Magic is a conventional word, and mannerism. In yours, you read Magical tales to your kids, unbelievingly. Skeptically.

You may be wondering why I've capitalized the word Magic. It's because that's the reverence it decrees. It is not just any wizard-with-a-wand kind of magic. It's Magic, the marvel that lets you live in a not-just-whimsical world but a world where you find miracles and 'signs' happening for you; especially when you need them the most. A virginal world that lets you dream, and then works miracles to make those dreams come true. A world of belief, of undefaced positivism. The world your children live in; the one you once lived in. The world where it didn't take much to make you cry, but then, neither did it take much to make you happy again. The world that you crave still. *Oh! How I wish I could have those days back!*

Irony dies a thousand deaths when you wonder where the Magical world went. Sir, I wish to inform you that the buck stops with you. *You* displaced yourself out of that world, by shutting your doors to the Magic; thought you're too mature for it. *You* stopped believing. *You* stopped listening to your inner voice; thought you are wiser. But then, miracles stopped happening for you. There were no more signs dropping from the sky. It made you all the more skeptical. You stopped looking up, not even to say *Why, God?* Or to gesticulate. You turned your back to the sky, burning all your bridges behind you.

That's a naked truth about you, for you to acknowledge. And own.

The crossover to the other side was smooth and swift; the crossover from being the character of a fairytale, to one who reads out fairytales, unbelievingly.

In all respects, the Magic didn't have to be lost. It *shouldn't* be lost, at all.

A classified secret I could share with you if you are so willing to have a listen: It's still in there. It's still inside you.

I see I digress from the main story. I confess I got carried away, in the need to fill you in on what you've been missing out in life; in the need to give you a gist of why things happen the way they do for you, when we're not around; in the need to get you back in.

For now, let's hop back into the story. The story that began with pills.

"Hey, it's cool! Won't happen again," Rock said, rolling his large self off of me. He left puddles of water wherever he spiraled. Me, he left soaking.

"Yeah, it's cool. Just that I would've been dead by now, had I not stopped to read your stupid replies," my saliva-laced anger spluttered in their direction.

"You kidding? You'd kill yourself for this idiot! It's the stupidest of all the stupid things you've ever done. And that too, over that shit!" Snippy's mocking eyebrow was doing what it was best at. "Frankly, I didn't think you had it in you."

Did she, for even a second, think that the condescension in her voice would go unnoticed by me? That too, at such a delicate moment? And *that shit!* Being humiliated and mocked by anyone and everyone wherever I went, being called *Li'l one* and putting up with muffled giggles, is *that shit?* Having to wear dark glasses and hoodies so I wouldn't be recognized, walking at a fast pace so no one could catch up with me and horse around, is *that shit?*

I know what you're thinking, sir. That it's so silly of me to consider giving up the life I have over a few snickers and giggles. In reminiscence, I do now, sit back and laugh, titter actually, at the entire brouhaha I created around it. But let me clear the air: I'm not stupid to kill myself over *that shit.* That incident was just the trigger. You remember what I said earlier? *When you are brimming over, just a tiny trigger is enough to spark a fire and burn the house down.*

The real reason was bigger. Much bigger.

YOU'VE RUN OUT OF TIME

The actual reason the first time around:

The photograph situation was only a trigger; my friends were only the catalyst. *You* were the one that had been tripping me up.

Yes, you, sir. Even the first time around.

Remember the time when the whole of mankind had been holed up? Ghosted? The un-walked streets, starved restaurants, emotionless theatres, soulless shopping malls? For once, there was fear in your eyes. What were you hiding from? Guilt? Sins you didn't want to own up to?

It took a tiny virus to show you where you had been going wrong; to show you the wrong you had been doing to your own world, to your own home. It took a tiny virus to pin you down, and prevent you from doing more harm. It took down lives like a bowling ball knocking down pins. Many lives were lost, millions of lives.

It was as though, Mother Nature finally got her chance to clear her debt, with a postscript in bold: REPAID IN KIND.

Tell me, what is it that you yearn for, sir? What is your biggest challenge? Clear blue skies? A permanent reversal of Global warming and Climatic change that have been the catalysts for unfathomable, irreversible, impairment of existence? Factors that have raped Mother Earth, repeatedly, perpetually, till she lost all desire to keep her soul alive. Is it unadulterated food? Food that has not been laced or injected to make it sweeter or plumper, or containing genetically modified organisms.

Didn't you have air clear of pollutants to begin with? Wasn't there a time when you didn't have to mark food as 'Natural'? You had it all, but you had no value for any of it. *Things that you have within reach or in abundance, you don't care for. Isn't that how it works? You would know very well, sir.* Remember me telling you this? You didn't value what you had because you thought you could do better than God? You thought you could create a better world, a smarter one?

Stop playing God!

It pains me to see what your world has come to. Where do I begin? What all do I undo? How can I undo, when even Mother Earth has given up on you?

Is Mother Nature really to blame?

The loss of those lives devastated me, and your deliberate attempt to avoid acknowledging responsibility for those lost lives pained me to no end. But you falling back into your detrimental behaviour, reverting to your negative patterns after all you had been through, was my tipping point. That, there, was the real reason for me to consider giving up my life the first around.

Let's leave it at that, for now. I'll bring it up in good time; although, you are running out of time to recondition your cosmos. But I have a story to complete first.

***

"I didn't think you had it in you. Tell me you were just pulling a fast one on us. You weren't gonna really do it, were you?" A dimpled cheek and half a wink weren't enough to let Snippy get away with her snide remarks.

"You can be really nasty. You're nothing short of a vamp!" I hit back.

"A vamp! How could you tell?" Rock couldn't let the chance to trip Snippy slip by.

"Oh, I've learned to recognize the signs. And you think you're any better?" I said, shifting my gaze towards him.

Rock's eyes squirmed with indignation.

Snippy's eyes narrowed, shooting venomous looks at Rock, and then at me. "Vamp, hunh!" She crossed her arms across her chest. "But you're the wimp. Just for one distasteful thing you don't commit suicide and write off everything we have had all these years. What about all the good times? They go unaccounted for? And you forget what we're here for, our purpose. How could you think of only yourself? How could you be so selfish?"

Sometimes, sir, you need to put in a little extra effort to control yourself from physically throttling the person across you when they, very articulately, exonerate themselves from all the guilt and aim the shit at you. But I did throw her a venomous don't-you-dare look. I watched the grip of her arms loosen, saw her arms drop. I kept my eyes fixated on her eyes till they, too, dropped.

Vulnerability trickled out from behind her ears. It flashed a timid smile. "Okay, I … I guess we were less sensitive in realising the consequences of our pranks." Empathy looked back at me through a frightened eye, "But why didn't you tell us it was affecting you to that extent? We were just goofing around. Things did kinda get out of hand, I do admit, but ending your life is not the way out, you hear?" She sounded concerned for me, almost.

"*Just goofing around!* It seems like a joke to you, doesn't it? And where does it end, this joking and goofing around? You call yourself my friends, then how come you didn't see what I was going through? And did you ever consider the fact that I could've done the same to you? I could've shamed you guys, but I chose to not reduce myself to such a degree, because true friends don't do that. No sane person does. The mental torture I went through was living hell. I would never put you through that. Not ever!"

My temperament was synchronic with the stormy showers outside; unwilling to recede. The rain's demeanor may have been unwarranted, but my thunders, louder than the ones in the sky, were justified. I had been through immense excruciating pain. The humiliation and the hiding, the planning of self-slaughter; the game plan itself had been sheer torture. And the execution part? Oh! That had felt like threading a screw, twist by twist, deep into the insides of a withered heart.

The lacy drapes on my balcony doors were belly-dancing, shimmy-ing their hips in tune with the rolls of thunder. Their bosoms heaving, with a sensual sway to the left and a smooth glide to the right, were alluring. Their fluid moves held my gaze, but they couldn't bring down my temper by even a degree. I got out a can of beer and took a long swig. With another swig, I half emptied the can.

"Hey, where's ours? Snippy screeched.

I stayed put. I didn't want them to have any. I didn't want beer to help them be at ease; I was not done with them just yet. Rock and Snippy looked at me, wide-eyed and stupefied. They had never seen my aggressive side. Hell, such aggression was new to me, too. But I was at my wits' end that day. I had just about downed the whole can and was heading to the chiller to get another, when they overtook me. How did I, for a split-second believe, albeit even in my most combative state, that I was any match for Rock's gigantic body and Snippy's snippety legs?

They were drunk soon, too. Soon, all three of us were smiling silly. Now, thinking back, I think it was just me smiling silly. The other two were just smiling.

At that *silly* moment I felt the need for a hug. *I know, I know! Gullible me!*

I gestured to them, arms wide enough for both to squeeze in, but the two stayed put; they were being cocky. I got up and made my way towards them. Snippy, all of a sudden, found a cuticle jutting out from her finger-nail. Rock started to cough the pre-vomit cough, as though he had eaten something that didn't sit well with him.

Tears, unable to stay contained, (besides all the beer, or was it because of the beer?) came trickling out; one at a time at first, and then, they burst their way out.

You must think I'm such a crybaby. I'm not, sir, not usually. It's just that my friends' apathy really got to me. Ethically, a person who forgets and forgives as easily as I did, should be put on a pedestal and worshipped till the end of days. The likes of me are hard to find these days.

I had just about half-turned, my misery talking me into leaving the room, when Snippy, in one leap, was all over me, hugging me, consoling me, wiping off my tears; beginning to sob some, herself. *I knew she had a soft corner for me!*

Rock didn't budge from his spot, not an inch. The only movement giving away his emotion was a peculiar twitching of a muscle in his left ear, as though his ear wanted to fan something off from his shoulder. Rock's ears were on the bigger side, but no way near an elephant's. He'd need more than a twitching ear to fan off his shoulder-devil.

His devil and angel, both on a shoulder each, were stoically poised to fight a duel if it came to that. The angel was telling Rock to get up and give me a tight hug, and his devil was like: *Dude, you kidding? They'll think you're gay. Just look away.*

And then, Snippy began wriggling out of my embrace. Damn! She had felt so warm. *Did she sense something stirring?* But with my hand still in hers, pulling me along, she inched towards Rock. Standing tall in front of him, eyes piercing his, daring them to look away, she gave him a tight whack on his head with her free hand. I could swear I saw a tiny black rock scooting away in a flurry. The white rock, with perked up shoulders and arms across its chest, perched high up on Rock's right shoulder, was smirking.

What choice did Rock have but to spring up and give me a hug? I was left gasping for air in the threesome hug. Arms entwined, heads linked, untold promises were being devised. I felt myself go limp, but I didn't take a fall—my friends had my back.

Then without warning, in a flick of a second, Rock and Snippy threw me to the floor; both on top of me, tickling, doing crazy things, all over again.

CONFESSIONS

REVELATIONS

THE RPS COMMANDMENTS

"I got a confession to make." The 'make' was as Brit as it could get.

Rock and I lifted our chins to look at Snippy. Snippy had her head down.

What is it? Shame?

She gave Rock a hasty half-glance before looking at the floor again.

Seeking permission? For what? My mind went into an overdrive mode, scrutinizing every gesture of hers. Her right toe was scraping something off her left one. *Scraping the surface? To unravel what lay underneath? A secret embedded within?*

I looked at Rock. His eyes were boring into Snippy's lowered face. His Adam's apple bobbed up, but as Snippy started to speak again, it got lost somewhere on its way down, making a sound like a distant knock.

"We … uh, screwed up!" Snippy said.

We screwed … you what? I remember seeing darkness all around. I must have shut my eyes. I have no inkling when I did, but it was just as well, because I didn't want to look at the two of them. *How dare they! I wish I could've shut them out of my life, totally. Why didn't I let her know how I felt about her? How could she fall for him, and not me? Oh, how I wish I hadn't puked out the pills!*

"We were so into it," she went on to say, "that we got carried away. We went beyond what was planned, and things, uh … got out of ..."

We were so into it … so into it … so into it. Why was my mind simulating a faulty gramophone? *Stop! Spare me the gory details …*

I looked at Rock. His eyes looked hard. Unblinking. *He doesn't want me to know? I wonder why. Now I* want to *know. Speak up, woman! Are you pregnant? I'll fuckin' kill you, Rock.* I was now glaring at Rock. The malevolence in my eyes could peel off the epidermis of his arms and face, dig through the dermis, and scrape off the connective tissues and sweat glands. It could melt the fat of the hypodermis to lay bare his bones. On them, I planned on etching intricate carvings, in detail, of the antipathy I felt towards him.

There was a pregnant silence; Snippy had clammed up. She wouldn't get her lips to part—glued together like a child's who had mistaken a glue stick for a lip balm.

After what must have been six seconds, I heard a chirping sound. *A cricket all the way up here? One that had found the silence in the room as deafening as I?* There was another sound. Rock's lower teeth were gyrating against his upper teeth. But there was no sound coming from where Snippy sat. *Is she going to tell me, or not?* My eyes were arm-twisting hers, to speak up.

A fact about Me:

I know a lot about a lot. I know a lot about you as well, for that matter. I know you much more than you know your own self. But when it comes to women, I lose ground; totally clueless. I do know one fact about them, though: they talk, incessantly, but when you want them to tell you what *you* want to know, they won't spit out a word.

Should I get her another beer? It's wondrous what quick slugs of beer can do. *Oh, but if she's pregnant, she shouldn't have any. She did have some earlier. Or was it pretense? My Beer Pregnancy-test will get the facts out in the open, for sure.*

She wouldn't touch the beer. *I knew it!*

"I, uh, need to have a clear head to tell you everything as it actually transpired. Beer, once inside me, has a tendency to speak an eccentric language of its own."

Liar! I chugged hers too. *I* didn't want a clear head; I was in greater agony than before.

I saw her watch me with a peculiar eye, like a lizard when it uses the sit-and-wait approach in anticipation of a passing-by fly. Snippy was using the sit-and-wait approach for the brew to get pally with my anger. She finally spoke, "Those photos of yours, we … uh, didn't just show them around to friends, we … uh, put them on … uh, Instagram and umm … uh, Facebook."

"How dare you! You guys are … are horrible. *So* … damn mean and *so* … *so* … mean." Why didn't hard-core badass cuss-words come to me when I needed them? I was seething; face cradled in my hands, eyes burning, I was yearning to hate the two, all over again. "I want nothing to do with you guys, ever. I wish I had gone ahead with my plans. I wouldn't have had to deal with this, all over again." I was, once again, abandoned.

Ideas of how to conceal my identity, now that I was 'infamous', were zipping through my head.

"Hey! It isn't all too bad. In fact, you're quite a hit, I must say. In just three days *Li'l one* became quite the hash-tagger. I gotta tell you, some comments were rather, umm … perky," cooed my Brit-accented, un-pregnant charlatan, in her attempt to cool my exasperation. "I was pleasantly surprised to know that girls find you and your uh … li'l package quite cute and kinda irresistible. They're really into you, Dude!"

Well, some good came of it; I finally had female following. *Yay!* I turned to look away. I didn't want them to catch the light in my eyes, or see my upturned lips, nor my shoulders that had arched towards the sky. Good news does that to you, it makes you smile, gets your whole body on the rise. A bull run! And the revelation that Snippy's confession wasn't about a pregnancy or about her having a thing going with Rock, felt like the coolness of torrential rain on a forest fire. My heart was happily playing in the muddy puddles. Howbeit my lips were not permitted to show even a hint of a smile; I wanted them to face the grave situation at hand. I feigned more anger than I felt at that given moment, "Don't you sweet-talk me. You think you can be coy and cute and I'll forget everything? Nothing … nothing you say can, or will, ever wipe off the humiliation and the mockery I have had to deal with. I'm ruined. You guys have ruined me for life. I was better off dead. And only after I was gone would you have recognized the consequences of your actions."

Snippy fell silent; remorse crept up her face. Ivy swamped its way up, penetrating every cavity, every crevice; forming mildew, germinating into mold. "I am so sorry. I'm truly, truly sorry. We should've thought about the consequences." Her voice was like butter on a warm toast—melted, savoury, and guilt-ridden.

There was a long silence. No one said anything except the cricket; it was tooting its own horn.

Snippy had her head tipped down; her eyes, preferring not to look into mine, pretended to find the chipped nail paint on her pinky toe engaging. Her pinky toe got intrigued by the sudden attention. It began twitching; something inside it was itching to get out. *More revelations?* "I, uhh… have another confession to make. Something you've suspected for some time but we … uh, didn't have the gall to tell you."

I knew it! I saw darkness again. *Did my eyes think that if they stayed shut, they could armour me from life's shenanigans?* I didn't want to know more, but inquisitiveness was getting the better of me. I cracked open my eyes and looked at her. A tug-of-war was going on between the two sets of eyes:

Are you deriving sadistic pleasure by torturing me with the suspense? Out with it!

I'm in two minds now.

I wasn't aware you had even one.

Cute! But with what I have to say I fear that cuteness might not last long.

Try me!

I'd rather not.

Shall I do the beer test on you again?

She cracked open her lips, almost instantly.

I knew it! The woman is *friggin' preg …*

"Remember when we … uh, moved out of the Tysons'?" she said, dislodging my thoughts.

"Uh …" I felt dizzy, as though, I was sitting in the wrong movie hall and, all of a sudden, was being ushered into the right one. "The

Tysons, yeah … of course." I cocked my head to the side; eyes far-gazing, recalling.

"That's been dead and gone, Snipps. Don't …" Rock intervened, but, was cut short.

"What? I cannot not let it out." Snippy looked like she had been holding in *wind* for far too long and it had to be let out; she couldn't be discreet about it anymore. She turned to look at me, "So while you were gone looking for your mom and dad, we hadn't been playing much with the kids. You weren't there, how could we? So, out of boredom, one night when the parents were out, the kids scrambled into their dad's library. While they were rumbling through his stuff, Rock …," she threw a fleeting glance at the person in question, but regretted her action instantly. Choosing to ignore his glare, she rallied on, "Rock … uh, saw a gun concealed discreetly under a drawer, and he, uh … nudged Pete to check it out. You remember Pete? The son?"

I nodded. But … *a gun?* "A gun?"

Snippy let her eyelids drop. "Well, uh … the next morning Pete took the gun to school to show off, and I guess, also to ward off a bully or two." She went on, with caution, "That didn't go down too well. The … uh, police were called in and the entire episode flared up into a news bulletin." Her Adam's apple was bobbing up and down, like Rock's. It was making the same knocking sounds too.

My fingers slipped off the can of amber brew. Its effect was wearing off. Fast. But I was okay with that; I didn't want to get groggy. Snippy and Rock deserved to feel my wrath. "What the …," but Snippy had more to say, and I wanted to hear it all.

"There were repercussions; he was taken into custody and kicked out of school. Everything got so messed up," Snippy was blabbering now, saying it all in one breath. The faster the bunkum words got out of her system, the faster her lungs would be cleared of the dead weight. "His parents became wary of his conduct. He had to go in for counselling. His life was in total shambles." Once done, she deflated completely; devoid of the baneful baggage that had been weighing on her.

"How could you be so stupid? You ruined his life. You made a mess of such a pleasant family. For what? Cheap thrills? You have absolutely no ethics, no friggin' morality. How do you guys even sleep at night?"

Rock, his head embedded in his chest, was a boulder of stillness and silence. Snippy wouldn't look at me either. How could she? How could she justify their fool-hardiness? "We know for sure he had no intention of using the gun to harm anyone …," she started to say.

That's her justification? "Just having a gun in his possession … that one move threw him into an existential crisis, ruining his life for good. Do you realise that?" I let my pitch vibrate. It wasn't the beer talking.

"It was a … a tiny misjudgment …," her voice trailed off. The ivy had crept further up, veiling her mouth, veiling her ears, her eyes; enveloping her every cell. There was no dearth of remorse and anguish on Snippy's face.

A *tiny* misjudgment? A gross understatement! I was fuming.

For a while, there was just heavy breathing in the room—three different levels of breathing—one, in the need to say more; another, in anticipation of stopping her; and mine, in the struggle to keep myself from throttling the two.

Rock hadn't said a word still; not a sound out of him.

I looked at Snippy. She was sitting upright as though she needed to burp. Undigested happenings of over the years, which were now, troubling her with their toxicity came burping out, "We thought we were on a break from our duties till you came back, thought we'd have some fun. But things went on another tangent. I … uh, went along like an idiot, 'coz you know me, I'm a compulsive, frenzied maniac, always ready for a thrill. And there was such an electrifying thrill in being around a gun. The feeling of power, of control, was giving me such a high …," her hands lifted to the height of her shoulders, palms facing upwards, eyes star-gazing, she looked delirious with wonderment. On seeing my *Duh!* look, she changed track, "But I wish better sense had prevailed. We, umm, sometimes have, uhh ... lapses of judgment when we're all not together, not guiding each other." Snippy's explanations were having a tough time staying afloat. Every single explanation, as it was making its way out of her mouth, was being muffled and flushed down the crapper by me, with a single look. Her upper lip was twitching in a funny way; there was more she had to say. "He then, did the most obvious thing—he kicked both of us out. It wasn't, umm, 'coz of you that we left the Tysons house."

My eyes halved; anger, disgust, hatred in dollops was weighing down my eyelids. My nostrils flared like submarine rudders; my jaw went taut. "Such a-holes! Such shithead twits. You've been lying to me all this time. You had me believe you were concerned for me, that it was for my betterment that we moved from there. But you were out to save *your* skins. Gawd, you guys are despicable! Selfish and unscrupulous and vicious. And how could you forget we were there to look after the kids; to make their lives better, not worse? We have duties, responsibilities, and you had the cheek to remind *me* about my purpose and call *me* selfish. Seriously?" Disgust was written all over my face.

"I … I … just wanted to, uh … us to not forget our purpose." Then, with the conviction of one who hates being cornered, she said, "The fact of the matter is that had you been there, all that would not have happened."

What? Is she blaming it on me?

Snippy went on the defensive, "What I mean to say is, uh … I mean … I, uh …" She turned to look at Rock.

Rock's face had softened a bit, like ice-cream in its early stages of a meltdown; but there was still not a word out of him.

Hangdog!

Snippy was speaking again, her voice soft; softer than I had ever heard, "Papier, we were so scared. Things weren't too pretty there. The mom was constantly snapping at the dad for having a gun in his possession. Pete's every move was being scrutinized by his parents, day in and day out. Lara, their daughter, was shit scared of being around Pete. The air was suffocating. There were no happy moments left in that house, any longer. It was as though the uh, … the house was waiting, anxiously, to steal its way towards the edge of a cliff, and at the next wrong move, off it would go tumbling down … taking its weighed-down occupants with it. Had Pete not kicked us out, we would've left on our own, soon enough. There was no way the two of us could've fixed things back to normal, on our own. By the time you got back, Pete had shut his doors to us, and it was highly improbable that he would let us in, any time soon."

"And why didn't you tell me this earlier?"

"We were too embarrassed to tell you we f … uh, goofed up." It took a lot for Snippy to admit that. Her voice had mellowed; her ears had crimsoned.

"After you left," Rock finally spoke, "Pete was, uh … giving me a very tough time." Rock's first few words sounded croaky; dehydrated, famished. They had been held captive behind bars, within the confines of his closed mouth, for far too long. "He kept pushing me out. You know, very well, how tough it was to get through to him. He was full of brazen nerves and unhealthy chutzpah. When you left, I was no match for him alone, so I thought I'd try some other strategy. I thought I would attract his attention by doing things he liked, things that gave him a thrill; thought I'd win him over by having some fun together. But I guess it kinda … back-fired."

"Having some fun! That is fun for you?"

"I guess, I … screwed up. I still have nightmares about it, sometimes." Rock's a-few-moments-earlier erect back had slouched. His voice had turned almost inaudible, "And now we kinda screwed up things for you too. I wish we could turn them around."

"I wish we had done none of it at all," whimpered Snippy.

"I'm so … so sorry." Rock's throat sounded guttural, like he had swallowed a warty frog, and now the frog wanted out. Rock had turned away from us, leaving us to face his back. I had never seen him cry. Watching his bent spine was making me mellow. I edged myself to the other end of the room, as far as I could get from him. I did not want to ease him of his pain.

Kids look up to us. People look up to us. We cannot screw up, Mr Umana. There was no way I would console Rock and put him at ease. Not yet. He had messed up, he needed to understand that. What may have seemed to him like a chance to look cool and smart-alecky, was, in fact, the very reason for him to be cut off from Pete's life for good.

"Oh, I'm so ashamed of myself, of so many things I've done without thinking." Rock moved towards my bed and slumped on the small ottoman at the foot of the bed. "People must think I'm sadistic. I've been telling myself that they deserved my belittling, 'coz they were such wimps. Well, they seemed like wimps to me. But now, I realise I've been so foolish and a jerk," Rock admitted; remorse writ large on his face.

I wanted him to pour it all out; it was therapeutic for him.

"I never let it really bother me. I guess I was running away from the situation so my conscience would not look me in the face and show me the person that I am. I've been hiding behind a mask of nonchalance." His tone had deepened, he was choosing his words. I could see a paradigm shift in him; this was not the Rock I was used to. Kingpin, Numero Uno, Mr. Perfect, was more him. Head hung, disjointedly, between his shoulders, arms thrown haplessly on his laps, he looked like a tree that had been brutally uprooted and left to wilt.

His cry for help was glare-blinding me, yet, my eyes widened when Snippy placed her hand on his knee. *She* does have *a soft corner for him!*

Looking at me, she said, "We were scared you would walk out on us if you got to know. We may ridicule you and may not say it to your face, but we know in our hearts that you're the sorted one. You have your feet on the ground. You keep us grounded, you keep our thoughts balanced. You're the sane one. We're hopeless without you, Papier. We need you. And this world needs us …"

She didn't need to say more, she had me at *Papier!* It was in the way she had said my name at that moment.

A Hidden Fact. Inconspicuous, masked in a Cryptic Language:

They needed me. Yet, pretended otherwise.

The world over, people know how prejudicial ego is, but they still let it come in the way of their relationships. People have lost many a genuine friend since they befriended their ego.

I was ecstatic. I felt loved. I felt I mattered. I felt like a winner. I was thrilled to know that Rock and Snippy valued me. They couldn't deal with my meek personality, my 'goody-goody' nature; they mocked me, substituted me for a punching bag, often enough. But that day, they acknowledged that I was wiser and better at handling situations. My rational decisiveness had paid off finally.

What a day it had been. Consequential! Nevertheless, we were all but done. If we had to stick together, we had a lot many amendments to make in ourselves. Each of us thought we were brilliant and had a license to resolve others' problems, oblivious to the fact that we were far from perfect ourselves. It's easy to see flaws in others, but ours, we turn a blind eye to. That day was a peep into some harsh realities. We needed a make-over of sorts. We had to become better versions of ourselves, both for the sake of ourselves, and others. So, we decided to have nightly discourses about the day gone by. New findings in our behavioral attitude would be discoursed and implemented. For that, a constitution was implemented—The Rock, Paper, Scissors (RPS) Commandments. Observations would be duly noted in it.

That night's discourse, the first of many, was a loaded one. My suicide fiasco topped the list, and rightly so. It wasn't a wise thing to do.

Standing there, that day, facing judgment in the court of conscience, I felt a sudden punch to the gut: *Mustering the guts to commit suicide had seemed easier and more rational than mustering the guts to confront the issue with my friends?* I must've been off my rocker! And what if I had gone through with it? I would never have gotten to know how much I was needed, how much I mattered.

Facts about Suicide duly noted in the RPS Commandments:

Suicide is not the way out.

It may seem to be the easy way out. It's not.

It may resolve the hot-button issue, may end it for good, but it ends everything else too.

If you have the guts to commit suicide, then you very well should have the guts to confront the situation, and all those that drove you to that point. *Spill your guts where they ought to be spilled.*

The next topic, was to address matters of conflict and misunderstanding between us right then and there, and not let them linger. There was no denying the fact that the three of us would, sometime or the other, argue over some issue or the other, be it a major one or even a petty one, but we decided to address the matter of contention before things went out of hand. And if, for some reason, no resolve would be found, we would agree to disagree. But we, unanimously, agreed to never again let the situation get the better of us.

Misunderstandings are like weeds. Don't you feel so too, sir? Do you make an extra effort to pull out the weeds? Do you just yank out the leaves or do you go deeper in and scoop out the weeds with the roots, making sure they do not sprout out again? Making sure they do not cause infestation? Do make that extra effort, sir. Misunderstandings, when not addressed at the root cause, weed out, making the mind prone to infestation, and become a major threat to the development of a relationship. Curating a misunderstanding from the root cause is essential for effective problem-solving. It is essential to eradicate the issues from the core, rather than merely addressing superficial symptoms. So that they do not sprout out again.

Next, was Rock's turn to bear scrutiny. He was reprimanded for being a bully. I couldn't let the chance go, it's not every day that Rock gets kicked in the butt. "So, tell me Rock, why is it that you bully only those who are weaker than you? Physically weaker, I mean," I was quick to add.

"Papier has a point," Snippy jumped in, giving me the much needed support. Alone, I was jelly; one rattle by Rock and I would be reduced to liquefied mush. Snippy was all about firmness and bluntness. She got the word across, loud and clear. I was glad for the intervention. "It boils down to the fact that bullies are scared of strong personalities. They only target the weaker ones 'coz there's a less-to-none chance of retaliation. Hmm? So, in reality, bullies are weak people who are out to gratify their egocentric selves. Tell me if I got this wrong, Rock?"

"That's the biggest bunch of bull I've ...," Rock came out all guns blazing, but stopped mid-sentence. He could find no terra firma to stand on.

Facts about Bullying duly noted in the RPS Commandments:

Bullies only target those that fear standing up to them; they do not target those that are stronger than them. Bullies are, in actuality, weak personalities, gratifying their egocentric selves by bullying those 'weaker' than them.

So, that was that! No more bullying, ever.

"And no more condescension, and no more mockery," I said, gaining ground from Rock's defeat. "We have no right to disgrace or mock anyone. Who are we to think we are, in any way, better or smarter than another? No one is perfect. If we can see faults in others, they can see faults in us too. If we can shame, so can they, but some choose not to. And it's not fear that's stopping them." I held my gaze; Rock and Snippy lowered theirs.

We were done for the day but we remained seated a little while longer, assessing our talk, familiarizing ourselves with all we had discoursed on; letting things sink in, letting things settle; simulating a jar being shaken to settle down its contents, to make space for more.

OF ARGUMENTS AND THEIR REPERCUSSIONS

Although having snuggled together all through the night, come morning, the curtain panels loosened their embrace by only a notch. A golden dagger, broad and long, stole its way in through the thin gap between the curtains. It extended its intrusion all the way to where I lay; its pointed tip positioned just above my right eyelid, forcing it open. The rays of the sun had their ways, devious ones at that, to wake me up if I lost count of time.

I looked at the clock; it was moustache-ing. *It's 10 past 10, and Robin is still in bed?* By this time of the day, on a usual day, the curtains would have been held open with tie backs, making them look like two annoyed ladies, with hands on their waists, displaying their annoyance at all those still sleeping.

Oh, of course! It's Sunday. Good, I don't want to step out yet either. I was still groggy from the previous night's frenzy.

Was it just yesterday that I was standing in the balcony? Was it just yesterday that I ...? I peered out from under the covers. Roo-mom was looking at me, her eyes beaming with love, but there was a hesitant fretfulness weighing down the sides of her mouth.

Are my jumpy thoughts of yesterday reflecting in my eyes? Or is it my forced smile that's given me away? How do moms just know? Where would I start? I sunk back into the covers; it was Sunday, after all. But sudden loud voices, that were getting louder, were ruining my lazy-day, and as warm and snug as the auburn quilt was, it failed to muffle the dreadful sounds entirely.

Ouch, ouch! I was being tossed around, because Roo-mom was being tossed around, because Robin wanted to go down and see what was happening. The sudden loud voices had awakened him, and without his kangaroo he wouldn't have been able to step out from the haven of his room into the scary cosmos that was drawing his attention. His mom and dad fought often, but that day's argument seemed alarmingly roaring.

Robin stopped at the staircase landing. Samara was sitting on the bottom step; she was hugging the banister. She must have heard the floor-board creak and looked up. Robin's eyes met her teary ones. In a blink, Robin was in near tears too. He wanted to go to Samara; he took a step down, lifted his other foot to take the next step but turned and climbed back up instead, and clung on to the banister at the top of the stairs. We were encircled within the grasp of his arms and the banister. Dangling mid-air, memories of a similar experience from yesterday, came rushing in. I pulled myself back, sinking into Roo-mom's pouch as much as I could. Peeping just enough from up there, I could see Samar in the kitchen, trying to pull his mom out of the kitchen. Arguments made him anxious. Arguments can make anyone anxious; they bring out the worst in everyone. Raised voices, distorted faces, banging doors, flying pans. Luckily there were no flying pans in the kitchen that day, but the mom, standing on the other long-side of the island from the dad, was trying her best to fling Samar away without taking her hard-glaring eyes away from the dad.

I couldn't gather much of what was being said; they had killed their loud voices and were using whispers to hiss out their spite, in monosyllables mostly. They had already disturbed the younger kids;

they didn't want to disturb them further with gory details. The mom, her one arm still hostage in Samar's hands, motioned him to take Samara and Robin to the family lounge. "We just need to talk about something important. Please take them and put on Brain games or something on the telly. I'll be with you in a minute."

Samar looked at Samara, and then at Robin. He dragged his hesitant feet to where Samara sat and tugged at her hand, while waving at Robin to come down. Samara held on to the banister even harder, while giving Samar a sharp look: *The kind of mood Mom and Dad are in, there should be someone rational to watch over them.*

Agitated, Samar jumped up the steps, two at a time, grabbed Robin and forced him down the stairs. He tugged at Samara with his other hand without looking at her, and led them both towards the lounge. The sudden jerk made Robin lose his grip on his kangaroo; Roo-mom and I went tumbling down the last of the stairs, crash-landing against the narrow wall between the kitchen and the lounge. Robin made to turn and pick up his kangaroo with his free hand, but Samar kept marching on, dragging Robin behind him.

I wish we had gone along with them. What transpired in the kitchen was not a pleasant sight.

"I wish I had left you years back. I was stupid to put up with you all this while. It was only because of the kids that I hung on, *and* the silly hope that you would change. But don't you, for a moment, think I will let you have your way any longer." Head held high, eyes unrelenting, the mom thought she was a sight of might, but her legs were jelly. She pulled herself up, "I'm done with you." Anger contouring the fringes of her words, hand hitting hard on the counter that served to announce the end of the conversation, she made her way towards the kitchen door.

"Oh, how I wish you *had* walked out and left me in peace. It's not too late now, either," the dad brought his voice to a rock-bottom low; the kids didn't need to know that side of him. The air around him was doused with a pungent smell. The smell of arrogance. He let his hard eyes fluster her, dislodge her, and then he walked out of the kitchen before she could. Storming into the lounge, in an unsavoury, crisp voice, he called out to the kids, "Anyone for Bigg Boys Cafe? The first one in the car will get a chocolate sundae."

***A Reality about Men*:**

Men will stoop to using bribery to win a score.

The dad scored low on my scale chart, though. Kids love sundaes, but they love their moms too.

I wriggled my way out from Roo-mom's tight hold, and from the nook of the door, eyes veering left to right, right to left, in the motion of a pedestal fan, I caught a view of the kids. Samara was in the about-to-cry mode. Robin, seated on the floor, with one bent leg in the direction of the commotion, and the other stretched out towards the TV, was trying to match the right emotions with the expression he had copy-pasted from Samara. Samar was looking at his dad: *Will just the winner get a sundae, or will we all get one eventually?*

All three were fidgety; they were on a sticky wicket: *Mom or a chocolate sundae?* Samara ran towards the kitchen first, "Mommy!" Robin tailed her. But 'Mommy' wasn't in the kitchen. I must've been too engrossed in the kids to notice her slipping out. They ran up the stairs looking for her.

"Mommy, please come with us." Sob. Plead. Sob.

"Yes, Mommy, pleeth come with uth." Sob. Plead. Sob. Robin's frontal lisp, on certain alphabetic sounds, didn't want him to let go of his babyhood just yet.

"Sweeties, you please carry on. I need some time to myself," the mom said, between bouts of cough, and failed attempts to hide her tears.

"Mommy, I wanno hab a thun-dae," Robin tugged at his mom's shirt.

"My love, you go with your sister and brother, please. I'm having a headache; I want to rest for a while. Samara, please take him. Have a nice breakfast and a sundae. And by the time you come back my headache will be gone."

Samara didn't budge. Robin, leaning on the edge of the bed, straightened himself. He had been a pleasant surprise when the parents were informed of his conception. They had thought they were quite done after Samara; that two were good to complete their family. Now, six years on, he was being a pleasant surprise yet again, manning up, consoling Samara, and leading her towards the door.

"Robin, I know you're a big boy now, but don't let go of Samara's hand for even a second once you're out of the car, you hear? And Samara, please put on your hair-band. Now run along you two, before Daddy leaves without you."

Although disheartened by the happenings since the morn, I was not distressed enough to not go for ice-cream. A gooey melt-in-the-mouth chocolate sundae with a double-shot of chocolate sauce was just what I needed to stomach the entire episode. Robin knew what I liked; he usually ordered what I wanted. I loved him for that.

We saw the kids head towards us. Roo-mom raised both her arms, making it easier for Robin to sweep her up. I clung on to Roo-mom; I couldn't risk being left behind in the rush.

And the kids ran past us!

Roo-mom and I, mouths wide open, were left gazing as the three kids rushed out the door. Rock, struggling to find his way out from the track-pants that Samar had dumped into a pile on the floor, had a similar open-mouthed look. "Now, that is mean! How could they go without us?" he shouted.

"They obviously forgot us in the rush. Besides, they don't need us there." They needed us all the more, to be honest. We would have diverted their minds from all that had transpired since morning. And I wanted my chocolate sundae. *Shoot! Hot damn! Shit's creek and every other damn thing!* My mind was screeching, but all I said was, "Yeah, just as well, we didn't go!" as I watched Rock give one last shove and roll out of the tracks' pocket.

Rock usually houses himself in pockets of lowers, be it of tracks or shorts or fancy pants. Perching up on shoulders is a big 'NO' for him. He can roll off and fall, well-rounded that he is. He can't cling on to any limb or clothing, bulky that he is. So pockets are his thing; a safer bet, peeping out of them, just enough.

Snippy has found her comfortable place on shoulders whenever she is not nestled in the crooks of elbows. She usually mounts herself on Samara's right shoulder, donning a glorious picture-perfect poise. She does, occasionally, settle on Samara's lap too. She has no restrictions; she can balance herself anywhere, being the sexy silhouette that she is.

I am usually up and about, fluttering around, fanning and cooling the strained air around people, when I'm not snuggled cosily in Roo-mom's pouch.

Seeing that we had been left behind, Snippy jumped down from Samara's shoulder. Of what use was she without us? Without me, she wouldn't have a good time, in any case. Hands on her waist, she walked past Rock in a reduced-pace stride; cast an uppity glance in my direction, and made her way into the kitchen. If I know her well, she was expecting acknowledgment for her sacrifice. And her sprint into the kitchen clearly stated her appetite for an explanation from the mom: *Why did you guys fight? Did you catch him cheating? That must be it. What else could it be? Ooh, I want details, every lip-smacking detail!*

The mom was, indeed, back in the kitchen. She was still; her left forearm resting on a counter, her index finger-nail tapping on the counter. Tap, tap, tap. Tap, tap, tap. Tap, tap, tap. *Sending Morse code telegraph messages? To God?* Her eyes sharp, very-near dispassionate, were transfixed on a charred egg that had been flipped over.

Her gaze shifted out the window, at the Petunias. As blue as they could get, they matched the blue of her mood. She made her way towards the kettle, putting it on more out of habit than need. She, then, made a grab for her phone kept on the kitchen island. Her phone, a fly on the wall, was tone deaf to the verbal exchange that had transpired earlier in the day, but in the mom's hand, at that moment, it couldn't turn a deaf ear, or play dead. It braced itself for what lay ahead.

The mom called her go-to person. "Hi. What're you doing? Free to talk?"

Her sister's voice was reinvigorating, palliating. It could set right the irreparable cracks too. Dilapidated parts of the mom had already begun to regenerate; indentations and bruises had already begun to ease out. She would be almost new soon.

Snippy hopped on to the footrest of Robin's high chair, nestled in a corner of the kitchen island. She somersaulted and landed on the seat. Chin in her hands, she was all geared up to listen in on the conversation. Rock wheeled himself in and tried, somewhat unsuccessfully, to roll up Robin's garden slide that had been pulled into the kitchen from the front lawn three days ago.

Robin had received the foldable slide for his birthday a couple of months back. It was still a point of interest for him. But it had been raining erratically the past four days, and when he wanted to go, he wanted to go. It was either pull the slide in, or deal with a totally-drenched-and-very-messy Robin playing outside in the rain.

Now, Rock wanted to perch himself atop the slide; he wanted an unobstructed view of the mom from up there.

Seriously?! I mouthed, stumped at his efforts to go up the slide the wrong way. *Go around the slide and somersault up the steps, you nut-case,* I gestured. "Oh, I forgot. You're too bulky to somersault," I smirked my cheeky smirk.

"Oh, yeah! Watch this." Rock saw an open drawer in the island,

and just to snub me, somersaulted into it. He landed on some very sharp knives. *Ouch!*

We saw the mom walking around the island, round and round, tea-mug in hand; her pace in sync with the pace of her thoughts, as though, if she walked out of sync, her thoughts would run ahead of her, and she'd miss out the meaty stuff. All of a sudden, her pace slowed down. She had caught her ghosted version in the glass of a tall stand-alone cabinet. Then on, every time she swung by it, she slowed down her pace by a couple of notches. Slender shoulders elegantly puppeteer-*ing* her slender long arms; a thin long neck, the perfect pedestal to showcase her chiseled face; hair whirling playfully just above her shoulders, lending only slight peeks of her tiny ears that looked like pink poking noses of baby mice out for a sniff—she sure made a pretty sight.

We caught her pouting at her reflection. The pout accentuated the creases under her eyes. The creases, like slimmed pleats of a skirt—intense folds starting from the outer edges of her eyes that softened as they stretched further on her face—were being evaluated: *This one sprung up when we had a major fight last year; I had raised my voice at him for coming home late every other night. These two wrinkles, when calling me close-to-cuss names became a habit. This one, here, seems new.* The new wrinkle's rebellion must have been super violent to have made a mark so soon.

She was lamenting somewhere in-between sobs and bouts of cough: *I know … I know he's a fabulous person. He's great with others, but not with me. He is gentle and thoughtful with others, but not with me.* The clock hanging high, above the scene-of-crime, had struck the XI mark a minute and a half after the mom had started sobbing out her sad story. Now, it was chiming with ecstatic grunts as its long arm mounted the short arm, but the mom's sob saga was nowhere near the end.

Snippy had been darting looks our way the entire time, teary-eyed looks, letting us know the mom was not the only one crying. Apparently, the dad had hit the mom. Actually, he had lunged forward to hit her. Luckily for her, and for him, he had missed. But the damage done was just as much.

PHYSICAL ABUSE UNDERMINES AND NEGATES THE VERY GOALS IT AIMED TO ACCOMPLISH FROM THE OUTSET

The sun had retired for the day. A million light bulbs had taken its place. Little did they know they could never take its place, even if a hundred million lit up!

The kids were seated at the dinner table on time; all three of them like disciplined soldiers in their positions on the PT field, ready to begin their day. The reason behind the sudden disciplinary conscientiousness? It had to do with them not wanting to disturb their mom more than she already was.

The dad always sat at the head of the table; the mom, on the other edge of the table, bang opposite the dad. Samar and Samara always sat on the long side to the left of the dad. Robin was placed on the long-side of the table to the right of the dad, all by himself. Not because he was messy, or that he would topple over a glass of juice or water or whatever was placed in front of him into his sibling's plates, but because he was left-handed. He would bang into right-handed elbows.

Every placement was the same that night, except for one less plate-setting; the dad was eating out. He had left after dropping off the kids post the ice-cream charade; it was a given he wouldn't return anytime soon. Whenever he had an argument with the mom, he went out, and stayed out till the wee hours of the morning.

Howbeit, that evening, the air in the room appeared to be untroubled, unstirred. Unruffled. The mom had gotten dinner ready without rattling the pans. She laid dishes on the table without making them sound disgruntled. There were no resounding thud sounds. She wasn't even doing the walking-corpse trudge she had been doing earlier in the day. The edginess was more noticeable in the kids. I wasn't getting tossed around or tumbled out of Roo-mom's pouch much, that evening; Robin seemed sombre. Less sombre than Samar and Samara, but, definitely, sombre. I was glad he wasn't hopping around as usual, but I was slightly un-glad, too. Kids don't look pretty without the naughty skip in their stride; without the playful, sinless look that fools us into looking forward to their naive devilry. That night, the looks were different, directionless. The looks had questions they dared not lend words to, had emotions they dared not express, and agony they dared not reveal. That was not how we wanted our babies to be. We needed to set things straight. But sometimes, *straight* things need to be set right, like straight lips that have lost their upward curve. We wanted their smiles back; smiles that had wandered off and were last seen, dressed in black, standing over a grave—the grave of their mother's smile.

With a wink, a thumbs-up, and a nod, the three of us got into action: Snippy cartwheeled, I flapped and fluttered, and Rock rolled his way in, as we positioned ourselves behind a kid each, and waited for the call. *Rock, Paper, Scissors, shoot!*

They played until they could play no more. The smiles were back. Three of the four smiles stayed up till bedtime.

Once the kids were tucked in and off to sleep, the signal for our nightly discourse was hooted, and out we came. No sooner had we settled ourselves into the family lounge than Snippy unleashed her outrage, "What gives men the right, or the authority, to hit their wives? Who the hell do they think they are? And is that their way to resolve things? Do they realise they are worsening matters, not sorting them? Not to forget the adverse effect it has on the kids. Men like these are setting the wrong examples. Our kids didn't get to know what their dad did, not as yet, but, eventually they will. I don't want to think of how hurt and disgusted they'll feel when they do."

Over the years, in the many homes that had honoured us, we fortunately never had the mischance to come across domestic abuse. But we've heard of it often. We know how it ruins families; how the children go through psychological trauma because of it. Many of the boys, who witness the men of the family physically abuse the women, assume that violence is a more effective way to resolve conflicts. They are later, as adults, more likely to assault their female partners. Girls, who witness the aggression, become averse to getting married, altogether. They fear commitment; they fear all men will be the same.

Rock and I don't ever want such power, such authority. Besides, we want girls running after us, not away from us.

A dark reality, not as loud and conspicuous as physical abuse, but definitely murkier, was that the dad cared least for the one person with whom he shared his most precious and most intimate moments—his life partner. The one he chose to have his children with.

To think that the mom gave up many a dream to make that wife-beating man's house a home!

What did the dad think he could achieve by being physically

violent, sir? That he could get his way with force? What about love and respect? Can he get that, too, with muscle power?

Facts about Physical Abuse/ Emotional Abuse duly noted in the RPS Constitution:

Physical Abuse undermines and negates the very goals it aims to accomplish from the outset. Abusers use power to command respect. Command! Not gain by manifesting solicitude. Love and respect have to be earned, not gained by manipulation. That which is given by obligation by the victim is not respect. It is not respect; it is not deference. Forced respect is compliance; it is submission. It is fear. Respect, in the attempt to be gained thus by the abuser, gets lost in translation, while the scars of physical or emotional abuse run deep.

Grandfather clock strummed twice a few minutes after the dad came home that night. He hadn't crept in—the main door, their bedroom door, and that of their en-suite bathroom, were all made unwilling accomplices to the announcement. He wanted to make sure the mom perceived, loud and clear, the emotion that is hinged on banging doors.

As the new day began, all seemed quiet. I turned my free ear towards the bedroom door to catch any unusual sounds; an argument, if any. Gladly, there was none. In fact, it was too calm.

The dad must have gone out again. Maybe the mom has. I don't want to know. I shut my eyes and my ears, and snuggled deeper into the covers. That morning, like most mornings, Roo-mom's pouch was like the early hours of an April sun, oozing with sun-kissed soothing.

What if the mom has done something to herself? What if the dad has done something … to her? Oh god! I threw back the covers and scooted down as quietly as I could, leaving Robin still snuggled-in and fast asleep. When the dad had banged his way in at night, Robin was jolted out of his sleep. I had felt him pull his quilt up till right under his chin, pressing Roo-mom and me hard against his chest. It was a while before his grip had loosened, and his breathing resumed rhythm.

I let him sleep in, and headed for the kitchen. The dad was nowhere in sight. I plopped myself on the kitchen counter. Hands under chin, humming to herself, was Snippy. Bright-eyed and puckering, she was all geared up to fill me in. *I should've stayed tucked-in!*

School lunch already packed, was sitting on a counter. The mom, standing by the gas-stove, was busy tossing something from a pan to a pile on a plate; her gestures, meticulous, precise. Too precise, actually. When the back is flexed and the arms are moving quickly, mechanically, know that the person is on the warpath. I decided to steer clear, but I could smell pancakes. I looked at Snippy. She was glaring at me, her eyes clearly stating that I would not get my hands on any until she got out the juicy gossip she was bloating on. Within seconds of me watching, she ballooned up like a puffer fish. She slid closer to me, coquettish; vexing me with her brazen eyes. They were saying: *Ask*. If I didn't ask, I know for sure, she would burst into a million tiny Snippys.

A million sexy Snippys! A million Snippys to flirt with. Nice!

A million Snippys to be tyrannized and dominated by? No way!

Snippy took my lack of response for egotistical reservation. She puffed up some more.

A million Snippys? I immediately threw her the concerned look.

Didn't take her a quarter of a second to get cracking, "I was disturbed all night! I was *so* worried!"

And a whole lot inquisitive, too, I'm sure!

"I came scampering down the minute I heard the mom walking down the steps. *He* walked into the kitchen a few minutes later," Snippy said, leaning in, speaking softly, as though she feared being overheard. "She went still, all of a sudden. I could tell she was preparing to unload. Didn't take her too long … as sarcastic as she could get, she tells him: *Why do you bother to come home to sleep? Do that out too!* What do you make of that, hmm?"

Oh, boy! was all I could muster. Snippy's cocked eyebrow, already-full cheeks getting fuller, pressed me to show more interest, "And … what did he say?"

"Oh, he told her she was being stupid and suspicious as usual; to straighten her thought process, and only then, to bother talking to him. She retorted that she was least interested in patching up with him."

"Oh boy! And did you get to know the reason for the fight?"

Did they need a reason to fight, sir? Tolerance levels had dropped; respect for each other had been lost. Aren't these reasons enough to set ablaze just about anything? To then, sit back and watch as everything that the relationship stands for, razes to the ground?

One by one, the kids came filing into the kitchen. Samara had taken on the responsibility to make sure they got ready for school on time; she wanted to take some load off her mom. She had rushed about, gotten ready in a jiffy so she could get Robin ready on time.

Three kid-heads—a soft side-mohawk one, larger than a neatly pulled back pony-tail one; a curly black noodle-y one, smaller than the neatly pulled back pony-tail one; and the neatly pulled back pony-tail one—were very *un*child-like calm; very *un*child-like stable. But their eyes were edgy, wandering. Searching. *Where is dad? Have things been sorted? Is it all okay now?* The kids were diffidently searching the mom's eyes for a hint of an emotion, and doing a feeble job at masking their own eyes—a glass case of emotions. I could feel for the kids; their struggle, their uncertainty, their dis-ease at the entire scenario. The parents had a disagreement, and the kids were paying for the damages.

Samara, while being walked to the bus stop later, tugged at her mom's hand, "Mommy, you remember you have to come to our school, tomorrow?" The next day was the last day of school before the summer-holidays started. It was also the School Annual Sports day. All parents had been requested to attend.

"Yes, of course! I'll definitely be there."

Before hopping onto the bus, Samara turned around and said, "Mommy, please remind Daddy, too." *Now, Mommy will* have *to talk to Daddy.*

The mom gave her an assuring nod. As the bus door closed, she turned, with the phone to her ear.

Nice job, girl! Samara patted herself. She even caught the glimpse of a smile on her mom's face.

The call had ended but the mom's smile still lingered on. She always found the office secretary pleasant to talk to, but at the moment, she was mighty pleased with herself. She had passed on the task to remind the dad for the school event to the secretary.

Come dinner, the dad was still not home.

"Mommy, will Daddy be joining us?" Confident Samara of the morning had shrunk to a thumbnail sized Samara; her chutzpah was taking cover behind her right ear. It was nudging her from there; it didn't want to stay in hiding, it wanted to make its presence known, which it could, if her dad would turn up at school. More so, if the parents patched up.

"He should be home soon. So, how was school today?" the mom said, wheeling the conversation in another direction, getting the kids huffing and puffing about their homework load; cribbing about their teachers.

"But, Mommy," Samara said, "I will miss Ms Atwood. I love her class. Even my friends love her class the most. She always tells us such splendid stories and teaches us manners and eti… etiquettes through her stories."

"Oh wow, sweetie. That's a new word for you."

Samara's lips widened, giving a cinemascopic view of her teeth. Her shoulders broadened. Sitting upright, she propelled her head from the mom to Samar to Robin; from Robin to Samar to the mom, like a periscope of a submarine, observing objects of interest within its range. With added crispness in her tone, she said, "Ms. Atwood told us it's a smart word for manners and she taught us how to remember it. She told us to think of a cat in the attic: 'attic' 'cat'. Get it?" Samara propelled her periscope again, waiting for laurels from her audience. Robin, too virginal for that kind of banter, kept munching on his rare treat of fries. Samar, with eyes fixated on the screen of his phone, looked indifferent. The Whistler's Mother, in the painting hanging on the dining room wall, didn't bat her only visible eyelid, either.

Samara's right eyebrow arched, lifting to a *just-as-well* stance. With a sharp turn of her head as though the periscope had detected its target, she looked at her mom and continued, crisper than before, "Anyway, the story Ms Atwood told us today was very nice, about a lion called Christian," her tone on the word 'lion' two notches higher than was required. She succeeded in getting what she wanted. Robin had let go of his fork. Resting his chin between his hands, elbows balanced on the table, he looked at her, eagerly, willing her to go on. Samar, although feigning to be too lost in a game, had on the sly, moored his ears in her direction. Samara could tell.

I was balancing myself on the rim of a bowl filled with French fries, trying every which way to prevent Robin from eating too many. Their mom had served French fries only as an appeasement for the displaced cheer and liveliness. Else, fried foods were always fighting a lost battle inside that household. Snippy was doing her bit by chopping the fries into many tiny pieces in Samara's plate, and in Samar's, hoodwinking them into believing that their plates were full of fries. Rock was lying on his back on the table, close to Samar, with one leg folded, the other crossed over; one arm behind his head, and the other dunking into the bowl of fries, every now and then. The guy could've been on the beach, for all you know!

"So, Christian was a baby lion, a cub," Samara continued. "He was on sale at Harrods. Two guys bought him and took him home. They looked after him like a baby, giving him milk and …"

"Weren't they scared?" Robin butt in. "Lions drink milk?"

"I guess they have milk when they are babies. Anyway…," Samara was itching to carry on but …

"Can we get a lion cub too, Mommy?" pleaded Robin.

"I don't think that's possible, my love."

"But why not? We can give it milk."

"Yeah, and he'd feed the lion his glass of milk every morning without letting the mom know. Clever kid!" said Rock, snapping out of his mental slumber. Rock needed a filter in his mouth. For once, I was glad the mom and the kids couldn't hear his mindless banter.

There are times though, sir, when the three of us wish kids, and adults too, could hear us. They don't even know we really exist. They think we're just playthings of some imaginary world they can pull out whenever they want, to pass their time with. Someday, maybe. Until then, we have our ways of getting our word across to them.

"Honey, it's not easy keeping a lion at home. Lions are strong and dangerous. They live in the wild, that's where their natural home is. If we pull them away from their home, they will get upset and might even try to attack us."

"But we see them on the TV, in the circuth, they do whatever that man thays."

"Honey, those men keep big sticks with them to ward off the lions and also hit them sometimes to make them obey. Would you want to keep a lion and then have to hit it?"

Head lowered, Robin whimpered out a dragged, "No."

"Soooo, they loved him and looked after him like a baby," Samara jumped in to resume her story.

"You've already said that," Samar butt in.

"I thought you weren't listening," Samara said, hooking two fingers, doing air quotes on the word 'listening'; a new mannerism she had picked from school. "Anyway, I'm telling the story to Mommy and Robin. Mommy, can you tell Samar, the Bummer, not to butt in?"

"I dare you to call me Bummer again," Samar hit back. His eyes, a wicked tease.

"Watch your words, Samara," the mom corrected her. She gave Samar the w*atch yourself* look.

Samara glared at Samar. His smirk troubled her, got her feeling angry, disgusted even, but it didn't dissuade her. She continued, albeit, a tone lower, "So, they kept him for nine months but after that they set him free in the wilderness of Africa because he had become too big to handle, and all their neighbors were getting scared." Robin's eyes widened more, but he dared not speak; Samara was already glaring at him, daring him. "Then, one year later, they went to Africa to find him. They went to the same place they had left him and called out his name, Christian … Christian! And then … they saw a big lion running towards them, and he jumped at them." She paused. She heard Robin gasp. She had been waiting for him to gasp. With heightened enthusiasm, she continued, "They were scared but he wasn't hurting them, he was hugging and kissing them."

Robin's full-moon eyeballs waned down to softened crescents. His mouth, left wide open, exposed fragmented glimpses of teeth barbarically entangled between tiny metallic chip-like pieces and zigzagged florescent green and orange elastic bands. One would think his teeth were convicts who often staged a jail-break and needed to be kept tied down.

"Ms Atwood told us this story to tell us that a lion, who is strong and fearless, if nurtured with love can be tuned to express love, then why can humans not do so? Nurture with love, leaving no scope for hatred. She also told us to be the first to show our love, that way we'll be the bigger and the better person." She looked at Samar to inspect the onslaught the daggers she darted in his direction had done. Pleased, she turned her attention to the massacred goods on her plate.

SNIPPY GETS TO THE HEAD

"Guys! Guys, do I have news for you!" Snippy came running to where Rock and I were. My eyes shifted from the book I was reading, to her face. Juicy tidbits of tittle-tattle were drooling down the sides of her mouth. "Well, what is it?" I prepared myself. Her gossip was always garbed up with psychedelic drama.

"Ahem! … Ahem!" She looked at Rock, waiting for him to show interest. But Rock was too busy poking a beetle with a toothpick. The beetle was lying on its back, its legs cropped to its chest. It didn't seem to mind what Rock was doing to it. It would have, had it not been stone dead.

"Well?" I asked again.

"Well!" she huffed, shifting her eyes on me. "The mom wishes she could be nine again."

"What? You're not making any sense, Snipps." I was running out of patience. *She's late for our discourse and now she's being a drama-queen, huffing and puffing with those chapped lips of hers.*

"Don't you have anything better to do than hang around the mom once you get off duty?" Rock seemed bored. "Get a life!"

There was a disgusted humph, a stiff flick of the head, and the chapped lips started moving again. "I did what you guys could get *nowhere* near doing. *I* got in; I made my way into the mom's *head*."

Rock and I yanked our heads up in a flash. *THIS. IS. NEWS!*

Needless to say, Snippy had our undivided attention; raised eyebrows, et al.

"I made it into her head and heard her say that … that she wishes to be nine again. She looked so starry-eyed and dreamy, so very wishful, one would think she sensed our existence. It was as though she wanted us to hear her and, with the snap of our fingers, make her wish come true. What she doesn't know is that we *can* hear her. We *can* make Magic happen for her. We're finally in. So, what d'ya make of that, huh? I got to hear everything from there-on, every thought, and every desire. Up until she started to snore, that is. And man, she can snore! I scooted the minute her Harley-Davidson took off."

It was a humungous breakthrough for us. Making it into the mom's head, after years of wait and struggle, was huge.

Into the mom's head, you ask, sir? *Why*, you ask? Well, haven't you figured it out yet? You weren't paying attention to me again, were you? See? I told you, you do that a lot, *sir*!

Didn't you wonder how I know so much about you? Things even you don't know about yourself? Well? Didn't you get it? That I am your inner voice?

I, Papier, along with my friends, Rock and Snippy, are *the* voices that you hear in your head. You know which voices I'm talking about, right? There's something you're interested in, something you want for yourself; a thing your heart is telling you to go for, but your mind is like: *Don't. Even. Think. About. It. It's totally off-limits!* But you still want it. You give your heart the go-ahead to overrule your mind. But there's a nagging feeling that tries to hold you back, a nagging voice.

That voice, that's us.

Yeah, we do get to be quite nagging at times. Yeah, like a wife (if this is the analogy that pleases you). And that's probably why you ignore us, all the time. Well, what can I say, we have to nag. Because you do not listen to us! You do not listen to your inner voice!

We are the voices that nudge you, that prod you; that give warning signals when something doesn't seem right. We are the ones that give you 'signs' left, right and centre to let you know he/she is the one for you. The bright ideas in your head? We are the reasons for those too. It's us that make you look brilliant. And you thought it's all you. Huh!

We are the driving force that gets you to do crazy, whacky stuff you wouldn't dream of doing. And all those things you could *only* dream of doing.

Do you remember the time when you were so disoriented because you missed your train for an important meeting, one day? Because of a silly goof-up? You looked up and you cursed, and cursed. Do you remember offering endless prayers of gratitude later on in the day? You remember why, sir? Let me jog your memory. It was because the train you were to be on, had derailed. All those on-board had died. We are that *silly* goof-up.

You wouldn't have known that the green fuzz you cross in a jiffy every day is grass, had we not given you a flat tire. You would not have figured that the fresh nip in the air, at a certain patch you zip by every day, is because of a river, had we not sent a black and white car with a cherry top, to slow you down. All of God's beauty, invisible to the untrained eye, if it wasn't for us. And yet, you doubt our credibility.

You keep chucking us out of your lives. It is rather demeaning, getting chucked out. And yet, we keep trying to weigh in.

Your inner voice is there for *you,* at all hours of the day. It's your subconscious self. It's the best friend you can ever have. Committed, non-judgmental. Totally unbiased. (Well, that goes without saying, it's in *your* head. It can't side with the other party even if it wants to.) Believe in it. Believe in us.

By acknowledging her desire to be nine again, the mom would be nothing short of a schizo or a hallucinator. But, in our world, she is a dreamer; someone who has held on to hope, and to her muses. She could fly on a magical carpet to visit Alladin in Agrabah, or she could make her world wonderful with colours and candies and butterflies. She could climb into a time-machine and go back to her childhood days, to her world of fairies and elves and kissing frogs.

But, in the true essence of things, we know that a 'dreamer' is just someone who is finding an escape from a world they find overwhelming; someone who is reaching out, subconsciously, to a world that feels pleasant and secure. Bogged down, timeworn, less revered, they are just someone in need of re-assurance.

Absurd that we are your inner voices? I told you, we existed much before we evolved into the Rock, Paper, and Scissors characters. The hand game is just a guise we took on, because more often than not, we are stranded outside minds; the blocked minds keep chucking us out. At times as those, the hand game assists in decision-making that would have otherwise been done by us. It is, hence, that we three are still here even after a zillion years, stuck in the same ole' job, adapting to varied forms as per the place and situation, working our Magic on whomsoever we can. But in essence, our inner sanctum, our work space is inside people's minds. We are your inner voices; your intuition, your archangels.

Finding it hard to accept, sir? Tell you what, take a look around you. Do you spot any vibrant, happy-go-lucky souls standing tall in a crowd, charming their way into everyone's hearts? See their radiance? Their sunshine? See the halo hanging above? Those souls are our fine works of art—the ones that have their doors open to us.

Let me tell you about one such soul, one amongst many of our most revered, Jonas. Jonas Rich.

Recently widowed, 63-year-old Jonas had been quite a sport all his life; traveling, golf, dance classes, and the works. But after his wife, things were not the same for him; he willingly relinquished the fervour within him.

One night, right after one of his routine calls with his daughter, he couldn't stop giggling to himself. His daughter and he had been reminiscing on older times, on better times. He sat up in bed, pillow propped up, arms crossed behind his head—he wanted a wide-angle view of those happy thoughts of his. *What I'd give to have those days back!*

That, there, was our cue to get into his head; we jumped right in. It was child's play after that. We got him venturing out more, catching up with friends. One time too many, we had him try out dance moves with the kids on his street as he passed by; even got him to throw in a couple of his own moves that he'd picked from his dance classes. We got him playing cute with his seventy-year-old widowed neighbour who would often eye him from her window, something that may have gone unnoticed by him till some time back; he wasn't the young Jonas anymore. But it was not something we let slip.

His neighbour, Mrs Sigel—Giggles for us, because she giggles like a little girl—had been watching how Jonas had slowed down; how he was letting go. She saw herself in him. She is an absolute darling but she, too, had actively disengaged from life after her husband had passed, refraining from being her normal beaming and effervescent self. It troubled us to see a person so full of beans while away her life in such a nondescript manner.

One thing she really missed doing was crib to her husband about a certain Mrs Whitmore who would call, at odd hours of the day, to crib about odd things that were happening on their street at odd hours of the day. Her husband had always listened quietly, nodding the occasional nod, which suited her perfectly. But then he was gone. Her stock was piling up. Ever since his wife had passed, Jonas missed having someone to make morning bed-tea for. We got the two hitched. Now, Giggles loves getting tea in bed. Jonas would forget to nod when she would rattle on and on about Mrs Whitmore, but it didn't take him long to get the hang of it.

Getting them together worked like a breeze, for them and for their respective families. The bothersome thing, though, was keeping them from whispers of malicious naysayers who sneered at their coupling.

Yes, there are people in this world who ridicule such coupling, sir. I fail to capture the finer nuances of their rationale. Don't they see it's not about physical attraction anymore? It's companionship one needs at this age; someone to talk to, more than anything else. Someone who can identify with the dense void of space looming large over them, the space between the longing for the vibrant youth that passed them by too fast, and the wariness of the slow ride to come. Someone to commiserate the matter of *when*. Who better to understand that, than two souls who are already facing the stench of the unknown?

Sadly, dysfunctional social stigmas bad-mouth them, intimidate them, taking away their chance to live a happier, and hence, a healthier and a longer life. And the naysayers call *them* senile!

A hard-hitting fact:

Loneliness is slow poison for the mind. Slow but sure, it destabilizes the assured attributes of mental attitude.

Loneliness is like an unannounced guest. It barges in even if you stand in its way at the door. *I thought some company would do you good.* It dumps itself on you, chews on your brains, hogs your productive time, makes you sluggish and inept; all the while empowering you with negativity. Negativity leads to grumpiness. Grumpiness turns the mind to gunk, making ground for disease. Many a disease is generated in the mind. If the mind is healthy, the body is healthy. If the mind is troubled, physical health takes a hit.

After losing his zest for life Jonas started walking with a hunch; his shoulders, as though left out in a storm overnight, exposed, vulnerable; willing to rot. Cynical resignation weighing down his body, his body weighing down on a walking stick. Gunk.

Giggles wasn't going to watch him rot that way. She grabbed the sucking tentacles of the gunk and peeled them off his back, one by one, before they could near-paralyze his muscles. In no time, she had him standing tall and straight. Now, the two pass their evenings dancing, without the walking stick, to sweet melodies of the '50s and the '60s, reminiscing classic movies of their favourites: Clark Gable, Cary Grant and Gregory Peck for her; Audrey Hepburn, Elizabeth Taylor and Sophia Loren for him.

There is a colossal difference in how Jonas and Giggles carry on with their lives since they've handed themselves over to us. Their days don't, anymore, wither away like autumn leaves; colourless, lifeless, worsted under uncharted feet. Resurrected, every day now for them, is the page of a vivid book written, word by word, to be compiled into a great classic. Every day, now, is a symphonic sound of newfound harmony. And their laughter—oh, their laughter! What a pleasant sight it is to watch, as their laughter pulls out the weariness in their eyes for a quick waltz, and with an over-sway, flings it away.

Do we really exist? (I know this question has been on your mind. Of course, I know. I know everything about you, which should be proof enough of our existence.)

Now, don't go asking me for proof, sir. Can you prove how, when and where the Universe came into existence? Some say God made the Universe from nothing. Some believe in The Big Bang Theory, that the Universe exploded out of nothing. No one has been able to validate any of these theories. Maybe the Universe is God's own creation, his artistry; making everything out of nothing. Visible appearing from the invisible. As is the case with us, everything out of nothing. We may still be invisible but we are, nonetheless, substantially present all around you, at all times. No need to go in search of magic lamps to rub and hope for a genie to pop out, no restrictions of only three wishes. We're your twenty-four by seven genies, in your heads, ready to roll out wish after wish after wish. That is, if you so wish us to.

Getting into kids' minds is no biggie. They don't have jammers blocking their minds, nor any pass-through codes. Sacrosanct, their minds are shrines, sans any hang-ups or inhibitions, bias or judgments. Ergo, kids do not make a big deal about every single thing; they do not hold on to things that do not matter; they do not set out to win every battle. *They do not let the little things bog them down. And, they do not go on ego trips.* That is until they mature. Then on, the alchemy of their young-ness gets lost in translation, in the rush to cross over to the supposedly wiser side. Maturity impregnates their minds, getting their beautiful pristine thoughts to come of age even before they can have a mindset of their own. Premature and underdeveloped, imperfect and unripe, it thrives unabashedly in its vainglory, overrunning and ravaging the innocence in those young souls, doing more harm than good. Once that happens, it gets difficult for us to get in.

We've been facing this problem with Samar as well. In his struggle to 'fit in' he keeps trying to shut us out. Most of the teens are doing that. It's the transitional age they're at, it confuses them. As long as they have not let go of the cognizance of their childhood, and the appetite for it, there is still hope for us.

There comes a time when kids are sending SOS signals without knowing it themselves. When we moved out of the Tysons' those many years back (kicked out, to be more precise), Samara was going through a very distressful phase in her life. She wasn't in her happy place. Her parents were fighting all the time; she feared they would get divorced; she feared having to choose sides. She didn't want to choose sides. She wanted her mom, and she wanted her dad. She would stay up till late at night, praying, hoping. It was during one of those moments, when she was wiping the last tear of the night; her head, raised in prayer, expectant, that we had jumped in.

After all, where there is hope, there is us. And where we are, there is more than just hope.

We need to bring every single soul alive from within, once again. We have to, no matter what. It's not just because we want to see them happy and spirited, and want them to live life to the fullest. Or, that we want the world to be one big happy place … that we definitely do. But it's more so because of Azraella.

THE YIN TO THE YANG OF GOOD

A*zraella.* Just taking her name gives me the jitters.

Azraella is clearly not one of us. She's the Yin to the Yang of good. She likes the easy life: *If you can't fix it, finish it.* We don't work that way, we fix the problem even if it's a tough challenge for us. Those challenging cases are the ones Azraella is always keeping an eye out for. The tougher they are for us, the easier for her. She knows which hearts we do not exist in, or are having a tough time getting into. She smoothly goes in for the kill, taking souls away, of adults, of young adults, and at times, of children too. Says she's relieving them of their unhappiness; they're aching and that is the only way she can make their ache go away. The thing is, sir, she doesn't have a heart.

I wish we could eradicate Azraella entirely, but we can't do it on our own. You could've helped in a big way. If I may be candid enough to say so, sir, you would've been helping yourself more than us. It is, after all, your life that's on the line.

A Hard-hitting fact:

The good souls go early.

God has His reasons. He can't watch bad things happen to the good souls. He values them more.

Some good souls are like candles, sir. They burn faster when the air around them is stirred; when they are faced with some untoward mishap; shattering their belief in niceness. They lack the hardiness and bulldog spirit of the rest. Once they lose hope, their hearts become sad, and they lose the will to carry on. They lie there, served on a silver platter, for Azraella to come and get them.

It doesn't happen overnight. It's not as though the minute they are sad she's rubbing her hands in eager anticipation, and comes scooting down. No. Millions of people lose hope every single day. She can only take them away, one by one. But once you're on that list, know that she will be coming for you.

I can well imagine the look on your face right now, sir. Yes, we do Magic and stuff. Yes, we do make miracles happen. Yes, we can get names off death-lists. Remember the Jamie Ogg incident, the newborn we brought back to life even after he was pronounced dead for over two hours? We do that kind of Magic, every so often. Yet, not as often as we would like to. The thing is that it's no easy task. It's a whole process we have to go through, a whole lineage of authoritarians we have to consult with.

Let's consider a hypothetic scenario where a Private of the Army has to, first, go through a Corporal and then a Sergeant, to send an appeal to the General of the Army. From there, he has to win his way through a Major, then a Lieutenant and then a Colonel before, finally, approaching a Brigadier to put forth his appeal to the General of the Army. *Phew!*

That is so like what we have to do to reclaim a soul. We have a Hierarchy of seven levels, starting at the bottom-most level with the Principalities, with whom we, first, have to confer if the concerned soul stands the test of deserving-ness and worthiness. We then, have to approach all the angels next-in-line: each one of the Dominations, and the Virtues and the Powers, and get the seal of approval from each one of them. It doesn't end there. We then, have to put an appeal to the highest hierarchy: the Seraphim, the Cherubim and the Thrones, to lay forth our earnest plea in the sight of God.

Imagine, getting on the lift of the Empire State Building and having to stop on every one of the hundred and two floors, floor by floor, before making it to the top. That's much like what we have to go through every time we consider reclaiming a life that Azraella has on her list.

What did you think? A snap of our fingers, and poof!—Magic happens? Or, one tap of our wand over evil, and evil vanishes? A lot of ink was spilled in forming strategies for the work we do. I've barely scratched the surface here. There's so much more to our world. It's a tough job we do. Unappreciated, unacknowledged, we still do it.

So, I reiterate, it's not easy getting you off lists. Besides, we don't want to get on the wrong side of Azraella. Nope, not happening! Never know what she could resort to; she resents interference in her work. The best would be for you to not get on that list, in the first place.

Before today, I would have told you not to stress it out; we've got your back. We'll do the dirty work, the elbow grease, so there's no chance of you getting on Azraella's list. We'll not let misshapen thoughts trouble you and get you feeling melancholy—no lamb, thereby no slaughter house, thereby no Azraella.

But not anymore! I am done with you.

An Oops! Moment:

I've strayed from my story again. It seems I have a habit of digressing. Here too, you are to blame.

Yes, you. Because I feel the need to crack down on you, every once in a while.

Let's get back to my tale-telling for now. So, where were we? Yes, Snippy having our undivided attention for getting into the mom's head. Right!

"Here, see for yourself, all the jibber-jabber that went on in the mom's head, right from the moment I jumped in." Snippy swiped her arm left to right, to display a three-dimensional virtual screen in front of us. A fuzzy image of a female figure came into view. She was standing statue-like in a bathroom with one hand raised to her left cheek; a grimy cotton swab pinched between her thumb and two fingers. Within seconds the image got less fuzzy. We got a clearer view of the mom, the Rais mom, Mira.

We saw Mira look closely at the woman facing her; staring with displeasure at the dark patches on her face—a few on the left cheek, a speck on the right one—that still needed attention. A solitaire, sitting prettily in her jugular notch, had caught Mira's eye. It was gifted to the woman by her husband. She tended to lose it, every now and then, when she would become carefree. But it would find its way back to her, every time; its route, having been frequently travelled, carved deep; making it impossible for it to get lost for too long a time. This time, too, it had started its route from her right eye and had come streaming down the steep descent. As it slid to the slope that lay between her chin and her neck, it met with the other one that had streamed down her left eye. The two merged into one, as always; their molecules entwined. When the woman looked up to question the author of her story about what more He had in store for her, the unified jewel slid further down, all the way to the dent of her neck and lodged itself there, safe and secure. Her gift, for the years she had put into her marriage.

By instinct, Mira touched her neck. Her jewel was still there. Moist. Tender to her touch. She felt a sudden upsurge of emotion towards the woman, an expansive burst that triggered feelings of sorrow for her; feelings of angst. Pain for her, for possessing such a jewel too.

We saw her direct the woman's hand with hers, to the blotched patches. They seemed to have increased, darkened further.

'I wish I could be nine again!' she was telling the woman, in the need to lighten her up.

'Have you gone bonkers?'

But Mira barely heard her; she was captivated by the un-tampered, virgin world her little kids live in. 'The sky in their world is blue, you know. Pink too. Or any color they fancy,' she rattled on. 'Purity, there, is still white. And God … He just loves it there.' She had lived there some years too; a lifetime ago. Now, she wanted back in.

We watched as her brows drew closer. 'Tell me, how on earth do I instill the virtue of pure, unconditional love in my kids when they grow up? To feel only love, to nurture with love? How do I stop their love from getting adulterated by hatred? By skepticism? And arrogance? How do I keep them from turning into another me? Or their dad?'

I'm sure Mira knows images in mirrors don't reply on their own; they need our help. But that didn't stop her from putting forth her concerns. She was beginning to confide in her re-found friend. She had lost her a long time ago, but now, she was retracing her steps. We found her opening up to her with as much ease, as she used to when they were close; when there was no one but her, to turn to for help; when she didn't doubt her inner voice. *Why the hell did I stop talking to myself? This is where I get the best advice!*

We watched Mira scrape the last few traces of turbulence from her flesh-and-blood face. She gave herself one last look before dropping the swab into the bin, and finish her cleansing regime with a final wash of warm water. She stepped into her room and stood by the bay-window, her go-to spot, which, on any normal day, is waiting for her with a hot mug of cappuccino or tea (depending on the time of the day) in one hand and warm, loving quietude in the other. With one knee Mira leaned over the daybed to look out the window, into the peace-coloured blackness. *Why can't I be a kid again?*

What did she want the Universe to tell her? That it's normal to feel that way? Or that she was going berserk? Or … that the butterflies in her chest set off by her naive question, are preliminary signs of awakening Magic? The very Magic she was a fool to stop believing in.

'I know I'm wrong at times,' she went on to confide, as she cosied up in bed and pulled out her night-cream from the side drawer. 'I know my anger crosses boundaries at times, but he pushes me to the brink and I … I lose control. I'm only human. And then, to rattle me more, he disconnects himself from me. It doesn't friggin' bother him if we don't talk for days.' Her cream-laden hands work deep into her face, massaging, kneading the re-energized turbulence, up and outward, pushing it out through her ears. 'Ugh, I hate that about him. I *hate* him. Ugghhh! I wish I could hate him. Ouch! Why did I bang my hand on the table?'

"He's only pushing her further away," Snippy grabbed the pause Mira took to throw in her two bits.

"But God, she's so whiny. She needs major fixing up. These guys really know how to complicate things," Rock said. "They want things to change for the better but are too stuck-up to talk it out and find a resolve. That's so friggin' messed up."

We heard Mira start to blabber again, 'I've forgotten how to laugh 'coz of him. We had such good times together, so many good times. Spain—was it two years back? Or was it three? That trip was so good, we couldn't keep our hands off each other. Robin was conceived there. Robin is now ... What? It's been six years since Spain? Six years? I'll be damned!' She closed her eyes and sighed. 'It was so beautiful between us.' She yanked open her eyes, 'When did talk about us move from *is* to *was*?'

'Oh, I'm so glad we moved when we did—new city, new house, new environment—a fabulous chance to leave behind things we didn't want to carry along, and to make corrective changes in things we couldn't leave behind; a rebooting of sorts, away from all the bric-a-brac and shenanigans of that place. It was getting to me. You're not who you really are, there. There, we had no time for ourselves, or for the family. No time to slow down and think of what was right or what was wrong. A pretentious life—living for others, dressing-up for others, clinking glasses night after night, wanting to be there, everywhere. Oh, I'm so, so glad we moved out of Dilliwood. Crazy rat-race, trying to get ahead of one another, and still not winning the damn race we were obliged to run. If we didn't take part, we were looked down on—misfits. Ugh! It was either that or become prisoners of a lifestyle we had created around ourselves. Ah, forget it, else I'll keep brooding. Alrighty, my dress is all set for the morning. Will these shoes be fine? Maybe I should go in for a flat pair for the school grounds. The pearl earrings and single string for the neck should be fine. Now, where's my book?'

We watched her pick up her book, switch on the bedside lamp and turn to the bookmarked page: *Every relationship has its tense moments, its ups and downs. C'est la vie! But absurdity is when we let the misunderstandings get to a point where we are willing to let go of the relationship due to skin-deep reasoning. Often enough, we become nonchalant and move away emotionally; make believe that the person does not matter to us, anymore. That's so unfortunate! We can make it work if we really want to, but we let arrogance come in the way. All that matters, at the time, is to prove ourselves right, so we let ego creep in and help us win the battle; which, in actuality, is not a win … but the biggest screw-up of our lifetime.*

'Hmm, has this book been reading *me*?' She looked at the cover of the book. 'Maybe I'll mail this author tomorrow.' She shut the book; holding it close to her chest, eyes closed, head on the headboard, she smiled. Within seconds her Harley vroomed off.

"I had bookmarked that page, deliberately. Clever, right?" Snippy flipped her arm; the virtual screen went out of view. She then, pulled up virtual collars—she was fishing for accolades again. "Well, now that we're in, thanks to me," she said, her words dragged, "we'll be able to fix her. Should be as easy as falling off a log, what say?" She sounded pissed off with our lack of response. "Oh, I'm certain I'll come up with a great strategy. Only a woman can really understand another woman perfectly."

Getting stoked by that provocation would be the death of us. I suddenly felt the sting of a cuticle threatening to poison me. Rock remembered a stunt he pulls off whenever he feels threatened—one that gives us the creeps, but gives him absolute thrills—seven sneezes in a row.

Is it true, Mr Umana, that six to seven sneezes in a row give the sensation of a mild orgasm? I read somewhere that sneezing produces endorphins, the feel-good chemicals. Just like orgasms. Although, the amount produced by a sneeze is far less than that of an orgasm. Rock rocked mildly, but I'm sure he was faking it.

DAY OF REDEMPTION

Bang!—the starting gun sounded. All those poised for the run, shot off; adrenalin fueling their zest, and shouts in the backdrop—*Dad, you can do it … Dad, hurry up, hurry up*—cheering them on. Many a fathers participated in the 300-metre race. Years of work-out were being put to test on the field that day; each dad pushing his limits to get ahead of the other. Some even risking getting disqualified by not watching their errant elbows that swung further back than needed.

Samar, Samara and Robin were sure their dad would come in first. He was almost there, lagging by only one. They rushed to the finish line where he was being cheered with congratulatory hugs. Teachers and other kids' moms were virtually all over him. He was beaming, although finally coming in third. The dad was still handsome, could still set many hearts aflutter.

Samar's look brought him down to ground zero.

"Hey, it's cool! There can be only one winner, right?" the dad said in consolation.

"Right dad, just like only one person can come first in class," Samar hit back; a comeback that was sure to keep the dad off Samar's academic record for a good time to come.

Samara was heartbroken. Once she was done with sulking, she moved on to strategizing, "Daddy, we need to get you into better shape for next year. You need to start jogging and working out. You have to … just have to win next year."

The dads' race was the last event of the annual day, after which they settled down to a hearty lunch of burgers and milkshakes. They crowned it with chocolate waffles topped by exotically colored sprinkles.

Right after, the dad left on the pretext of having work at the office. He had come straight from work. Mira had come from home, picking Robin from day-care, on the way. The dad had called Mira before leaving for the school, to ask if he should pick her up. She hadn't answered, or called back.

She didn't because she couldn't. Rust had eaten up important elements within her. Rust, formed by the dirty work-play of oxygen (in her blood) and water (the water content in her brain that helped brain cells to communicate with each other) reacting with the iron-clad stance she adopted often, had corroded the electrons that were responsible for giving her a sound judgment.

An entire revamping of Mira was not going to be easy, we knew that, but for things to get rectified, we needed to find a way to get into the dad's mind as well. So, with the way things stood at the moment, he had come to the school on his own.

We missed the kids' school event. We got a full replay of the events of the day from Mira when we were in her head again, later in the evening.

There was somewhere more important we had to be that morning. It was to be a day of redemption for us.

It was after 10pm that the dad finally made it back home. Sloshed, zonked, and trying hard not to look it.

Samar, Samara, and Robin were sprawled all over the place.

Samar, on his tummy, forearms propping him up, remote in both hands, continued making *bam-bam* sounds while playing the Dragon Quest Heroes -2; totally unperturbed by the loud bang of the main door.

Samara had knocked together an ambience of her own. Brilliantly-coloured books, in two stacks of four each, were piled very neatly in front of her. To her left was her I-pad displaying a spectrum of psychedelic colors moving in waves from left to right, pumping equally psychedelic sound-waves into her ears through the too-big-for-her florescent pink headphones. On her lap was a mayonnaise and peach donut-shaped pouch out of which she was choosing nail paint befitting her mood. She was too engrossed to say more than a quick 'Hi' to her dad.

They were getting used to not having him around much.

It was just Robin who ran up to him. He wasn't one from the 'mature' clan. Yet. Besides, he needed someone to applaud his colouring, which no one had offered to glance at. We should've, but we weren't in the best of moods. Our day hadn't gone as expected.

***

Standing outside the structure that was once home to us, we were nostalgic. Benumbed and paralyzed. We had gone to make amends. We were on the verge of turning back just about a million times but we managed to stand our ground. Our apologies to the Tysons had been long overdue.

There used to be three ivory-colored baskets, about a foot-long each, hanging on the outer side of the gate, with overflowing kaleidoscopes of blooms, greeting anyone who came their way with illuminated smiles. That day, we were greeted with forlorn looks from wormy clutters; some dirt-brown, some deep grey.

The fencing around the lawn was paler than before too. *Where are the crimson and blush, orange and burgundy vines that had adorned the façade of the house? The ones that gave the house a perennial plush complexion? The vines that had thrived, not on water and soil, but on the love that seeped through the walls from within.* All we could see were webs of withered twines—all brown, no blush. I didn't want to know the emotion they were feeding on. I felt unsettled. I could sense a similar unease in Rock and Snippy. We walked through the gate, one by one, each, urging the other one on. Given the situation and a preceding bad reputation, we thought we would try to sneak in through the back door and assess the situation. But all side and back entries had been bolted shut. We had to make a front door announcement.

I slowed down, willing one of the other two to ring the bell. I saw Rock emulating me, so it was on to Snippy to do the honors. She dilly-dallied for a bit, glowered at us, huffed, then glowered some more, till she realized her huffing and glowering maneuvers were ricocheting off us like bullets bouncing off a bullet-proof jacket.

"Seriously? You guys are pathetic!" She huffed one last time and turned to face the door. She heaved, walked up the two-step porch, and rang the bell. She stepped back almost instantly, "Shoot, there's no moving back now!" She was a bundle of nerves. Rock and I, a short distance away, were buzzing like exposed, overloaded, high-voltage cables.

We waited, and waited, but no one came. At long last, it became clear that Pete and Lara didn't want anything to do with us anymore. They had shut their minds and their hearts to us, forever. What were we expecting anyway? That they'd forgive us? That they'd hug us and beg us to move back in?

We stood there for a few moments longer, just stood there—three heads looking like three bowler hats hanging limp on a coat-hanger—not ready to believe, not ready to accept that the Tysons didn't want to meet us. Could we really blame them? They had been compelled to forgo their youth because of us. We had stuffed Pete's naiveté into a sack, tied it up with rocks and slung it into the depths of a lake. We hadn't spared Lara, either. Her innocence had been lured into a dark, dilapidated house, and left there all alone. Stranded.

As we turned to make our way out of their lawn, Snippy caught sight of the neighbour's daughter, Tiffany, peeping out the window from the first floor of her house. She had her doors wide open. We slipped right in.

Was she a world of information!

Apparently, Mr Tyson had gotten into some raunchy business under the wrong influence of an acquaintance, who had recorded every move. Soon, blackmailing and extortion ensued. Threats got murkier and greedier. Ashamed, drained, embracing a meltdown, Mr Tyson decided to put an end to his life, once and for all. He got a gun and was waiting to muster the balls, but Pete beat him to it. Mrs Tyson, although relieved her husband was alive, never really forgave him for getting a gun home, or for monkeying around.

What about Pete? Where is he now? And Lara?

Pete was sent off to Michael School in North London—a newly set up organization believed to be the most disciplined one in Britain. Lara, after months of home tutoring, eventually started regular school. Apart from her painting and Casio practice, and an occasional outing with her mom or a cousin, she keeps to herself. Tiffany misses going for a soda or to the movies with Lara, but she knows it's only in her best interest that her mom doesn't let her.

Standing there, outside the Tyson's, facing the stench of truth, we came to the realisation that was too brutal for us to embrace: *We don't deserve the forgiveness we came seeking.* With it came the realisation that self-condemnation was a sack of stones that would have to be carried on our shoulders, day in, day out, for life. No wizard would fly down and zap off that load. For once, we—Rock, Papier and Snippy—could not take the load off each other. We couldn't tell each other, *'It was done on a whim, in a silly moment. It's okay'.* Because it wasn't okay—duties had been overlooked, an error was committed. One that was inexcusable. One that would haunt us for life.

***

"Great job, kiddo!" said the dad to Robin, as he pulled out a bottle of chilled water from the refrigerator. "Man, you're getting to be a big boy. Look how well you did that!" he said, with as much interest in Robin's colouring skills as he would have in choosing a dress for his wife, yet, feigning as much interest as he would have in a football match. Not that he didn't love his son or wish to invest time in him, he did. He was just going through one of those moments when you don't want to connect with anyone. Mostly, because your mind is not in a very good place, and not relaxed enough to focus on any one thing. And partly because of the intoxicant you have guzzled to make sure your mind is not in a very good place.

A thin stream of water dribbled down his lips and a tiny droplet lodged itself in the cleft of his chin. His dimpled cleft was not as pronounced as John Travolta's, but it was something. And now, the droplet had found its safe spot there. It peek-a-booed at Samar and Samara from where it sat; bobbed up and down within the cleft as the dad inquired about their holiday homework, and then slid out and jumped off the cliff of his chin when he stomped up the stairs, without waiting for their replies.

"Are they talking? Can you hear them?" Samara tried to pry Samar from his game. She needed to shut him up. His 'bam-bam' was drowning any sound she hoped to gather from upstairs to know if their parents were talking to each other, or arguing, or still practicing the silence-*asana.*

Snippy scooted up to the parents' room even before Samara could get there. She was too antsy. I had nothing better to do so I, too, followed suit. We found the dad rumbling through his stuff in the last drawer of the bachelor's chest. The chest, a beautiful lemon vintage-printed cabinet, standing arrogantly against the wall between their bedroom door and the door leading to their dressing room, added just the right touch of distinction to their room. The dad had been allotted only the last drawer in the *bachelor's* chest for his stuff. As he straightened up, he stole a fleeting glance at Mira through the mirror above the chest. *In the hope to catch her looking at him?* She wasn't; her eyes remained lowered. He quickly averted his. *He didn't want to get caught looking at her!*

Mira was on the day-bed reading her book; supposedly reading. Her eyes were not doing the smooth glissando—gliding over the exotic amalgamation of words, word by word, all the way to the last one. Rather, they were zipping from end to end of the page, left to right, right to left, as though keeping track of a ping-pong ball in a very intense table-tennis match. Not a word had sunk in since the dad walked in. And then, the corner of her eye caught him leaving the room. It, instantly, blasted SOS signals to her brain. Her brain went into screeching mode: *Don't just walk off this way. Can't* you *ever try to sort things out? Show some remorse. Do something, damn you!* Any louder, and the dad could've heard her. *Please!*—her mind shouted, in the desperate bid to be heard.

I could tell what was coming next, and I would've stayed on to do the needful but my inquisitiveness got the better of me. I followed the dad into the library, leaving Snippy behind to knock some sense into Mira's tears. Just because they're tears—they're super flow-y and always in the ready-willing-and-able mode—doesn't mean they can come, as and when they please. But they came then, as they pleased. Also, because they saw a head held high, a jutted-out chest and a very stiff back, as the dad made his way out the door.

On entering the library, that very head dropped, plummeting at breakneck speed like a faulty elevator losing control. The jutted-out chest deflated, ribs jammed into his spine, making him look like a compressed vacuum-packed pillow. The stiff back collapsed like shattered, spider-webbed, toughened-glass.

Much later, around midnight, I entered the kitchen to find Snippy pouring beer into two mugs.

"Hey, where's mine?" I asked.

"One's for you and one's for Rock," she lamented.

She doesn't want any? Is the woman preg …? Before I could think further, she lifted the bottle to her lips and guzzled a mouthful. *Ah yes, my hottie likes to drink straight from the bottle!*

The beer was a dip in the lake on a sweltering Indian summer afternoon. The kind of day we had had, we had hit rock bottom. I watched the bubbles as they sizzled up to the surface of the mug, pulling me up along with them. Their effort was duly acknowledged.

"Mira was very mellow again, today. The dad should've tried to make amends. He was in the wrong so obviously he should've made the effort," Snippy said, setting the bottle down. "He's so snooty … so damn arrogant. He needs major working on."

"Yeah, but in the library, he was a whole new person from what he was in front of her. He was in shambles; mumbling to himself about what an ass he is, that he crosses boundaries sometimes and needs better control over himself. He kept banging his fist on his forehead—*thump, thump, thump.* Reminded me of a slot machine … you know, how we keep thumping our fist on the button of a slot machine, in wait of a jackpot—thump, wait for a win to pop out. Thump again, wait again!"

"And his anticipated jackpot … a brilliant idea that would pop out and help resolve the issue without it looking like an apology," Snippy retorted. "So very narcissistic of him! He knows it's his fault, wants it to get rectified, but will not bend over to fix the mess."

Snippy did seem biased, and had I not watched the dad that evening, I guess I too, would've had the same viewpoint as her. But I could only be fair, "I don't know … after what I sensed today, I feel the dad is not all too bad. He did do wrong but the realization is setting in. He may be waiting for the right way and the right time to do it. Something's gotta give soon. What d'ya say Rock?"

Rock shrugged. His skin had taken on a blanched look. The Tyson thing had really gotten to him. He had never felt the need to ask for forgiveness, ever, but now the hunger for it was nibbling at his insides like termite, eating its way from inside out, making him hollow, making him prone to crumble.

"Hey, let's go for a movie. It'll lighten our moods," I said. A nice rom-com seemed like the perfect thing to fix the mood in the room. It was either that, or we'd drink ourselves crazy. "Kate Winslet's *The Holiday*, what say? Love her Brit accent … ooh … super sexy!" Luckily for us, there were a few movie theatres that still ran some much-in-demand classics.

"Super idea! Let's! Jude Law is in it, right? I love *everything* about him." Snippy's accentuated accent sounded jealous.

"I don't know. I'm just too fizzled out. Let's do it another day," Rock suggested, dampening our moods.

I lifted my mug and took a big gulp. I felt I took in more than just beer. My alter ego, had clambered up the rim of the mug, unnoticed. It went straight to my head and started spewing bewitching ideas into it: *Just Snippy and you at a movie together … late at night!* I was getting tempted, *What the heck! This could be the chance of a lifetime.* But a more practical, sober-sounding voice in my head sounded concerned: *Do you have what it takes to ask her out? What makes you think she'll agree? And will Rock stay behind even after she agrees?*

I did. She did. And he did.

We juggled through knees and feet turning this way and that, to get to our seats. Oh, how I hate centre seats! That's what you get in last-minute bookings, but how could I miss out on the opportunity of having Snippy all to myself, sitting next to me squashed between seats, elbows grazing, with even a chance to put my arm around the back of her seat.

Watching Kate cry was making me teary. I must have watched every movie of hers. Some twice, thrice even. I looked to my left; Snippy was munching away from her bucket of popcorns. For her, 'movie' means 'popcorn', and popcorn means 'no sharing'. I extended my hand towards her. *Don't worry, I'm not gonna hold your hand,* and dunked my hand into her popcorn. She jerked the bucket away from me so quickly that a load-full of popcorn landed on the lap of the guy sitting to her left.

"See what you made me do?"

"Me? Look at you. You couldn't give me any but gave half a bucketful to a stranger."

She shook her head in disgust; she turned her head to the guy to her left and smiled sheepishly, mouthing a *Sorry*. Her emotions were in the periphery of humiliation, but more so, on greed—she wanted her popcorn back. She looked at the popcorn plopped in his lap, looked at the knees and feet she would have to cross again if she went for another bucket, looked back at his face, and smiled again. *Friggin' fiddle-sticks!*

I looked over at the guy; he was flashing all his teeth. I'd have bet a million bucks on that guy's thoughts, right then, but I didn't need to. He proved to be easier to get into than I thought. He was a piece of art: *Is this too odd a time to ask for her phone number? And the popcorn, now that they're on my lap, can I eat them?*

The audience in the hall was doing what audiences do when a comic scene comes on; their heads bobbing like bobble-head toys.

Are they, by any chance, laughing at us?

SORRY … IS ALL IT TAKES

I was awakened, abruptly, by loud noises coming from downstairs. Not human voices. They sounded more like pans rattling—metal against metal. *They've resorted to fighting with pans now?*

I threw myself out of the covers and sprinted out of the room in a mad but as-quiet-as-I-could-be rush. Robin was still asleep; he was better off asleep. I didn't want disturbances from downstairs getting him upset again.

Halfway down the stairs I could smell burnt toast. *Oh, the dad is cooking! Hmm … sweet! He's making amends.*

Sizzling and crackling, the eggs and sausages smelled yum. I could already visualize it—an English breakfast (no bacon of course; he wants Mira to cut down on more than just a couple of calories) plated and set on her favorite carved tray; to the left of it, a purple hyacinth in a single-flower vase, adding an aura of loveliness and warmth to the setting; on the right, a soft-pink card.

Awww!

I peeped into the kitchen. *Oh! Okay* … I could see an abandoned bowl on the kitchen counter with a quick-fix breakfast emptied halfway through—a mix of cereals and bits of nuts and seeds; some floating, some dunking, in leftover milk. *He left them to drown.*

I looked over at the sausages and eggs he was devouring from the pan itself; the pan still on the cooking station, him halfway over the station. There were two burnt edges of toast lurking on the lid of the butter dish. He may have made one less plate to wash but sure made a whole lot of mess otherwise.

And he didn't cook for her! No tray! No apology cards! Nothing!

Samara came rushing into the kitchen soon after. Her ears had been aching to hear the waking-up sounds of a household. A bad dream had kept her on edge since the early hours of the morning. Disturbed, she had tried to hold herself together for fifteen-odd minutes, tossing in bed, but when she felt she couldn't contain herself any longer she had gone to Samar, of all people, to be comforted. The cold war between the parents had worked as a catalyst in creating camaraderie between these two perpetual foes.

Samar had wanted to sleep in till late, it being the first day of the summer holidays. But there she was, at his door—a double knock and a muffled *Samar,* alternating at equal intervals, till he let her in.

Dad might not have come home last night.

How d'ya know?

I couldn't hear his snoring.

You can hear his snoring all the way to your room?

No, silly! I was trying to hear from outside Mommy-Daddy's room.

You stand outside Mom-Dad's room listening to the sounds coming from within? Gross!

Shut up! I had a bad dream about Daddy and wanted to make sure he was back home.

I'm telling Mom you said 'shut up' to me and that you eavesdrop on them!

And I'm telling Mommy you … you … she stopped herself. She couldn't piss Samar off, she needed to tell him about the dream she had had. *If only I tell someone my dream, I may jinx it.* It was too odd an hour to make a call to Beverly, her best friend. Taking into consideration the too-ghastly-an-hour to wake up a friend, even a best friend, and that, too, on her first day of summer break, Beverly was out of the question. Samara certainly couldn't tell her mom; she didn't want to freak her out with the goriness of the dream. All the more, if the dad hadn't come home at night.

Let me summarize Samara's dream for your perusal, sir:

Her mom—rather unusual for her to do so, so late into the night—had left not just the front door but also the back door and all the windows of their house wide open. When the dad came back from work the front door shut with a loud bang just as he was about to step in. He tried twisting the knob but found it locked. Samar rushed to open it from the inside but it wouldn't budge. So the dad went around to the back door and the same thing happened: the door shut with a bang and the knob wouldn't budge. After a few more failed attempts, he stomped towards the window which would let him into the family lounge. But it, too, shut with a sharp rattle. Samara rushed to open it but, just as with the doors, it remained jammed. The mom rushed to help. Surprisingly, the doors and windows opened only to the mom, but every time the dad made his way towards the opening, no matter which door or window, it would shut again with a loud bang, preventing him from entering the house.

Something was terribly wrong. It was making the walls quiver. It was making their bodies rattle, some parts fragmenting. Robin had begun to cry, tiny sobs at first, which went on to become loud wails. Samara, too, let her tears address her fears. All through the night, her mom, as well as Samar, had been frantically opening the shut doors and windows, extending their hands to pull the dad in but they couldn't get him in. He was right there, in front of them, yet couldn't be with them. After innumerable failed attempts, they stopped trying. The dad, too, stopped trying. And then, Samara saw him fade away. Gradually. At first, she thought her tears had formed a thin veil in front of her eyes and hence, he seemed blurry. She rubbed and rubbed, but the dad only paled more till he became translucent. And then he was gone, blended into nothingness.

The dream, brutal and merciless, had Samara wide awake. Sobbing, face drenched, she stood outside her parents' room in the wee hours of the morning, seeking assuagement in her dad's snoring. On a usual day, his snoring would've been the butt of their jokes. It would be content to get their way with him: *Take us for a picnic/ Legoland or we'll put the recording of your snoring on the family WhatsApp group.* But that day, she was hungering for it. Panicked and antsy on not hearing any, she had reached out to Samar to unburden her soul.

Finally, after what had seemed like a million minutes to her, comforting sounds from below had wafted up. She had rushed out of Samar's room and came crashing down to find her dad standing in the kitchen in his boxer shorts and usual ragged T-shirt. She let out the breath she was holding-in all the way down. *I jinxed my dream! I jinxed my dream!*

Soon after, Samar came scampering into the kitchen; hands placed irately on both his hips, eyes vigilant, sharp, taking it all in—

the dad, Samara, the mess on the counters, his mom's absence. His eyes went back to Samara, instructing her, commanding her to belly up and get on with the task. He had voiced his opinion in his room, earlier: *Dads listen to their daughters.* Besides, she was the one having the petrifying dreams. So, it was all on her to tell the dad to come home on time at night, every night.

Samara turned to look at her dad. "Daddy, what are you cooking? It smells so good," she moistened the parched mood in the kitchen. "I'll pass you more eggs and bacon." Ingenious, I must say! Mira had presumed there would be just cereal for breakfast, but Samara turned out to be a smart cookie. She toasted the bread; laid the table with plates, and forks and knives, and salt and pepper. She was Super-girl. Although, she did spill some salt on the counter, but she made it disappear with one efficient swipe.

"And something for Mommy too, Daddy? We can take it up to her."

"She's had her coffee," he was guesstimating, "and I'm getting late for work," and dodging.

"I think Mommy's still in bed, Daddy. Last night she said she wasn't feeling too well. She needs to eat; she'll get even sicker. Then there'll be no one to look after us, Daddy."

Samar was idly nibbling on some almonds Mira had soaked in a glass bowl the night before. He gave his dad a look that clearly said: *When Samara advocates something, it's best to yield, sooner than later. Might as well just do it and get it done with.*

And that's how a tray, set with delish looking breakfast, was lying on the kitchen island, waiting to be taken up to Mira. It was too heavy for Samara to take up, and Samar was engrossed by his phone, while downing the remains of his breakfast. His nonchalance, for once, worked in Samara's favour. "Daddy?" she said, looking her dad in the eye; her puppy face mouthing the word *Please* was too tough for him to combat.

Samar, lifting his eyes from his phone after the dad had drudged his way up with the tray, whispered "Good job, girl! Mom won't touch it, but great going."

Samara's wide smile of victory halted in its stride. "Stop these negative thoughts. Ms Atwood says that the Universe is listening to every thought of ours, all the time. Think negative thoughts and negative things will happen. Think good thoughts and good things will happen. Don't you want this to work? Don't you want Mommy and Daddy to be friends again?"

"Really?! Is that *so*? Let's see how right your Ms Atwood is. So, from this moment on, I'll think just this one thought *very* wholeheartedly: for you to vanish off from the face of the earth, forever!" Samar said, simulating a magic wand over her head while making 'poof-poof' sounds.

She looked at him, all set to stick her tongue out, tilt her head and present him with the cross-eyed look, but she let the moment pass. She had bigger concerns for the moment. Him, she could—correction—*would* tackle another time.

Samara had thought she would wait for about ten minutes before going upstairs on the pretense of clearing the tray, but not a minute had gone by and she was heading her way up, with Snippy tagging along; and me tagging along Snippy.

The dad was fumbling through his stuff in the walk-in closet. Mira was nowhere to be seen.

How is he looking so composed? Almost thrilled? I looked at Snippy. Snippy looked at Samara. Samara looked at the breakfast tray. The breakfast tray looked back at us, crestfallen. Laying abandoned on Mira's side of the bed, it was too shame-faced to whine or whimper about the haste with which the dad had dumped it there to avoid a face-off with Mira.

Tell me, Mr Umana, why was it so difficult for the dad to present his wife with the breakfast tray? That gentle gesture was a brilliant way to do the job without him having to apologize verbally. He couldn't do even that bit?

The dad grabbed a pile of his clothes and made his way out of the bedroom the moment he heard the washroom door-lock click.

"Daddy made breakfast for you, Mommy!"

Mira beamed; glistening diamonds sitting pretty in the rims of her eyes, added to the spark in her smile. She snipped a piece from the egg and a chunk of the sausage with her fork, and offered it to Samara.

"No, that's for you, Mommy. Daddy made the same breakfast for us too," but Samara still took the bite. She was famished; she hadn't eaten her breakfast. It was laying, untouched, on the kitchen counter. She had been so involved in setting the tray for her mom that she didn't get the chance to eat her own breakfast.

Samara had set the tray as I had envisioned it; a good-enough make-do, considering the circumstances. She had been quick to catch on to the parable I engraved for her in the salt she had spilled-over earlier:

A flower to bring on a smile,

A loving card on the side,

Set on her breakfast tray,

She shall cherish with every bite.

Getting a card on such short notice was too far-fetched, I must admit, and a mason jar was a good-enough make do for the Petunias she plucked from their lawn outside; on the whole, it was a job well done.

Samara watched as her mom savoured every morsel with her eyes before downing the first bite. "Mommy," she said in a low baritone, "it's Beverly's parents' Twenty-Fifth Anniversary next week."

Mira could sense Samara's concern. Beverly's parents, Kayla and Reuben, had been planning a bash for their special day. It was eight days down the line; RSVPs had been sent out; the caterer had been booked. It wasn't a big one but guests were coming and they didn't, necessarily, need to be enlightened about the cold war between her mom and dad. "Yes sweetie, we will *all* go and have a great time. I've been planning it with Kayla, so don't you worry, okay, love?"

Samara beamed. Her mom was Super-mom.

"And Samara, say *Thank you* to your dad. And tell him just that, no mention of any tears or anything, okay?" She started to cough, just then; a deep-throated cough. She got out a strip of Strepsils from her side-table and put it in her tray to take after she was done with breakfast. She had been relieved, earlier in the week, when her tests had confirmed that her cough was not due to the virus.

Why is Mommy coughing so much all the time now? "Mommy, Daddy has been smoking a lot again. Beverly's dad smokes a lot but I think Daddy smokes more. Ms Atwood said that even if we do not smoke ourselves, we are still passive smokers if those around us smoke," she said, doing finger quotes on the word 'passive'. "This means that when anyone in the house smokes, the cigarette smell gets into the curtains and the sofas and the carpets, and then we inhale it all day, so we also get the smoke into our lungs. I don't want to be a passive smoker, Mommy."

"No, baby, you won't be. It's true what Ms Atwood said. We'll make Daddy stop, but tell me, why was Ms Atwood discussing smoking in class? Is it a topic in your syllabus?"

"No. Tyler asked her. You know Tyler, Mommy? That tall guy with a slit in his left eyebrow?" She began to chuckle then, and digressed to explain why she and the rest of her class called the slit in his eyebrow 'The Strait of Sweat'.

The Strait of Sweat. That's so funny!

"Because sweat beads from his forehead slide down from the slit, from The Strait of Sweat, and stream down onto his eyelid. Anyway, so he asked Ms Atwood why, before a movie starts, there is a note claiming that none of the actors support smoking, although they still smoke in the movie. That's when Ms Atwood explained it all to us. She said ..." Samara rattled on. Mira's nodding may have misled Samara into believing that she was listening, but she was far from any such thing; she was plotting, and making a note to call Ms Atwood for help in executing her plan.

Once Samara was satisfied with her discussion with her mom, she and Snippy went looking for the dad, with me fluttering in tow, of course! We came across him just as he was stepping out of the library, shutting the door behind him. The smell of smoke wafted out with him.

"Daddy, you were smoking again. Ms Atwood says it's not …" Samara gasped, while trying to match her steps with her dad's.

The dad was striding. He wanted to deflect Samara away from the library as fast as he could. "Sam, sweetie, I haven't smoked in a *very* long time."

"But Daddy, the smell of smoke?"

"Oh, that's just an incense stick I put in there. It's to calm my mind."

"But Daddy …"

The dad stopped in his stride, turned around in one swift move, bent down on one knee and faced Samara. "Promise not to tell your mom. She'll just get another reason to skin me more. Please, baby? I promise I'll cut down. Do you promise?" He had to come clean, what choice did he have? Once Samara began to advocate on what she believes ...

Samara was about to say something but the dad turned around and headed off towards the kitchen. We trailed him and found him taking out Samara's favourite ice-cream, Cookies and Cream. He scooped some into a small bowl without asking if she wanted any.

Snippy arched her right eyebrow. When a kid gets served ice-cream in the early hours of the day, it's not ice-cream, it's a bribe.

Samara climbed up onto the high-stool and grabbed the ice-cream; her first meal of the day. What a way to start a day! Of course, it was a well-deserved treat; it was no easy task to sort out parents' fights! The dad took out another spoon from the drawer and leaned over to scoop out a spoonful from Samara's bowl. He lapped it up, scrunched his nose, finding the ice-cream too sweet for his palate, let the spoon leave a trace of stickiness on the counter and turned to make his way out of the kitchen.

"Daddy, Mommy said to say *Thank you*. She ate every single bite."

He slowed down his pace. Half-turned.

"She loved it, Daddy; I could tell. And Daddy, Mommy was crying when she was eating. She didn't say anything but I could tell those were happy tears. She has been very sad and she's been crying a lot."

"Uh-huh!" he let out, avoiding her gaze, and turned back to head out.

"Daddy … Daddy?"

"What is it? I'm getting late for work!"

"Daddy, Beverly's parents' anniversary is in a week. And Daddy … you need to come home early. I don't like sleeping without getting a hug and a kiss from you." He looked at her, smiled, mumbled something, and walked out of the kitchen.

Was that the sound of agreement? Or was it a grunt? Samara toyed around with mixed thoughts for a while; fragmented visions of disconnected conversations, of grunts at the dinner table, of banging doors; the untroubled pillow on her dad's side of the bed; the wet stain of a droplet on the pillow on her mom's side of the bed; her dream. So much that had sucked out every pinch of colour from her soul. The super-charged, super-enthusiastic Super-girl felt like a full-blown balloon left out in the hot summer sun.

THE UNIVERSE IS ALWAYS LISTENING

Summer holidays crash-landed into the Rais' house, and planned on staying for the whole of six weeks. For the kids though, lay a plethora of exciting times, for the whole of six weeks. There was much to do; many plans to be made, of late nights and sleepovers, of Winx fairies and Barbie themed play-dates, and Star Wars and Dinosaur themed ones, too. Paint-balling, skateboarding challenges, splash parties. The entire paraphernalia! Watching them had me feeling excited, obliviating, no, not obliviating, but turning a blind eye to the challenge of having the kids at home for more hours than one had bargained for. The odd waking hours, and the not-ready-to-bathe-yet moments; the most dreadful of all being the no-bathing-at-all moments. And how does one shut eyes to the PS4 remotes and skateboards and Lego blocks and books and contents of a kitchen play-set that are strewn all over the place?

In the midst of it all, a project, one that was planned by Mira, was of utmost priority. Ever since we had gotten access to Mira's mind, she had been thinking brilliant thoughts. (Just saying!) The project, with just seven days to its deliverance, left the kids with only six days to practice.

Near-empty bowls of popcorn and crisps were eyeing us from where the kids had left them, after a fun day of practice. Before Mira could clear the mess, we hopped into the bowls and settled down to have our nightcap discourse. The very first discussion, that day, was on positivity. Positivity was big on our list; it should be big on everyone's. You attract what you think. *Think positive and positive will happen. Think negative and negative will be called in by the sub-conscious realms of your mind.* This is how the Law of Attraction works. Take note, when you wish for something to *not* happen, you're still thinking about it, be it out of fear or in the hope that it doesn't happen. But, by the same token, you are, nonetheless, attracting it towards you. Furthermore, negative thoughts bog you down and slow down your rationale. On the flip side, with a positive frame of mind, you see opportunities and subtle blessings even in travails that come your way. Positivity helps you think straight, it helps find a solution. When you are a positive person, it's not that you do not think negative thoughts, you do, but the positivity in you does not let negative thoughts take charge.

Rock made a mental note to banish certain thoughts from Samar's mind. Of course, Samar couldn't make anyone vanish by just thinking it, but … *the Universe is always listening.*

Next, we discussed the breakfast tray that was set for Mira. An act of benevolence, no matter if it is big or small, can make a world of a difference in the ambience. Even tiny gestures: a hug at a tense moment, a wink, a smile; anything to streamline the situation, anything to lighten the mood, bring the temperament down by a zillion notches and break down bulwarks that get built against one's better judgment. They help overcome emotional overloads, sustaining one's sense of rationality. There's one more attribute to their credit, the most benevolent one, in fact: these kindly gestures, unseen-ly, take on the role of the word 'Sorry'.

Sorry.

Mr Umana, does the word 'Sorry' instill feelings of fright in you? Does it leave you shitting in your pants? Does it blackmail you? *If I ever get to know you've used my name to clear your name, you'll never get to see the light of day again. And if, for any instance, it becomes imperative that you use my services, don't you dare be the first one to do so. Let the opponent do it first. I like to know what I'm up against.*

Is that how it threatens you? Is that why you refrain from using the word 'Sorry'?

"The dad did go along, with a bit of a push; a huge shove actually, but he's not up for any appreciation. Well, not from me, at least. He was like: *I help set the tray, took it up. Not my fault she ain't there!*" Snippy was infuriated at the way the dad had dumped the tray on the bed and scooted. "He could've stayed on, let the mom relish the gesture. If nothing else, he could've looked at her with empathy. Had anyone shown me that kind of concern, I would've surely buckled under, and the entire squabble would've been unremembered for life."

"Not for life, you would never! Only till the next fight came up," Rock butted in, rocking her boat.

"Is that so?" Snippy's face turned into a red balloon, inflated to the point of bursting, "You always have to pass some cheeky remark, don't you? Remember last month when you kept saying I'm …"

"And there she goes," Rock was in splits. He raised his hands like a lawyer who had just won one of the easiest cases ever, saying, "I rest my case," with the conviction that it would bring an end to her rattling.

But I knew better. Snippy's outbursts, if not checked, could spend the night with us. I quickly steered the matter away, "I'm glad the kids didn't realize their dad hasn't been sleeping in his bedroom the past few days. It would disturb them to know that the fight has come to that."

The dad had been shuffling between his library and the sofa-cum-bed in the family lounge. I was especially concerned about Samara. The untroubled pillow had not gone unnoticed by her. It wouldn't be long before she figured things out. And then, she'll be crying every night, anticipating a divorce and whatnot. Her heart will become sad … *an open house for Azraella!*

"Yeah, but on the downside, the scenario will be pretty much the same for a long time to come if the kids don't intervene. We can only work on Mira. Getting the dad to make amends is not gonna happen anytime soon, not until we get in. So that's that, for now," said Rock, giving his point of view. "But if the kids are in the know, they'll crack down on their parents and make them patch up. If nothing else, they can stop their parents from sleeping in separate rooms. You know what happens when the parents make sleeping in separate rooms a habit: they move away emotionally too. I think Samar should be in the know."

"Hmm, I guess you're right." I agreed Samar was big enough to recognize the grim reality of the situation. With the go-ahead from Snippy and me, Rock couldn't wait to let Samar in on it.

Samar woke up all charged, the next morning. *Why the hell didn't I think of this before?* He waited just enough to pat himself before letting Samara in on his brilliant plan. She found it super too. Had to. Who doesn't like going on a trip? Visiting new places, going to theme parks, Al fresco dining every day and every night. Not that their mom is not a good cook, but eating out every day is fun. Staying at hotels meant open access to pools and fun sports whenever they wanted. An extended buffet of desserts only added to the lure. And room service!

Once Samara was sold on the idea, Samar craftily threw the task at her once again, bringing the discussion to an abrupt end with his favourite remark of late: *Dads listen to their daughters* …

The next few days went off in boisterous merriment, practicing for the project Mira had assigned them. On one of those nights, Mira and the dad went over to the Clives' to finalize the minutiae and beyond for their upcoming event. No, they had not patched up yet; their cold war simply goes on self-activated *pause mode* when around outsiders.

Reuben Clive grabbed the opportune visit to launch his plan he had been scheming all afternoon, ever since the Rais let him know they would be dropping by later in the day. Kayla was pig-headedly insistent that he partner her in a dance performance. He'd never danced centre-stage before, with all eyes supposedly scrutinizing his every move. But it was their silver jubilee, and if he had been dancing to her tunes for the last twenty-five years, a dance performance after all those years should have been mush. But he was apprehensive; couldn't trust his nerves. Every time he was faced with more people than he was comfortable with, his nerves would throw a fit and threaten to walk off, leaving him to face the music alone.

So, as soon as the Rais settled in, he suggested rather innocently: "Hey, why didn't I think of this before! Just an impromptu thought … why don't you guys do the dance skit along with me and Kayla? That'll be so cool! Don't you think?" He would have someone to copy the dance moves from if he fumbled, which he knew he would. Above all, he would not be the only one being scrutinized for goof-ups.

That night at dinner, Samara was inquisitive to know her parents' decision, "What song are you dancing on? Are you doing the skit with Beverly's parents or are you dancing on your own? Do you want me to show you some moves?"

On cue, Robin quickly got off his chair and began showing off fancy moves while singing *She Move It Like* in his cute lisp-y dialect.

"Sweetheart, I don't have time to practice for any dance performance. Besides, I have two left feet," the dad said, getting up from the table. He patted Robin's head and left the room, leaving him mid-dance, and getting Samara troubled, yet again.

Mira gathered the fragile ware and made to leave the table. Fragile things, as the ones she was holding on to at that moment, would've been too delicate for the kids to handle. If dropped, disgruntlement would come pouring out, blotching the tablecloth with its pigmentation. Stubborn blotches, as when a thick Indian curry spills over, are impossible to remove entirely, even after many washes, leaving the tablecloth stained permanently. Fragile things, if shattered, would make way for misery to come marching out, and command loudly: *Chest out, chin up! Left, right, left, right!*—and stage a parade for hours on end. Lastly, would come out pain. Pain; most extensive, most unbearable, as it takes down everything that comes in its wake. Even mighty things as the breath of a soul.

A woman, a wife, a mother, knows only too well how to look after her family. Mira gathered her fragile possessions and put them away.

Somewhere in the background, she heard a faint lisp-y: *Dad hasth three feet?*

IN THE DAD'S HEAD … FINALLY!

The grand night at the Clives' finally arrived, like an idling sneeze that couldn't be waited on any longer. The moon had walked the grand night in, like a father walking his daughter down the aisle, leading her to the wonderful life that lay ahead for her. And the night, like an eager bride-to-be, shone with charmed brightness and enthrallment.

But the brightness beamed more from the Rais' than from the Clives'. The insides of the Rais' house were fully ablaze and abuzz, as though the party was at theirs and not next door, at the Clives'. And that was because Samara was like an energy beam, sending off taser-like impulses in the directions of her dad, her mom, Samar and Robin. She wanted her family to look perfect for the party with not a stitch out of place.

As for the Clives' house, that night, it was the moon itself; a full moon radiating with the glow of the glimmering hearts and bright smiles of those within, illuminating the Rose of Sharon blooms spread across its front lawn, giving an illusion of violet stars, dropped from a wizardly sky. It was illuminating the lane it lived on, its trees, its pavement, and its streetlights too. Illuminating even the moon in the sky.

Of the Rais', Samara was the first to enter; she was entitled to. It was, after all, because of her that the two families had such great camaraderie. She and Beverly have been practically conjoined at the hip for the most part of the day, every day, ever since the Rais moved next door to the Clives. Ever since Samara turned up, Beverly no longer missed the pleasures of sibling bonding: shared secrets, reading with flashlights under a make-shift tent, and mid-night ice-cream treats, which she didn't get much of from her brother, Graham. Samara was an angel in disguise; the two did not need a reason to be together. They just had to be, like peanut butter and jelly.

Being on the duskier side with deep-set facial features, about two shades deeper than the rest of her family, Samara looked as though she hailed from further south of India than them. In a knee-length dress, the color of mulberry, with an intricate cut-work ivory lace on her delicate collar, in the likeness of a necklace; her dark, lush hair held up in a high pony with a polka dotted scarf of the same mulberry colour, Samara felt like the guest of honour.

Samar strode in next, walking his walk. A party at Beverly's meant Beverly's friends would be there too. Sprinting into his thirteenth year in a few months' time, Samar was having a tough time containing his tween-feet from tripping into teenager-dom. Cropped hair, sleeves rolled up, collar pulled-up, sagging jeans; he was almost there.

The first time he had seen Beverly, he had realized it would take a great deal for him to not fall for her. With a paralysed gaze, all he could do was stare at her. Her lips, like two petals of a deep pink tulip, had the perennial pout ready for a kiss. Her mellow honey hair, some dribbling on to her shoulders, some cascading down her back, bounced delectably when she walked. Her walk, at times, was a glide like a swan's, and sometimes, a skip, a hop, a sudden twist, as though she had springs under her soles. Gorgeous, slender; she was early-teen Veronica and early-teen Betty molded into one.

As he entered her house, Samar felt the familiar twinge, yet again. Every now and then, he'd recognize a familiar glint in Beverly's eyes too, but he didn't approach her. He couldn't. She was his sister's best friend. Bestest friend.

No! I don't think decency or decorum would keep any youth of that age from pursuing their heart's desire. Nah! It had more to do with the fact that Samara would tag along with him and Beverly wherever they would go. And if, by any chance, luck would have it that she didn't tag along, she'd still get to know everything from Beverly. And Samara, being Samara, wouldn't miss a chance to wind him up on it. *So* not happening!

Robin, although he had been holding his mom's hand all the way to the Clive's, let go of it a second before he stepped in. Pulling down his navy checked summer blazer, flicking a hand over his jelled hair, he looked less the little goblin that ran between legs all day long. Without the cap he had on usually, to hold down his unruly hair, he looked quite the chap, I must say.

The dad and Mira looked spectacular too. They needed to, to camouflage the mess inside; the one they had made with their aching hearts and troubled minds.

All five looked resplendent. As did we.

Snippy, in her razzmatazz hot pants teamed with a wine colored off-shoulder top was a looker that night. I couldn't keep my eyes off her. *Hot!* would be an understatement.

Rock was looking great too, but the added flab, thanks to all the French fries and stuff, was playing peek-a-boo from in-between his shirt buttons. As a matter of fact, one of the buttons was waiting, quite anxiously, for the hors d'oeuvres to begin their rounds. One single bite was all Rock had to take, one bite, and the button would go *Pop!*

Don't think Rock will be dancing with Snippy tonight! As for me, I just might. Without wanting to sound too full of myself, I would like to say I was quite a head-turner, that night. Not that I'm not every other day, but that day I had outdone myself. Looking dapper in a grey plaid blazer over a crisp, high-collar slim-fit shirt, the color of lemonade-pink, French cuffs et al, there was absolutely no chance in hell that Snippy's heart wouldn't miss a beat. Much pleased with myself, I sat perched haughtily on Robin's right shoulder; my immodest smile reflecting in my shone-to-perfection shoes.

Roo-mom didn't want to go. She usually skips parties; she feels out of place. Ethically, we three should've stayed home too, knowing the kids didn't really need us there, but who can resist the temptation of a sparkling bubbly and jiving to the latest tunes?

Samar headed straight for a dimly-lit corner where a few of his friends from across the road, and a few from school were gathered around Graham. Samar wasn't particularly great friends with Graham. Graham was a good three years older, and considered Samar still too wet behind the ears to hang out with.

Robin hung close to Mira for a while, and then tagged along with Samara till he sighted a set of twins more his age, both girls, and headed in their direction. He was hugging and planting kisses on their cheeks. I am certain I heard a whisper: *He's a chip off the old block!* coming from the direction of a three-seater sofa that was being weighed down by fleshy chit-chat.

Mira found herself next to a friend she had got acquainted to a couple of months back. Kayla and she had come across her in the super-mart a few blocks down and had hit it off, immediately. It was nice of Kayla to invite her over.

Their new-found friend was a bit too bling for that evening. It was probably one of those nights for her; a first time meet where you can't figure what to wear. Go subtle and risk looking under-dressed, or bling it up and look over the top. The friend was not familiar with many faces there so Mira kept her close. *How do I keep her entertained? What shall I talk about? I'm so pathetic at striking a conversation!* "Work good? Kids doing good?" *Great. What next? Too much detail and she'll start telling me how she makes mashed bananas and oats for her little tod.* She motioned her new-found friend towards a group of four ladies. Two of those four ladies were talking simultaneously. The third, so as not to seem any less intellectual, kept dropping in her inputs, midsentence. The fourth one was nodding profusely; her head like a bobble-head toy, bobbing in the direction of the talking ladies, from one to the other.

"Hey y'all! This is … uh … umm … a very dear friend. I'll leave you to introduce yourselves. Please make sure you girls look after her drinks." Mira dumped her new-found friend on the simultaneously talking, nodding ladies and darted off.

Snippy noticed how Mira left out her new-found friend's name while introducing her to the gang.

Gawd! Why does this happen to me?

Age! Best to blame it on age. Snippy tried to console her.

I'm not that old! Mira shuddered.

The shudder had Snippy very nearly falling off. She was sitting on Mira's shoulder that night; she wanted to be noticed. What she told us was: *I can keep a better eye on the kids from up here.*

As though we can't read her mind!

After some formal greetings and intros (or lack of them) Mira darted off to the kitchen to add an extra set of hands to Kayla's, in getting the hors d'oeuvres and tidbits around. "Tosh … that's her name! Finally! What a nitwit I am," she blurted out, between setting trays. *Too late to have a replay of the introduction, now!*

Snippy got tired of Mira's rambling thoughts and moved on in the direction of three women settled snug on a three-seater sofa. The three women were bobbing their heads, every now and then. They reminded me of the Drinking birds, the red-beaked toys that kids amused themselves with years ago. The birds would, in a timed manner, bob their red beaks, one by one, into a glass of water. These women were bobbing their heads, one by one, into dollops of gossip. Snippy plopped herself on the backrest of their sofa.

Call it intuition or gut instincts, but I sensed someone watching me. I looked up and caught Snippy looking at me. *She's checking me out! Nice! What's the word she's mouthing? Peaches? Aww! Or is it … bitches? OMG! She's calling the women bitches. But I'm sure she's checking me out too.*

Apparently, the *bitches* were more interesting than me. Snippy had already turned her attention back to them. I, too, turned back to the men's conversation on my side of the room. The men had their own trip going. Some serious talk about making wills and stuff; why it is imperative to make one well in time. A person known to one of the guests had not made a will, and when he suddenly passed, there was mayhem and utter chaos over the inheritance of his assets. He had remarried some time back, albeit, with a reluctant go-ahead from his kids. In the absence of a will, with a major of his assets going to the new wife per the law in that state, things between her and his children had taken an ugly turn, bringing out the worst in all of them.

The mood in that part of the room had gone dense. There was pensive mumbling. Submissive nods. *So not* party-like. It was making me gawk. I humph-ed, considered getting another drink, when all of a sudden, the Rais' dad let out a throaty shriek. Someone from behind him had grabbed him and swung him around, and was throwing playful punches at him.

"Girish! Girish Reddy. Pleasant surprise!" the dad exclaimed. "Been years! What're you doin' in this part of the world?" The dad and Girish had schooled together since the eighth grade. But once out, they had both made no effort to stay in touch. The dad never thought he'd ever come across Girish again. Even so, there was endless stuff they talked about and reminisced for the next hour or so. All the memories: the goofing around in school with his schoolmates, pestering his professors, getting detention for horseplay, and at times for none of his doing, made the dad gush with delirium and yearning. A pinata bag from his younger days had been ripped and all his childhood and teen memories had come bursting out. He made a grab for as many memories as he could; he was nostalgic, wistful. He wanted to live the stories he had already lived, all over again.

Our antennae were, all of a sudden, going *beep … beep … beep.* Rock, Snippy and I looked from one to the other. We detected the source emitting the signals. Without losing a breath between us, the three of us made a dash to get inside the dad's head.

And we finally got to know what Victor was all about.

'COMMON SENSE IS A FLOWER THAT DOESN'T GROW IN EVERYONE'S GARDEN'

"Hey, I never got to know why I was called Crabbie," Girish Reddy looked Victor in the eye.

Oh, wouldn't I just love to tell you why! The way you were grabbing and groping every girl passing your way, you looked nothing short of a crab flexing all six of its claws to grab as much prey as it could. The name was so friggin' right for you.

"Ooh, Victor sounds vicious!" Rock's face lit up. He had been bored out of his mind hanging around Samar. For most part of the evening all he had done was try to keep Samar from getting buddy-like with Graham and his friends. Now, inside Victor's head, the party was really rocking. "I dare him to say it out loud. Let's see if he has what it takes."

"Do you remember 'Sentimental'? Dev Mintal, his name was, right?" Victor said, instead. "Remember how he'd be so sensitive when we'd call him 'Mental', so we started calling him 'Senti-mental' and he stopped fussing? What an idiot!" This was as audacious as he could get. "What became of him, anyway?"

Glib talker that he was, Girish found several listeners in no time. "When I was in Mussoorie last … Mussoorie in India, not Missouri in the US … I think it was last August that I was there, I came across this very interesting quote outside the JW Marriot hotel that read: 'After women, flowers are the most divine creations.' I don't know about flowers, but …," and he got a riot of comments on the matter. Not all agreed that women are divine creations, but all agreed, in unison, that women are definitely the most sensual of creations. Almost on cue an attractive blonde walked over, looking a bit lost.

Victor's pulse started drumming wild beats: *Look at her! Caramba! Now the evening's really going places!* He was drooling, I tell you, sir. It was a struggle keeping pace with the goings-on in his head. His thoughts were, unabashedly, unreservedly, cheating on Mira. Sure, he can admire beauty but he didn't need to drool. And to think he'd been calling Girish 'Crabbie'.

Victor inched closer to her; thought he'd begin by offering to get her a drink, when he spotted the host walking towards them. "Reuben, this is uh …" he paused. *How silly of me. Obviously, he knows her, she's at his party. I'm such an idiot. This woman, she's making my mind Jello.*

"Lovita dahlin', where is your drink? I don't want to see you without a glass in your hand." Reuben clinked his glass with Victor's. "Vic, make sure Lovita's drink is topped up through the night, will you love?"

What more could Victor ask for. He had started weeding out his best chat-up line, was going in for the kill when he saw Girish walk towards them, leer at the woman, and make a grab for her waist. *Crap, Crabbie!* "Girish, this is Lov …"

The woman extended her hand to Girish, "Lovita Reddy."

"Reddy? Oh!" Victor looked from Lovita to Girish, to Lovita. *Friggin' daft, I am. Yeah right, take the piss out of me, both of you. Damn you, Girish!*

"Common sense is a flower that doesn't grow in everyone's garden. This was another quote I had read outside the JW Marriot in Mussoorie," Girish said, giving a hearty chuckle, and pulling his wife even closer.

Mira was clinking glasses with Tosh, doing small talk; saying the latter's name out loud at every opportunity. *Can I get you another drink, Tosh? So, Tosh, did you manage to get an appointment with my dentist?* It was the best she could do to cover up her faux-pas from earlier. In-between conversations, she was scanning the room for her herd: Samar—check; Samara—check; Robin—nowhere-near check. Robin looked like he was itching to pick on his nose. Mira watched, with a very controlled breath, as he took his finger right to the edge of his nostril, and then steal a quick glance at his mom to see if she was watching, which she was, and instantly retract his finger, giving her a cheeky smile. *That was close. But I'm sure he'll have a go the minute I turn my head away.*

Mira knew she should have been relaxing and enjoying the evening. She turned to look in Victor's direction and understood the real reason why her antennae were up: 'Red-alert, danger threat. I repeat: Red-alert, danger threat.' (Courtesy Snippy). The lanky looking guy next to Victor didn't seem familiar, and he didn't seem to be a threat of any kind, but as Mira's eyes fell upon the lady standing next to the lanky looking guy, her antennae went *bong bong bong,* swinging to and fro, like live-wires.

Victor sensed Mira's eyes on him and motioned her to join him.

So, Mr Umana, this thing about *sensing eyes on you*—ever given it a thought? You're busy doing your stuff, totally engrossed, and all of a sudden, you get a ping in your head that you're being watched. A tinkle, a buzz, a notification; call it whatever you wish. That's us. It's us that get your antennae buzzing. How else would you know if someone from the other end of a packed room is watching you? How, when totally engrossed in a book on the tube, you get an eerie feeling of someone watching you, you lift your head and lo!—there is someone watching you. And you seriously thought you had extrasensory perception on your own account. That ESP of yours, sir—that is us.

As she walked over to them, Mira's first impression of Girish was bang-on—lanky to bits. His too-small pants clung on him so tight, she figured the only way he could have gotten into them was by putting them on and then going through a Heat Shrink Tunnel machine. His limp blazer didn't help any, only accentuated to his lankiness. Also, he laughed too loud.

As for the woman, from up close, her persona was not as much of a threat, as it seemed from afar. Not that she was bad looking or anything, but—how does one put it subtly? She had worked on her pretty looks so much that it made her look un-pretty! Ghastly, even. An unnatural blonde, flaunting shoulder-length hair paired with unmatched color brows—fashion statement or fashion gone wrong? A figure-hugging dress on heavily pronounced curves; gawd-awful dangler earrings doing more harm than good; a bright peach lipstick combating desperately with the rest of her to be the centre of attraction, she was the kind of woman, who, walking into a room, turned heads for all the wrong reasons.

How could Vic have even the tiniest bit of interest in this mobile chandelier?

From Girish, Mira later got to know things about her husband she hadn't known in all the twenty years of being with him. Every misunderstanding, every disagreement, over the years, had made her feel she did not know her husband at all. That night, she realized that she, indeed, did not know him. He was not a dreary, insipid, angst-ridden critter, after all. He was not a grouch or a mutant alien or an ogre (don't think Shrek; Shrek is an exception). Neither was he a kill-joy. Rather, he was very much the man she would have wished to love till the end of time. *Why did he have to change so much after marriage? Couldn't he hold on to his interesting bits? What happened? Was it life's pressures? Was it our marriage that changed him so drastically? Nah! I'm sure I have nothing to do with it.*

She could hear Girish saying the words 'lamb biryani', over and over. He was recalling how, on seeing lamb biryani, Victor would make a weird wheezing sound; his salivating tongue, unwittingly, rendering a delighted whistle. No one dared ask him for a share. Thinking back, Mira did have a faint memory of him making a peculiar sound in the initial few months of their marriage whenever biryani was served. She remembered glaring at him every time … *People are watching!*

At the other end of the room, Kayla and a couple of her friends were discussing big fat Indian weddings, and dowry, which still existed now in the name of 'security for the newly-wedded couple's future'. Snippy had forfeited her delicious spot on the three-seater sofa to go back on Mira's shoulder when she spotted Victor near Lolita. Now, from all the way there, her ears were stretching themselves too thin to pick up every detail of the wedding shenanigans—designer clothes, extravagant flower decorations, exotic menu spreads. Although the background music was not loud enough to drown the gossip, Snippy did not want to miss out on any of the juicy stuff so she nudged Mira to bail on Victor and his company, and towed her into the heart of the chatty circle.

Kayla was relating the tale of a couple who threw the most buzz-worthy destination wedding in Tuscany. With no expense spared, the two families entertained guests from all over the world to a grand series of ceremonies, ensuring they left with unforgettable memories. But, as three months whisked by, the euphoria of the lavish wedding began to fade. Things didn't seem fancy to the newly wedded couple anymore. A backlog of overdue debts from the wedding celebrations strained the relationship between them and their families. Debts, because the couple had insisted on a lavish wedding, had mounted. The dowry was used to clear the debts. That didn't go down well with the wife and her family. The result? Divorce, sadly. That meant more expenditure in divorce proceedings. Ironically the dowry, which supposedly, was to be an asset for the couple was, in fact, the actual apple of discord.

"So, the thing that could have secured their marriage, ended up being the very thing that led to its downfall. But that's just me thinking out loud," Kayla said, downing her entire drink at one go. There were some topics she was overly sensitive about.

Mira turned to look out the window, seeking her peace-coloured expanse. What she saw was a woman reflected in the glass of the window, looking jaded in a sea of glamour, in a knee length dress, the colour of a moonless night. The woman was wearing the same pearl earrings she had worn to the kids' school event, but it was clubbed with a longer necklace string this time. Mira walked to the window. *How many years till our kids get married?*

Still a lot many.

Ah! I'll have another glass of wine to that.

Meanwhile, Rock's expressions were screaming, *somebody get me outta here.* He was back on duty with Samar and wasn't happy with where the conversation between the boys was going; inappropriate for Samar's age. He tried to nudge him away from Graham and his friends: *Nature's call.* But Samar kept shutting him out. How long can one hold their pee? Samar finally did excuse himself, and headed upstairs. By the time he was done, a sudden commotion from below made its way up. The lights had dimmed and the *Bruhemaayush* soundtrack came on. It was the entry music to announce the commencement of the much-awaited event of the evening. Samar knew his co-conspirators would be looking for him. He rushed down, two steps at a time, and found them ready in their costumes. Beverly and Samara had wrapped *saris*, Mira's outdated *saris*, over their dresses. Robin had taken off his blazer and had his shirt out of his pants. Samar didn't need to alter his attire; he was to stay as he was.

Samara took centre-stage by the fireplace, microphone in hand, "Good evening, ladies and gentlemen … boys and girls," she added, looking at the younger lot; she paused for a look at her mom, received the assurance she was looking for, and read on, "Day in and day out, we children are learning lessons in our lives; learning from experiences, learning from our teachers, learning from our parents. But today *we* wish to impart an important message through our play called 'Children are a Reflection of their Parents'. The role of the father is enacted by

Samar, the role of the mother enacted by Beverly, that of their eight-year-old Son, Troy, by Robin. I am the narrator of this play. Hope you all enjoy it as much as we enjoyed practicing for it."

A huge round of applause gave the kids the much-needed encouragement. For the next fifteen-odd minutes, they had everyone in the room glued to their act.

The play delved around a family where the father (Samar) ignores spending time with his son, Troy (Robin), due to his obsession with watching the news and smoking. When Troy imitates his father smoking, the mother (Beverly) scolds the father. The father promises to quit smoking but doesn't keep his word. He falls seriously ill and passes away, leaving the family in grave distress. Young Troy drops out of school to help his mother, but the burden becomes overwhelming, leading him to pick up smoking and substance abuse. The play highlighted the devastating impact of the father's actions on his son's life, and on how broken promises could lead to severe adverse consequences.

Another round of applause announced the end of the play; some applause in contemplation, some in remorse, and some in assurances. A great message was put across brilliantly. Our babies had made us proud.

Mira had called Ms Atwood right after Samara had complained the previous week: *Daddy has been smoking a lot again* … Plotting for the play had started that very day, with Kayla in the loop.

On his way out, after the dinner, Girish asked Victor if he was free to meet in the coming week, before he and Lolita flew out. *With the wives.*

"Sure! But let's go stag. I'm better off without my better half," replied Victor, a second before he tripped at the threshold; right after he thought he felt a smack to his head.

The minute the Rais stepped out on the street, Robin burst out, "Mommy, was I good? Daddy, did you like my acting?"

"You were great! You all were superb!" Victor couldn't resist clapping; directing his claps towards all three of his kids, one by one. "FYI, I got the message, loud and clear."

"Daddy, you could be superb, too, if you gave up smoking," Samara said.

"Hmm, so you mean to say I'm not superb already?"

"You know what I mean, Daddy." Somehow her dad always managed to steer away from the seriousness of the topic.

"I'll definitely try. It won't be easy, and I'll need some help from you guys; a little leniency, now and then, would make the going not so tough. Is that a promise?"

Mira gave him a side glance. *Aren't you the one who has to do the promising?*

Victor took out his phone and entered a reminder: *Dump cigarettes first thing in the morning; all but one.* He also dropped a message to his lawyer: *Would like to meet you some time soon. Something's come up.*

"It was such a lovely evening," Mira said, unlocking the front door; getting rid of her heels, just inside of the door, before she stepped in. "Great ambience, great music. The play was a nice add-on to the celebrations, and Reuben's promise to give up smoking was the perfect return gift to his family. And the food … yum. Hey, did you guys have the chocolate mousse? Absolutely yumm."

"Ooh, I thought I'll have some but Beverly called out to me and I forgot. Will they have some leftover tomorrow, Mommy?" Samara was in two minds to rush back and get some before the Clive's lights went out.

"So, you're just gonna go over there tomorrow and say: *Aunty, I forgot to have the chocolate mousse last night. Can I have my share now, please?"* Samar said, mimicking Samara's voice. He slumped on the sofa, legs crossed beneath him, with his shoes still on.

"Leave her alone, Samar," Mira butt in. "And head up to bed."

She peeped at Robin snuggled cosily in the nook between Samar's back and the sofa. He was fast asleep. "Take him up, will you please. You too, Samara. Up you go."

"Good turnout, wasn't it?" Mira said to Victor's back. He made no move to turn; let his back speak for him. Mira wanted to strangle him. "With the number of bottles they received, today, they'll need a wine cellar!" she tried again. Still no response from Victor, not even his patent grunt. You'd think those shallow caves on both sides of his head were ears. *I'll get you talking, all right.* "Didn't you find Girish's wife a bit too … garish?"

Victor turned, then; his eyes holding Mira's with a piercing look, one that could cut through things, dissect them, split them apart. But, in a flash, his eyes dropped. Because her look proposed to slice into his insides with a very sharp knife, twirl the knife, mess up whatever came in its way, his guts and his stomach and his lungs; sparing not even his heart. And only when satisfied, would retract; stitching him back up with his guts sprawling out some.

"Food was good," Victor retorted. "The tiramisu, absolutely yum. Lip-smacking. You should learn a thing, or two," he said. His chutzpah was back in place.

Whoops! He shouldn't have said that. Bitterness came lashing out just as the kids scaled the last step up. The perks of being married to a thoughtless husband! A perceptive husband would've figured out, on taking the first bite of the tiramisu, that it was made by his own wife.

Samara fell asleep the minute her head hit the pillow. The evening had gone off well; the Clive's, or the guests, did not sense anything amiss. But nothing goes unnoticed by an astute woman's heart. Kayla had messaged her concerns to Mira, before calling it a night.

"Long day, hunh! Samar kinda had me on my toes, today," Rock said, downing an entire bottle of water, as though he had just braved a fiercely parched desert.

I was exhausted. I just wanted to hit the bed, but Rock wanted to talk.

"He kept shutting me out. It's that company he was with, Graham and his friends. He wanted to show them he is one of them; not a kid, anymore. Was trying to be as smart-alecky as them; talking their language."

"It's the age he's at. He's walking a fine line between the pleasures and perils of being a teenager, in the want to cross over too fast. Adolescence! We have to work on him fast," I said, stifling a hippopotamus yawn.

"Yep, yep!" Snippy added-in. "But I can't get over the major breakthrough we had today," she said, upbeat. "Victor is finally in. That's huge."

"Cheers to that," Rock said. "Now, every time he thinks wacky stuff, he'll get a whack on his head. Did you guys notice how I tripped him as he was stepping out of the Clive's? For the remark he passed on his *better half*?" Rock winked.

"Neat move, yeah!" Snippy said, with a contemptuous snort and a very unladylike snicker.

"That's your way of fixing things?" I hadn't found Rock's move tasteful, but sometimes, diabolical ways are the only quick fix for the bullheaded ones.

TWO TENDER HEARTS A PERFECT MARRIAGE MAKE

"You sure you're okay with this, Mira?" Kayla picked out the mushy greens from the salad of the previous night before serving it to Mira. The salad was the first thing that needed to be checked; it wouldn't last another evening.

"Of course. By the way, Vic loves your cooking. He just loved the tiramisu, told me to learn it from you."

"Seriously? These guys really are something. After creating Man, God must've been like *Oops! Even I can err?"* Kayla winked, as she handed Mira a fork and the two began digging into the salad. "Something's on your mind." She noticed how Mira acknowledged her remark with a half nod and a strained smile. "What is it?" She had an inkling a response wouldn't come easily. "There's something I should tell you, but you go first. I want to see if we're on the same wavelength." She tipped her head to meet Mira's eyes.

"It's just … uh … he … Vic is just so difficult, at times. So distant. Lately, he's been …" *What do I tell you? That he's sleeping with another woman. I don't have any proof, and I don't know if I should be saying anything at all, but I want you to tell me these thoughts cannot be right. I, so, need you to hug me and tell me I'm being a fool!*

Snippy was a bit down too. (Oh, yeah! She had tagged along.) She had tried every which way to put Mira's mind at ease, but such thoughts are not chased away so easily. They need explanations. They need facts. They need nothing but the truth.

"I was in two minds all of last night but I feel it's only right that you should know," Kayla stopped herself for a moment. She looked at Mira; considering the aftermath of her decision. She took Mira's hands in hers, ready to address the elephant in the room.

Kayla's hands were sticky to the touch, moist from sweat, but Mira could feel only their warmth. It was only when Kayla picked up the soft, almost inaudible, release of breath from Mira, that she spoke up, "Last night … I heard Norah, Sophie and Andrea talking. Apparently … Andrea saw Vic's car parked outside the Country Club, a week or so back," Kayla paused there, letting that bit of information stay adrift. It was loaded, and would take time to settle. "You okay, babe?" She got two half-nods from Mira. In-between the two half-nods, she saw Fear facing her, white as a ghost. She saw Hope, that didn't want to acknowledge what Fear claimed it had heard. She heard a Plea say *Let it go.* And another Plea say *Go on.* She took a deep breath and spoke again, "I had my back to them. I don't think they saw me; they were so hooked on to their crappy talk. I balanced my phone on the backrest of the sofa and recorded every word they said while I pretended to chat up other guests. You wanna take a listen?"

With a few taps on the phone, Andrea's squeaky voice could be heard saying, *yes, I remember clearly, it was a Friday night before the last. And … there comes Vic trotting out of the lift, sprinting his way out of the club. So, I looked around for Mira. But, lo! She was nowhere to be seen.* Andrea's voice was melodramatic, adding the right amount of pepper and sting that would get anyone with a piquant palate to lap it up. There was a '*Oh my*' and a '*Ah ha*' added into the background, by Sophie and Norah, undoubtedly. *Well, you know me … I immediately dropped a message to Mira that I was hoping to meet her, on seeing Vic there. Was she not well? How come he was there alone, so late at night? I'm guessing she figured out what I was trying to hint at. And I'm guessing it couldn't have died out, just yet. Do you see any stiffness between the two?*

Another voice, Sophie's or Norah's—Mira couldn't tell, clearly—purred, *if she's throwing, I'm ready to catch. I've always carried a scorching flame for this hottie. Me too,* Andrea said, and then there was a round of giggles, and snickering, and more bitching.

All of Mira's fears gushed out along with her tears. Neither of the two, not her tears, nor her fears, need hide anymore.

"I … did question him, that night. Initially, he told me he was at work all day with back-to-back meetings; didn't keep tab on time, so got late. When I mentioned him being seen at the club, he, very conveniently, said it skipped his mind; that he'd gone there for a meeting with a client. The next morning, when I tried to extract the truth out of him, he lunged at me."

"What? How dare he!" Kayla spat the words out through spittle teeth. Instinctively, she leaned forward to hug Mira. Mira stayed in the hug. She would've taken it home with her, if she could.

"It's been going on since then? And he's not given any explanation? Those witches could just be making a thing out of nothing, for all you know. I wish I hadn't invited them, but our husbands get along so well."

"He could be telling the truth about the meeting but I don't know. And now, the kids are insisting on going on a trip."

"Hmm! A trip may be good for you guys, actually."

"A trip with this cold war on … I don't know, although …" Mira, went on to recall a trip they had taken for Victor's birthday some years back. They were in a warring mode then too, but tickets and hotels had been booked well in advance, and the kids had been looking forward to it; canceling was out of the question. So, what choice did they have but to put their fight on pause mode for the trip? With the promise to resume it, once back.

"And did you? Resume it, once back?"

"Oh, I don't remember! Probably not."

"Perfect, then. Listen woman, Reuben and I, we're not the perfect couple, you know that. But we pull along. Bit of an effort, but ... what do you do? Not much of a choice, is there? There are the kids we need to think about and the life we've shared together. I'll let you on to a secret. I talked sense into …" she pointed both of her thumbs at herself, "moi. Told myself: *This Reuben, the one I have to deal with after a fight, is worse than the one I started with in the first place.* You get what I'm saying? He was always getting on my nerves, doing things the wrong way, saying the wrong things at the wrong time. Basically, being a nitwit. But I realised when I'd fight with him over that stuff, it only worsened things. He would still not acknowledge his mistakes, forget about rectifying them, and to top it, he'd start avoiding me. Even started cribbing about me to his friends. So, I thought: *I can't change the man, so I better stop being the nagging witch he says I'm being, and learn to deal with the old Reuben who is just messy and a jerk, and not push him further into becoming the impossible person he becomes after I'm done with him.* You can't change a person if they don't acknowledge their need to change. They think they're fine just the way they are. And who says I got it right? Trying to be perfect all the time? Now, I don't waste my energy picking on him; I just turn a blind eye. It's not easy overlooking things if you're the self-proclaimed perfectionist that I am—I want everything to be just perfect, immaculate. That's how I am, but I can't impose that on him. Not all people can be the same, or think alike. So, I checked myself rather than trying to check him. And now, things between us are so much the better. We're comfortable with each other. In fact, we quite enjoy each other's company. What is imperative is that your spouse's smile doesn't fade when you enter the room, their upper lip doesn't twitch to one side as you begin to speak. What is imperative is that they do not look for a friend to have a drink with in the evening, and rather, find that friend in you. Let him goof up. Allow yourself to goof up. You, each, don't *have* to give a hundred percent. It's the sum of your efforts, his and yours, that will find the happiness, and the peace, that should add up to the measure of bliss; the panacea to how 'two tender hearts a perfect marriage make'!"

She gave Mira's hands a reassuring tug, "I'm sure there's a fair enough reason for him being at the club the other day. I have a gut feeling he wasn't cheating on you, babe. So, chill. And you're going on that trip." She grabbed her phone, tap-danced her thumbs on its screen, "I'm thinking a cruise would be just ideal. My cousin, half-brother actually—but I pass him off as a cousin—was a cruise director on the Celebrity cruise-liner. He's retired now, but I'm sure, he can get you a good deal," she said, as she packed the remaining of the chocolate mousse for Mira to take home.

WHEN THE INNER DEMONS COME CHARGING

That evening the family lawyer came over. Mira led him to the library. *Why is he over? What's Vic up to?*

Victor sensed Mira's apprehension. He snickered: *I'm not dying just yet, woman. Just making sure things are sorted and in place, for when the time comes.* The discussion the guys had had at the Clive's the previous night had hit home. Living in a foreign country and being unfamiliar with the legalities, Victor didn't want to take any chances.

The lawyer always delighted in meeting Victor at his house, particularly because of the library; the handsomest one the lawyer had ever been in. On every single visit, his eyes luxuriously consume, and revel in the sight of the mahogany and midnight blue, black and emerald green leathered walls that mask the mysticism of a transcendental saga, or a timeless love-tale, or a whodunit cliffhanger. Cryptic magical realms concealed behind spines; behind thick spines, behind thin spines. Spines with clues—single-word clues, maybe two, or even one-line clues—a few words capturing the entire essence of thousands of words. Some have engraved on them, the names of the authors in gold. Gold on leather. Leather on walls—mahogany and midnight blue, black and emerald green—commingled with a distinctive aroma. The aroma, an amalgamation of breath and body; matured, musk-sweet. Cedar-*y* too, of wood and smoke. A seasoned culmination of fresh and old, from newly born paper and aged paled ones; from cigars and cigarettes, smoked two hours ago, two years ago, or ten.

"Could we have some coffee please, Mira?"—was Victor's way of telling her to leave them to their business.

"I didn't know what you had in mind, so I got your entire file," the lawyer said as he heard the door click behind Mira. "I dropped you a message you but I didn't get a reply."

"Oh! So sorry about that. I did see your message. I was in a meeting at the time and meant to reply right after, but it must've skipped my mind. My bad." Victor was very involved in his work most part of the day. Gladly for him, he was doing something he was passionate about: books. (That goes a long way to explain the huge collection of books in his library at home.) Back in Dilliwood, Victor was very dissatisfied with his work as an architect, although a high-ranking one in a top firm. He would feel frustrated; a lack of motivation; a lack of sense of purpose. It was diminishing his creativity and his resilience to work. It was killing the drive and zest in him; all work and no play, making him a dull boy. He needed to do what he was passionate about, for the right balance. When he moved from there, he stood by his decision to make his passion his work. He opened an indie bookstore, *Our Nights Together.* Mira and he, together, had come up with the name of the store. Within a span of less than five years, he had taken it to unimaginable heights.

Minutes later, Mira walked in to find the lawyer crumbled on the floor. Victor was crouched over, his hands on the lawyer's neck.

"What the …?"

"Call an ambulance, immediately!" Victor screamed out. "He's had a stroke!"

While backing down his driveway to follow the ambulance, Victor called the lawyer's office and explained the situation to the secretary.

Mira stood at the window, watching. *Hope he gets okay soon. His wife and kids must've gotten to know by now. They must be so worried. Life is so unpredictable. He's not much older than Vic.* Mira moved away from the window before she worried herself sick. She picked up the coffee tray. There were some papers scattered on the floor. "Samar, please help me clear the mess," she said, heading out.

"This is so freaky!" Samar was equally shocked; his hands were showing his uneasiness as he placed the papers in a folder, one by one. After only a few seconds, he rushed out of the library, howling "I knew it! I knew it!"

Mira dumped the tray on the kitchen counter and ran to him, "What is it, Samar?" But he dodged her and ran out of the house. Mira was left there, standing mid-walk, wondering if she could try going after him, or stay behind with her little ones. They were rattled enough with the lawyer's episode; the loud voices, the ambulance siren, the paramedics. She rushed back into the library, instead. *What happened? What got him so agitated? He was supposed to clear the papers, not make a bigger mess!*

Her phone rang, just then. It was Victor. The lawyer had fainted due to hypoglycemia and not a stroke. That was worrisome, too, but his condition was under control and his family was with him.

Should I tell him about Samar walking off? I'll just get him worried. Let me try calling Samar first. But Samar wouldn't answer her calls. *What the hell happened? Why won't you answer? What is it, baby?*

Rock had zipped his way through the doorway and jumped into Samar's pocket as soon as he saw him rushing out. Now was not the time to let him be on his own. Samar was clearly disturbed about something. The goings-on in his head weren't making any sense to Rock; too many waffling thoughts, drowned by loud banging noises. Rock could pick up only bits and pieces of jumbled fluff flying everywhere. *Why me? … why? … loving only those two … throwing the shit at me! That aunty in Dilliwood, she had mentioned … they shut me up. All true! … effing true! I hate …!* Then, just as suddenly, everything stopped. Rock could hear only white noise; Samar had kicked him out.

And then, Rock saw Samar break down. The air around Samar had thickened; gotten pungent. Muggy. It had taken the form of a white-faced, bloodless carcass and was creating unrest all around Samar; a hungry insurgency feeding on resentment and distrust and abhorrence, spitting out wretched versions of him. Out came Confused Samar and Troubled Samar. Terrified Samar, too. It was Terrified Samar's violent tears that Rock had felt, a moment back.

"Fiddlesticks! Now what do I do?" Rock felt vulnerable. Ambushed. All of them, together, were too much for him to handle. But he had no choice; he couldn't let Samar get consumed by his inner demons. Rock pulled himself up, and as though in a war zone, fiercely braved the three faces of Samar: Confused Samar, Troubled Samar and Terrified Samar.

They must've shuddered. He had felt the earth beneath his feet tremble.

Samar got home much later, sneaking in through the back door. He heard no sound coming from the kitchen and presumed everyone was upstairs. But as he entered, he found his dad seated at the island, sipping tea. His mom was leaning by the refrigerator, a cup in her hands. They were speaking in hushed undertones. Samar stood still, watching them from just inside the door. Mira was telling Victor about the happenings at home, giving curt replies to his queries: *I've been calling … No one seems to know.*

They hadn't heard him enter. If he had to make it up to his room, he would have to cross them. He had no choice; he stepped out of the dim space and dashed for the stairs. Mira turned, made a move to stop him but he was already at the top of the stairs, leaving her calling after him. He wasn't interested in what she had to say. He wasn't going to make it easy on her, or on his dad. He was troubled, and he wanted to see them troubled too. He couldn't help it; he was in pain.

Mira went up to his room and knocked at the door. "Samar, can you please let me in. Can you, at least, tell me what's bothering you?" She waited; her head and two hands on the wooden impediment that was keeping her from her son, urging it to let her in. Something told Mira she would find herself outside his room, knocking and pleading, endlessly, for days to come.

Over the days, she noticed a seismic change in Samar's behaviour. He was picking fights deliberately; his tongue, sharp-edged and brutal; finishing off discussions before they could start off. Samara, he refused to acknowledge, altogether. Robin was too small to hurt, but he still kept him at arm's length. He had lost interest in video games, playing only to kill time, unlike before, when he would rush through his homework or house chores to play until he dropped. Now, all day, he would have rock music blaring in his room to drown any knocks and requests from the other side of the door.

Rock would drag Samar to the breakfast table for some family time but all he would do was sit there, totally unresponsive, totally evasive. Right after, he'd head out and stay out till late; having dinner with his friends on most nights. Things he had picked up from Graham on the night of his parents' anniversary but was too scared to do, he was willing to give in to now, unreservedly; reveling in the rebellion.

The mood at the Rais had gone from bad (thanks to the parents) to worse (thanks to Samar). Getting things to snap back into place was entirely on Samara. She had been dropping suggestions to her parents for a trip, but wasn't making any headway; Samar only added to her woes. Samara caught a hold of him one day, as he was heading out, "You were the one who suggested the trip. Now you don't want to go. Don't you want things to get better between Mommy and Daddy? Why are you troubling them even more?"

Samar had already walked out the door.

"Ugh, why did Mommy and Daddy even have to have you?" Samara shouted out loud; loud enough for him to hear it even at a distance; loud enough for it to go ramming through his rib, shattering it; stopping just outside of his heart. The heart, it couldn't pierce through. It had thickened, toughened.

"Whoa! This is crazy! The task now isn't to convince the parents for the trip, but Samar." Snippy's head swung in disbelief at the ongoing flux of complications. Complications that were behaving like acne lesions; before one would die out, a new one had cropped up.

That night after dinner, Victor waited up to have a man-to-man talk with Samar in the library. "What's going on with you, kiddo?

What is it?" He waited for a few seconds before giving it another try, "What's all this rebellion about?"

Samar was like rain clouds: thunderheads; built up, full of pressure, ready to explode. But he let the pressure remain contained within him.

"Can you not tell your own dad? If something is troubling you, tell me, I'll help you sort it. Did Mom say something to you? Was it something I did? What is it, goddammit? Are you into drugs or anything? Is it to do with a girlfriend?" He cut the formality of in-between pauses, kept the questions flowing; he knew the answers weren't coming.

Samar remained still. His face showed no signs of anxiety or fear or vexation. He just stood there, looking away from his dad; looking just nowhere. After, what could've been seventy-two heartbeats of nothing from his end, he started to pull off his shoes without as much as bothering to untie the laces; peeling them off with his feet, kicking them off. One flew a few feet away from him, and the other slid under the study table.

Does this mean he is settling in? I'll finally get some answers. Or is this another form of rebellion? Can't tell with kids these days! Victor was getting edgy; his fingers were getting fidgety. He opened his drawer and slid his hand onto his one and only cigarette, rolling it, within the confidentiality of his drawer. "I am asking you one last time and I want answers, right now. I've had it with this attitude of yours."

Samar looked at him then.

Members of a family know each other only too well. They know where it'll hurt the most, when it'll hurt the most and how much; never letting their eyes off the target. Anger and Hostility, having lived with Samar twenty-four by seven for the past few days, knew what was needed of them to kill whatever fight was left in his dad. Samar left the task to them, and walked out of the library.

TO-DO LISTS

"Mommy, can I have a hamster?" Everyone at the table jerked their heads up. Everyone but Samar. Ever since the lawyer episode, nothing anyone said extracted a reaction out of him.

"You want a hamster?" Victor asked, making sure he had heard Samara right.

"Or a puppy or a kitten. At Beverly's house the other day, Avril told us her parents got her a hamster and she keeps it in her room at night. Her dad got a nice two-level cage for it. She has named it Coco. It's a female. Please, Daddy?"

"Mommy, Daddy, pleeth, pleeth!" Robin wasn't sure which one of the three he was rooting for; he could go in for either one, or all of them.

"Daddy, please!" said Samara. "We can name it Chocolate."

"Chocolate?" Mira was totally averse to the idea. "Not happening. I'll have cravings to eat chocolate every time you call out its name."

"Hmm, in that case, we should name it Macallan, or maybe, Dalmore," Victor said, cheekily.

The kids didn't seem keen on the names their dad was suggesting, but if that's what would get them a pet, they were okay with whatever name.

"Since we're going on a trip, we can't keep one yet, can we? Who will look after it? So, let's talk about this when we get back. Okay, sweetie?" said Victor.

"We're going on a trip, Daddy? Yes! Yes! Where? Where, Daddy?" Samara screeched.

"Yay, yay! We're going on a trip! Samar, we're going on a trip" Robin screeched, but Samar had already got up from the table and walked off.

Victor was beginning to get worried, especially after the previous night's emotionally disengaged discussion in the library. He had confided in Mira. After much contemplation, both concluded that a trip may, after all, be a wise step—a cure-all for things as they were.

They were to leave in nine days' time for an eight-night cruise to the Eastern Caribbean islands from Fort Lauderdale in Florida. All in all, it was an eleven-day trip. They had been lucky to get the cruise bookings at such short notice, courtesy Kayla's cousin. There was euphoria all around, but a bit of worry too. Samar still hadn't agreed on going. There seemed to be no way to convince him; we were still out in the cold.

Mira's cough had got worse. It wasn't a virus, that had been ascertained, but it had lasted for too long to ignore. She visited her physician; she wanted to start medication well in time, so as not to be a dampener on the trip. Tests were done. Preliminary results were inconclusive so the physician had suggested further investigations. Results of those were due in a week. Although the physician had not voiced any concerns, he looked worried.

Mira didn't want to mention anything at home yet. Everyone

was in *vacay* mood. Besides, the frigid precipitation between her and Victor hadn't thawed completely for her to discuss her concerns with him. So, she used Kayla as a sounding board.

"I'm glad you convinced me to go on this trip. You never know, it may be my last one with the family. You think it could be 'coz of Vic's smoking? Am I jumping the gun? Of course, it could be nothing, for all I know." She needed to stop rambling; she needed to calm down. Everything Kayla was saying, and all the hugs she was offering, didn't feel enough. Mira loved her friend dearly, leaned on her. And Kayla let her. It was with her that Mira shared her intense moments. It was with her that Mira discussed all her ups and downs. But that day, the comforting words, the hugs, the assurances were wanted from someone who meant more. That *more* was her husband. During such times, in the shadow of an impending illness, even perfect-friendships as Kayla's and hers, tend to fall short.

Mira gathered her wants and needs, and took them home to where they belonged. She pulled out her cookbooks; she was going to make a nice Chinese meal. Victor would like that. Samar would love it. And it would keep her from going crazy. *What if it is something? A malignancy? God, what about my babies …?*

A fly was buzzing around. *Or is it a mosquito? Too large for a mosquito, too small for a fly. Don't you dare inject me with any of your bacterial infections or … viruses! I've got enough going on. And I have a trip to go to. So, shoo!*

Samar walked in through the back door, just then. He saw Mira flailing her arms. He was only too eager to be shooed back out. Mira caught sight of Samar's back. She rushed to make a grab for him and clung to him. Samar tried to pull free, pushing and shoving her away.

"I'm making Chinese for you tonight. Won't you like that?" The only response she got was from the buzzing fly (or mosquito, whichever it was). It sounded thrilled. "Sweetie, please talk to me. What's happening with you? You need to get it out. Let me help you, please," her voice broken, pleading with Samar's back.

Samar stopped struggling; he stood there for a moment. Then, his arms dropped, taking his shoulders with them.

Victor, from behind the closed doors of his library, heard a shudder. Then another. The walls of their home were shifting, leaning in. They were talking in whispers, about tears and fears. He stepped out of his library and found Mira holding on to Samar's waist from behind him; Samar had his right hand on the knob of the kitchen door.

"Samar, can you listen to your mom, she's concerned for you. We all are. Can you open up to us? Let us, at least, know what's going on in your head so we can work it out together. Will you speak up, God da …?" His lips were still three-fourth of an inch apart from each other; there was more to be let out, but he had a feeling 'more' would push the wrong buttons. He went with a 'tad less'. "Okay, stud! Tell you what! Let's go for the trip. It'll help cool things, and in a new ambience, we could work things out. You cool with that?"

"Who're you to tell me what to do. You're not my dad. And she's not my mom."

Say what? Say what? My head went into a tizzy. I looked at Rock. His mouth was gaping with *What?*—suspended mid-air, dangling between his jaws like a forest trekker that had gotten caught unawares in an Ojibwa trap.

"What? What?" *What did he just say? What's wrong with him? What made him say that? What was in the library that …?* Thoughts were running amok, colliding with each other and falling into Mira's arms, smearing her clothes and her face with their pissed-off blood and the ugly insides of their guts. She was screaming, throwing them away but they kept coming at her.

"What are you talking about?" Victor shouted through his bared teeth. The forced delicateness, the 'tad less' of before, had been rolled into a ball between his tongue and palate, like about-to-be-discarded gum, and was spat out. His next words came out with a fleshy bite. Madly. "What the hell's gotten into you? Why would you even say such a thing? Who has put this nonsense into your head?"

The walls of their home began to rattle, then. Disturbing emotions were questioning their might. Walls are not strong enough, nor are foundations of houses strong enough, to take such a load. Every disturbing word uttered was causing a fracture in the floor, making it uneven, crooked; making the floor loosen its grip on the walls.

"Yeah, I know the truth now. I'm not your son, I'm adopted. Why else would you wait for seven years to have me? No Indian couple would wait so long to have a kid. 'Coz you couldn't have kids back then, so you adopted me. Yeah, I know what you want to say … and how do I explain Samara and Robin being birthed by you? I looked it up, that when you can't have kids, sometimes the presence of a child in the house has a good impact on the hormones. It brings out motherly emotions and stuff … shifts the imbalance or something, and then you can conceive. Or maybe you had some treatment done and so had them, I dunno! What I do know is that you always favor them over me. And that's because I'm not your real son. I'm adopted! I know I'm adopted!" Samar's voice was broken; his eyes, shattered. His face was ruptured, bitterness gushing through the cracks. There was nothing left in his face to justify his age of thirteen-*ish* years.

"Oh, my baby. That's not true! Why would you even think so?" Mira was hugging him. He tried to push her away; he managed to get out the back door, with her still attached to him like a suckerfish. He was struggling. She was struggling to hold on, even more.

"And what gave you this … this … stupid thought?" Victor followed them. His mind was racing. *The day the lawyer was here … library … what? … what?*

"I saw the adoption certificate in the lawyer's papers, the day he was here."

"Adoption certificate? Oh, Samar! It's not … it's not … true. How do I convince you?" Victor turned to look for support from Mira. She would know how to hold the walls together. She had the strength.

But Mira wasn't there. *How could she leave me alone at a time like this?* Then he saw Mira rushing back to them, leafing through a photo album. He felt the walls regain their posture, align themselves, get back on their own feet.

Mira pushed the album into Samar's hands. In it were pictures of the day he was born—of the hospital, of him cuddled up in her arms, and in his dad's arms, and in his grand-dad's, and in his grand-mom's. Samara, in the meantime, on her mom's behest, had brought down a collage from Samar's room that was put together on his 10th birthday. In it, too, were pictures of his birth, all bundled up in blue. There was no mistaking Samar was their own.

"But the certificate? It said …" Samar was ready to question his own conviction just so his fears wouldn't prove to be true.

"It was probably somebody else's, nothing to do with us. The lawyer must have brought it, by mistake." Victor hugged Samar tight, very-near suffocating him, suffocating all doubt and resentment that Samar had been harboring the past few days. Standing there, lowering kisses on Samar's forehead, Victor looked like a feeder pipeline, pumping not oil, but an endless supply of warmth and love.

"I don't know. I've obviously seen all these pix all these years. I knew it couldn't have been true but when I read my name on the certificate, I … just lost it." He still asked, "Can you get that certificate from him? I just want to see it once."

"Your name? How is that even possible?" Mira looked at Victor.

Victor's eyes were darting back and forth; from corner to corner. They were looking for a place to hide. A place where he could be alone for a while—to think, to cook up an answer. *If he saw our names too, how will we get out of that?* "Yes, I'll get it, love. He's still recuperating. It wouldn't be right on my part to disturb him, just yet." He had saved the day for the moment. "But I will get it once we are back from our trip, just so you can be at ease. Okay, love? Now, we have a trip to go to. Let's go get wild!" Victor shouted, rattling the walls once again.

Excitement had taken care of the tears, and half assurances had assuaged the major part of the fears. Victor heaved a sigh of relief.

Mira heaved a sigh of relief. The three of us heaved sighs of relief—we had access to Samar's personal Wi-Fi, once again.

The Rais could, finally, get down to making preparations for the trip in full swing. There was much to do. Mira got out her phone and started making her To-do lists.

The woman loves making lists. She has lists on her phone, so her lists are at hand when she's on the move. And she makes copies of those lists on paper, two copies each, because she loves ticking things off her list, physically, as they get done; one copy to go on her dressing mirror and the other, on the fridge in the kitchen.

You have to check-out her lists, Mr Umana.

For the (nine hours) flight to Miami:

Comfy blue dress.

Gucci sneakers and Gucci travel bag.

Passports.

Travel bag list:

Passport folder/ ~~pen~~ 2 pens/ Shades/ small sunscreen/ Wet wipes/ Cough expectorants/ Hairbrush/ Samara's hairbrush/ Dry fruit in zip-locks/ Hand sanitizers. Mask?

Check-in baggage:

Outfits/ sun wiser/ swim suits/ shoes/ socks/ beach slippers/ belts/ camisoles for under dresses/ toiletries/ big bottle of sanitizer …

Comfy tracks and T for the flight back.

To-do list:

Call the gardener.

Empty out fridge the night before.

Put out the garbage just before leaving for the airport.

Set the alarm.

Call Kayla from cab to tell her to check on the house, now and again.

Toothpastes!

A To-do list for the gardener.

Lists for the kids' things; a list for every kid individually.

A list for things to shop for the trip.

A list for things to shop during the trip.

Her lists were endless. Phew!

MONKEY POSE

"Stop staring," Samara snapped at Samar.

Samar had been eyeing a girl seated at a table next to theirs. She was angling her phone in every possible direction, at every possible arm's length, pouting her lips to every pose she could possibly make.

"Do you girls realise you look like monkeys in snaps?" Samar said, in a low tone. "Why can't you'll have a normal smile? Pose naturally? Someone please go over and tell her she's looking hideous. She'd look much prettier without that silly pout."

While Victor waited in queue for coffee and chocolate brownies, Mira managed to find a large table where she could have her three brats seated, in her line of vision. She didn't want to lose anyone of them; the trip had just begun. She wanted nothing to come in the way of her long overdue and much deserved fun.

Mira had one eye on her kids, the other was trying to catch the name of the book a guy, not too far from her, was reading. In the attempt, she didn't realize she had tilted too far for comfort. "The Immortals … of …" tilting, she stopped, just short of falling. *Oh, of course! Google to my rescue. The Immortals of … Meluha.*

Robin was getting bored. He wanted to check out the toys at Hamley's.

"You're staying put, for now. Once we're done here, we'll head there, okay love?" Samara and Robin crammed large chunks of brownies into their mouths; dusting their hands, they looked at their mom with expectant eyes.

But coffee is not to be devoured or hurried. It is to be savored, like love; unrushed. It has to be relished; letting the roasted, smoky fragrance, rouse and vivify every sensory nerve. A double shot of dark roast, full body, without sugar was how both Victor and Mira liked their coffee; this was one thing the two absolutely agreed upon.

The actual euphoria of their trip kicked in once they had made a beeline for that part of the airport booming with brilliantly lit-up and colourful duty-free stores, and aroma oozing cafes.

Airports have what they call 'the golden hour'—the idle time between security check and boarding, in which airports strategize to tempt confined, *captive* passengers to shop and feast. Everything from soothing, well-designed walkways to the beautifying of the airports with fresh green and brightly-coloured plants is a strategy to play with the passengers' psyche to relax them after the stressful security check-in, and spend more. The no-doors-strategy is to not restrict the in-flow of buyers. Did you ever notice, Mr Umana, how the walkway through the duty-free usually curves to the left, which leaves more space for merchandise on the right because passengers, a majority of them being right-handed, subconsciously look to the right while walking on the left?

Their flight was uneventful, besides Mira throwing annoyed looks at Victor. He had forgotten her neck pillow in the cab. She had had her hands full, what with holding her younger kids' hands while keeping her eyes on their kiddie trolley bags; also making sure Robin wouldn't drop his kangaroo, or a shoe.

Mommy! Mommy! Samara's voice was trying its best to penetrate Mira's world.

Mira had been juggling between two books: *The Immortals of Meluha,* a last-minute buy at the airport, and *Ikigai,* which she had asked Victor to get from their bookstore. She settled on *Ikigai* for the flight journeys and in waiting areas, whereas, *The Immortals of Meluha* was reserved for the cruise, where she would get longer stretches of time to get on with the story uninterrupted. She was an avid reader, and that was one of the reasons why Victor and she had hit it off immediately. So yeah, that is another thing, and probably the last, they have in common.

"Mommy?" Samara's tuneful voice was giving it one more try. It would give one more, and then another. And then another.

"Yes sweetie. Sorry, I was ..."

"Mommy, I told Samar what Ms Atwood had told us about wishing for something with all our heart and the wish would come true, and he said he would very, whole-heartedly, start thinking about me vanishing from Earth. Will I vanish, Mommy?"

"No baby … it doesn't work that way." As Mira spoke, her tongue caressed slight abrasions on the inside of her right cheek that were caused by popping too many cough drops.

"But Ms Atwood said *think positive thoughts and positive will happen. Think negative thoughts and negative will happen.*"

"She's right in a way, we should think positive thoughts. But negative thoughts don't work that way." Mira struggled with the right words to put her daughter's mind at rest. "Sweetie, Samar won't really ask for such a thing, he would never. He was just pulling a fast one on you. So, relax my love. Tell me what is the first thing you want to do as we get on the cruise?" With ease, Mira managed to take her daughter into another world.

As for her, *Ikigai* had to wait a little longer; she was deep in thought. *Does the Universe really listen? Is it listening to everything we say? Is it listening to us all the time? So, if I send out prayers into the Universe for Samar to forget about the adoption thingy, will it work?*

One by one, the kids dozed off.

We, in the meantime, thought it best to take a nap while the tiny tots slept. We needed to conserve our energy; we were on a trip to Miami, and the Caribbean and Virgin Islands. We couldn't wait for beautiful Miami. Beach bodies. Sun, surf and sand. Glitz, pomp and glam. Luxury and lavish indulgences. Home of the rich and famous. The Millionaires Row. The Kardashians. The Versace mansion. It was another world altogether.

Once in Miami, in the cab midway to the hotel, Mira got out a packet of nuts from her handbag and passed it on to the kids and Victor. It would be a while before they could grab something to eat. There was first the check-in into the hotel. Then the kids would want to do a quick tour of their whereabouts: the pool, the kiddie's pool, the play-area.

We finally settled down to dine at the Pinocchio café on Ocean Drive. Victor and Samar had looked up the reviews of the place and had found them to be top-notch. The kids wanted to eat there because of its name!

We had had a long day and were to head off to Fort Lauderdale early next morning, so we thought we'd call it a night. Back in the hotel, Victor got a hold of Samar. "Mom's just tucking in the little ones. Then, she and I will slip out for a bit. Keep watch till we're back, okay, mate? Just one drink and we'll be back before you know it." Victor was not going to let sleep deprive him of the pleasures of Miami. He was finally in a world he had seen only on screen. *Miami, get ready to party!*

But Samar didn't seem game. It was only when Victor's clenched hand emerged from his pocket, extended towards Samar, and Samar's clenched hand went into his own shorts' pocket, that he gave his consent. But, as fate would have it, Robin wouldn't sleep without his mom in the new place, new bed. So, Victor went out on his own.

Perfect start to the holiday! Mira thought to herself.

Perfect start to the holiday! Victor thought to himself.

Next morning, after a quick breakfast, we caught the coach for Port Everglades in Fort Lauderdale to meet the cruise liner that was waiting for us.

And there it was! In all its magnificence and extravagance: the Celebrity Equinox cruise-liner. We were mesmerized.

After checking in, we rushed to check out our rooms. Once we had *ooh*-ed and *aah*-ed enough over the expertise with which so much had been fit into so little a space, the kids wanted to check out the four pools that spanned between sixteen decks.

On our first and second days on-board, we were to stay at sea. Just as well, as there was so much to explore and do on board; the cruise-liner stretched vast, akin to an endless ocean within another. On the third day, we were to dock at San Juan and the next day at St. Maarten and, so on. We were so ready to take on each day as it came.

As expected, the very first thing the three kids did, with their mom and their dad in tow, was splash into the first pool they came across.

That's when I saw her …

Rooted atop a bar stool, Pina Colada in his hand, Rock had been eyeing girls walking by. Snippy had settled herself on the edge of the pool lounger that Mira had reserved for herself—a book left spread-eagle on the lounger, or anywhere for that matter, almost-legally reserves a spot. While the book was making the most of it—lazing on its belly, soaking the sun with its upended rear-side—Snippy, with one leg crossed over the other, was eyeing girls too. Her skeptical eye was checking-out their fashion style.

I was flat-out on a lounger on the far-end from Mira's. Victor's crumbled towel, lying next to me, soaking-in the lazy humor, didn't bother to stretch itself out. It knew it would be wet again soon.

I could see kids diving in and out, closer to my end of the pool. Splashing, dunking, screeching their joy; least bothered that stray splashes were finding their way towards me, wetting me, leaving me limp; making me uncomfortable. It's not that I have anything against kids splashing in the pool. In fact, I love watching them enjoy themselves, but I wasn't in the mood to get wet, just then. Luckily for me, they were quite done and soon headed out; their moms had laid out burgers for them. I let out a relieved sigh and stretched myself, end-to-end, on the lounger and closed my eyes. *Aahh, bliss!*

The sun was just getting there, warming me up to near wafer-crispness, when there was a loud splash again. I was drenched, through and through. *I'm not going to let these kids get away with it this time.* Sloppy, wobbling, I leafed myself forward, to give them a piece of my mind, but stopped mid-step. I felt flutters in my stomach, like the flapping of wings of a butterfly that had just pulled itself out of its cocoon and was trying its first flutter. There, before me, was the sexiest girl in the whole wide world, coming out of the pool. Silver droplets glistening down her svelte silhouette, she was heading in my direction. She was the one responsible for splashing … life into me.

Yes, I agree, Mr Umana, I should be writing *splashing water on me and ruining my day* but don't you see there's been a change of heart here?

My heart was crying in dollops. I was flinching at the thought of her first impression of me—faded crispness, utter limpness, looking nothing short of a paled-out disposable table wipe. I held back my whimpers; didn't want her to hear me. I couldn't risk her seeing me. *Where do I hide? Where do I hide?* I lay flat on the lounger and shut my eyes.

A beautiful aroma—a touch of vanilla infused with amber and musk on skin—told me she was close. Her hotness was warming my cheeks. *I will be crisp in no time.* But then the aroma was fading away. She was headed towards the bar. *Rock is at the bar.* I saw Rock's eyes walk arm-in-arm with her, guide her to him. *No! No! No! No! Noooo!*

Apparently, her splash in the pool had caused Rock to notice her too. *Why isn't he watching over our kids? Snippy alone can't keep an eye on all of them.* I rushed to the bar; Rock was already offering her a drink.

"Charmaine," I heard her say, as she put her hand in his. "So, what kind of a name is Rock?"

"Papier! How do you do?" My out-stretched hand compelled her to pull her hand out of Rock's and put it in mine. "I couldn't help but overhear your … uh, amusement … over my friend's name. Solid, smooth, and as round as a …" I said, cheekily, looking Rock straight in the eye. *There is no way in hell I'm gonna let you win this girl over. I saw her first. One blow from me and you will be rolling off to the edge of the deck.*

Blow me *over? You? Now, that is a challenge.* Rock would have done his sarcastic-laced belly laugh at that, but he was in the presence of a beautiful lady.

"Interesting! Well, I am highly sought after, for bonding friendships," Charmaine said, just then.

Wait a minute, can she hear us? Did she say what she did in response to our banter or was it just a remark she happened to pass? Rock and I, both, tuned out and immediately put on our sound filters—only that what we wanted heard would be heard by her. *Perfect.*

Charmaine, a three-wrap friendship band of Lima-beads in varied shades of aqua, was definitely worth putting up a fight for. She even had a heart-shaped charm dangling by a string. *Charm-ing Charmaine*! Her parents had named her very thoughtfully. Unlike mine, Papier! *Will I never forgive them?* But when she held my hand and said, "Papier, charmed!"—accentuating the French-ness in my name, I not only forgave my parents, but felt earnest gratitude towards them.

I was hopelessly, foolishly, shamelessly, and in many other silly ways, falling in love. Charmaine was the girlfriend material every guy dreamed of. There was a spunk in her eyes. Her lips were fuller than any I'd seen; fuller and most sensual. Her hair in beaded bangs—so Cleopatra—added to her charm. I won't even start about her figure ... well, maybe just a bit! Hourglass; voluptuous in the absolute required places, finely slim in the others; perfectly toned, long-boned slender legs from thigh to slim ankle, with just the right touch of curve outlining her outer thighs; sweetly-widened hips giving a delicious swing to her swagger. Yes, it would take a lot of me to not fall for her.

***

After a wild first day of activities and exploring, and a hearty dinner at the Silhouette, it took but a few minutes for the kids to conk off. Samar and Samara in their room; Robin with the parents.

We thought we'd find a cozy spot on the deck and catch up on stuff. We hadn't had our nightly discourse for some time, but Snippy was in a weird mood, mooring on the edge of paranoia. "What did you guys see in that girl, Charmaine? Did you see her lips? Blubbers! What's so great about her? She doesn't even have great legs." Saying that, Snippy stretched out her athletic-like legs, crossing and uncrossing them, and jutted out her chest while pretending to adjust herself in the bean bag.

Rock and I looked at each other, *Gawd, come on!*

TWELVE YEARS OF TOGETHERNESS DEMANDING IT'S DUE

"You should try the Eggs Benedict. It's delish," a man being served at the egg station was telling Mira. He had two of them on his plate and suggested she grab one, too.

Mira had come across the same person earlier, while getting the kids their choice of goodies at the candies cart. They had exchanged small talk—great weather, fascinating ship and stuff. Now, she noticed how charmingly handsome he was, with slivers of grey gracing his mane. She had a thing for salt and pepper hair.

"Can't believe you're a mom of three," he was saying to her, while plating her the Eggs Benedict.

What she heard him say was more on the lines of: *I'm interested in you.* "I didn't mention I have three kids." *Is he stalking me?*

"I … uh … saw you enter with them earlier on," he was quick to check himself. "Trust me, you will love this. Another one?" She refused a second one, although she could see how the Eggs Benedict made everything else on her plate look uninteresting.

She did love it and went in for a second one. *I'll write off today as binge day.* She'd go on a diet another day; she was on holiday.

Sensing eyes on her, she lifted hers to catch the Eggs Benedict guy looking over from a seat not too far from them. She mouthed a 'thank you' to him. As if on cue, he grabbed the chance to come over. *Is he really gonna … did I prompt this? Oh boy!*

It turned out that he was Kayla's cousin, Zaydan. Zaydan informed Victor and Mira that he would be looking after them, making sure they made the most of their stay. Victor was full of gratitude, more so, because Zaydan had reserved their seats on the cruise at short notice. Mira was flushed, *Kayla had said he was retired. I wasn't expecting to meet him on-board. And here I am, letting my imagination run wild. Huh!*

Zaydan affirmed that he was in self-imposed retirement. He was, though, invited on-board, off-and-on, pro bono of course, whenever trainees needed his guidance. And he was entitled to certain privileges, such as reserving seats for family and friends on priority basis. He had, after all, worked on that very ship for a good twelve years.

"So, tell us, what are the things on-board and in San Juan that are not to be missed?" Victor was anxious to get the mundane queries out of the way so he could ask what was uppermost on his mind: "How about some tricks to strike gold at the Fortune Casino?"

Right after breakfast, the kids headed for the play-areas; Fun Factory for the little ones and X-Club for the older ones. It made perfect sense for the kids to play indoors while the sun was blazing. Victor ventured off on his own after a while, leaving Mira to settle the kids in. So, Mira found a cozy wicker day-bed in a nice corner right outside the play area and plonked down with her book. The spot was perfect. It overlooked the pool. A melodious symphony, composed by a buoyant cruiser slicing through the buttery *mer,* reached out to her; rhythmic and soothing. And she dozed off.

She must've been knocked out for quite some time because Robin was hungry again and it was only ice-cream with crushed Oreo cookies and M&Ms, lots of M&Ms, that would satiate his hunger. On their way back to the play-area, Mira came across Zaydan.

"You're a cute little thing. How old are you?" Zaydan asked Robin.

Robin's hair was speaking the language of the breeze; untamed black streamers were springing out of his head. "Four years, four months and two days," he replied, his smile smeared with chocolate bits, end to end.

"Wow, that's very precise," Zaydan said, amused.

"Kids these days." Mira, too, was filled with wonder at her son's promptness. "I didn't know you keep tab so well," she said to him, kissing his free hand.

The fact of the matter was that it was just that morning Robin had seen a kid showing off his glow-in-the-dark watch. Robin wanted one too, but knew his parents would not get him one before his next birthday, which was going to be a long wait because, according to his calculations, his last one had gone by just four months and two days ago.

The kids were up earlier than usual the next morning. They weren't wasting any time on sleep, not while they were on-board a cruise-liner. It's only back home that they hated getting up; a task on a school day, and an even tougher task on a holiday.

Samara had her day planned; her detailed itinerary pinned in her head. Samar went by mood and the kind of crowd around at the time. Robin was the simplest to manage and look after. He just tagged along with someone or the other. Victor and Mira thought they would relax in a Jacuzzi and maybe after, bask in the sun for some time before they docked at the first port of their trip.

San Juan, breath-taking and overwhelming, was a world of its own. The capitol of Puerto Rico, with its psychedelic-colored buildings—a string of candies splashed over blue cobbled streets—was a wondrous delight.

I didn't know Puerto Rico was home to the Pina Colada. It's no wonder that the people there are so high on life. It must be in the air; a sweet mix of coconut cream and pineapple and white rum. What else could explain the *merry* moods wherever we went?

Back on the ship, even though it was past eleven p.m., we were ready to take on more. The younger lot, Samara and Robin, though, were done for the day. Their arms slush, with legs lagging behind them, they looked like wet cotton mops that had swept a floor too many. In no time, they were snoring in their room.

Samar was not ready to hit the sack, just yet. He wanted to venture out for a bit. Victor and Mira wanted to try their luck at the casino. A deal was struck. One hour was what Samar got before he had to head back to his room to watch over his siblings. For Samar, that one hour ended before it really began to take off, and for Victor, the same hour dragged by in sixty minutes. Not fifty, not fifty-nine, but sixty whole minutes; one minute at a time.

Once set free, Victor went straight for the Black Jack. Mira tried her hand at the slot machines. Three minutes gone and forty of her blue tickets-to-a-lottery had already been chewed up by the hungry machine. It burped back only three tiny ones, which it eventually chewed up too. She went in search of Victor; she would coax a few out of him. But Victor seemed to be spending more time at the cashier than at the tables. His wallet had lost a few hundred pounds within minutes, power walking, to and fro, from the cashier to the table. Mira figured it wasn't their lucky day. She decided to head out, to the bow of the ship. Victor could catch her there on his way back. She stepped out onto the deck and took in the rugged expanse that lay before her. She could distinguish the robust ingredients of the cryptic darkness that lay beyond: briny, fishy, mouldy. Unrefined pureness. The unpretentiousness of the waters made her sigh. Strolling, taking it all in, she reached the bow of the ship. She found Zaydan there.

Zaydan was letting out thick white fumes of carcinogens from his mouth. He stubbed out the cigar on seeing Mira. "Sorry about that. I don't usually smoke. One of the passengers was so insistent I try this brand, I thought I'd give it a shot."

"That's alright. Victor is also finding it tough to give up smoking. So how come you took early retirement?" Mira asked. "If you don't mind my asking?" she added quickly.

Zaydan's forced smile, silent sigh, half-smiling eyes gave Mira the impression she would have to figure it out herself.

Does he have a terminal illness? Gosh, he's so good-looking. Why him? Was it a #Me-too thingy? He must be aware of his good-looks. Bummer if it was that. Something at work? He's still on the same ship, so it's not that, for sure. Just plain lazy? Wants the easy life?

"It's … a long story. But the short of it is that," Zaydan let out, eventually, "I needed time to myself. I kinda … complicated … things in my life." He paused. Sighed; a bit of reserve, some guilt and a fleshy chunk of remorse came pouring out with the sigh. He shifted his weight on the hand-rail, stood a little upright-er. "I needed to fix myself." He thought he would stop at that but Mira's frog-eyed look, and her parted lips in the set-to-ask-questions mode didn't leave him with much choice. "I, uh … was married to this beautiful woman. She loved me like crazy and I … loved her. But then … I don't know why I wanted out. Was it boredom, the mundaneness of years into a marriage, or what? I don't know. So, I divorced her. Then I got married again but after some time, I wanted to get out of that marriage too. After that divorce, I thought I'll get back to my first wife, but things weren't the same anymore. It's not as simple as our minds make it out to be."

Mira felt the need to say something but couldn't figure out the right choice of words that would erase the lines on Zaydan's forehead. She let the moment pass, but a few seconds later, her eyebrows arched, and her eyes opened wide like space capsules, impatiently awaiting the arrival of astronauts. She wanted details.

Zaydan knew the look only too well. He directed Mira towards the only bench there; if she wanted details, she had to stick it out. "I hit a low point. Kind of went under, lost interest in my work. Made excuse after excuse for not being on duty. You should've heard the lame stuff I was laying out there, and they were buying it. At least I thought they were. I later got to know it was only because of the mess I was in; they had been watching the cookie crumble. I wasn't ready to acknowledge I was messed up until I'd gone under. I needed to do something about it." He stopped for a breather there, in the hope that all he had shared so far would satiate Mira, but she remained quiet … a clear indication that she was hoping for more. "It took a lot of shoves and pushes to get me to work on myself. There was a lot of introspection; a lot of retrospection. It needed time. I thought it best to retire so I could work on myself, which was more important than any other work I was doing. If I'm not sorted from within, I'm only gonna make a bigger mess outside. And this job of examining one's soul, I've come to realise, is a lifetime thingy. There's no retirement there. So, you see I'm still a work in progress, in the quest to be, at least according to me, a better version of me," he said. His sheepish smile added a pinch of cheer to the intense talk.

But now she doesn't want me back. Zaydan's words kept ringing in Mira's head as she lay in bed, that night. *Serves him right though.* Even with sleep weighing heavy on them, Mira managed to roll her eyes.

Zaydan had told her he had begun comparing his second wife, Olivia, with his first wife all the time, in his mind. Olivia had lost her appeal very soon; she fell short in comparison with his first wife, Zeenat. He'd try to go over the things that had attracted him to her, that had been enough, then, to make him leave Zeenat. But eventually, the attraction was not deep enough to hold him for long.

The twelve-year bond that he had shared with Zeenat was, unawares or by design, ghosting him with sand-soled feet from a trip to Greece they had taken many years back; it was making him tread on the path he thought he had long forgotten. It was hounding him with the three words she said to him as he had turned to walk out the door, bags in hand. Three words—I need you—that had, then, made him feel conceited and swollen-headed. Those three words were now rehashing, not in hers, but in his voice. In the washroom, when he was alone, the bond was, callously, provoking ghost-impressions of her love-bites, revealing them on his neck, and shoulders, every time he looked in the mirror. And at night, it would creep up on him from her side of the quilt; her fragrance, teasing, vexing, even after a hundred washes.

The twelve-year bond was weighing the score of the arguments she had lost, not because she was in the wrong, but because of his pride. Twelve years of togetherness was demanding its due.

WE CAN NEVER GLORIFY OUR STATURE BY DEMEANING OTHERS

"You said she didn't want to take you back. Do you resent her for that?" Despite having a restless night, Mira had made it through the morning routine with her family; getting them out of their beds, heading for breakfast together, and moving them on to their places of interest. The ship was to dock at St. Maarten by noon. Victor and the kids wanted to take a leisurely dip in the pool before that. After a few laps, Mira had pulled out of the pool and settled on a spot nearby. Her smile had let Zaydan know it was perfectly fine to come over.

"I did, initially." Zaydan spoke in a low baritone. "I hated her and blamed her for everything, accused *her* for pushing me away; bad-mouth her all through that phase. I simply didn't picture myself as someone who had wronged her. I got away with throwing the blame on her, with my friends and family, but facing Zeenat after all those false accusations was not easy to do." He paused, his breathing shallow; deep in thought. "Besides, how long could I lean on stolen honour? We can never glorify our stature by demeaning others. Rather, in bringing them down, we are taking our selves down, too; we show our ugly side. And for what? Throwing the muck at others can't turn things around for us. Believe me, it only worsens matters. I told myself that she pushed me to it. But over time, over days and days, even months of intense soul-searching and half a million conversations with her in my head—strolling by the beach; sitting in a coffee shop, gazing out the window, downing coffee after coffee—I realised I was the one who drove Zeenat to the point at which one is bound to snap. Thinking back, I realize I was never there for her. Her wants and her desires were never taken into account; never given a second thought. I guess I didn't value her enough. Not until I had lost her." He paused, there, and took a big sip of his smoothie before continuing. He had emptied out a large part of his guts; he had earned the chilled calm of the smoothie.

We do this all the time, don't we, sir? Over time, we begin to overlook or forget to value the things we have. That's because they're right there, like a painting that's been hanging on the wall of our room for years. We pass by, without giving it a glance. Only when the painting is gone, and the wall-ghosting—the line of dust where the painting had been—showcasing the emptiness left behind, hits us in the face, do we realize the value of what we had.

The air around Zaydan and Mira had gone dense, weighing down heavy on them. Every breath taken was an added effort. Mira was silent; her eyes, downcast. That is what is expected of one, who, having let inquisitiveness get the better of them without considering the consequences, digs out sores and pangs that have been trained diligently, over the course of years, to lie low and unstirred.

Mira grabbed the quite moment to cast a fleeting glance at her kids. Robin was hugging the edge of the pool. She could make out he wanted to take off his water-wings but she simply smiled at him. She needed him to keep the water-wings on; they were doing her job—keeping her child afloat. Samar and Samara seemed sorted, doing laps and stuff. Victor was stretched out, knocked out on a lounger nearby.

She turned her attention back to Zaydan; her eyes, space-capsules again; once again, compelling him to go on. The reason wasn't just curiosity. It was more to do with the fact that she could relate to a lot of things he was saying; things that she often had a tough time figuring out on her own. Zaydan's talk made sense of those things; it was therapeutic, even. All the while, she had been strawberry-picking-and-pickling—picking the plump and ripened pointers from him and preserving them for future use.

He understood her wide-eyed look, "When realisation struck, I wanted to retract my steps and go back to the life I had with Zeenat. But, comes a time when you realize that life is not a walk on a beach, where waves wipe off the footprints you leave behind; but rather, like walking on wet cement. Before you can cover your misstep, the cement runs dry and imprints of your mistakes are sealed for life. By the time I wanted to go back she had learned to live life on her own terms. I guess, in the face of adversity, you learn to stick it out. I couldn't accept the fact that she didn't want me back. I was hurt, humiliated; hated her for putting me through that. It was a long time before I learned to free myself of the resentment and anger—things that would've eaten me up and eventually made a living corpse out of me. I needed my past to make me better, not bitter. Life is definitely calmer and more meaningful since I sorted myself out. Yes, it's not the life I would've chosen, but I didn't leave myself with much choice, did I? I respect Zeenat for the person that she is today. I let her be, while living in the hope that someday we may get to reconnect again. If not, I shall accept it as my Karma. What troubles me most, is not about losing what we had, or what has become of us. It's about her being content with where we are at now, and not wanting more."

"I … I don't know what to say. I can relate to her feelings. Often we wives crave respect more than love. Love comes where there is respect. I really hope things work out the best way for you, both."

Zaydan's smile began on a note of gratitude, but ended with resignation. His shoulders had shriveled; coiled. "The actual fallout happened … when our son passed away in an accident." He stopped; took a long pause. He knew Mira would need a minute to digest that; the sudden jerk of her head had said as much. "It was probably he who had kept us holding on to our relationship, until then. But suddenly he was gone. Things got ugly when I suggested I wanted to donate his organs. Someone out there could see the world through his eyes. Someone could keep his heart beating. That someone would feel love, and share love as my son would have. I would have had him with me for longer. But she was dead against it; said there would be cuts and patches on his face; that she couldn't bear to see him that way. But our son was so mangled up, in any case, after the accident that …" Zaydan closed his eyes; he continued softly, "that a few more cuts on his face wouldn't have made much of a difference." He broke off there, leaving the rest to Mira's imagination.

Mira shut her eyes. If only she could shut her mind, too. But what good did her eyes do by staying shut? Tears had still managed to find their way out.

Just then Victor came looking for her. His near-smile vanished on seeing her. *She's telling her sob story to a stranger? She barely knows him.* "Shall we grab the kids? We're going to dock soon." Victor didn't bother with small talk; one formal nod at Zaydan, and he walked off in the direction of the kids.

Gawd! Where are his manners? I can never figure what ticks him off. "I'm sorry, we need to make a move." Mira tried to downplay the apathy Victor had shown. Her conversation with Zaydan, about his son, was not one to be left midway, and the ache in Zaydan's voice was not one to be appeased on its own, but she was left with no choice; she had to leave. Zaydan had to deal with the melancholy he had fetched out, at her behest and then left him with. He had to, singlehandedly, lift it, shake it, dust off any lint it may have gathered, lay it flat, face-down, fold it neatly and place it back into the closet it came from.

She would have to air it another time.

In the meanwhile, the kids had had a wild time in the pool, going down the water slide, splashing. They would've stayed in longer had they not docked at St. Maarten.

We had a blast of a day, too. Charmaine looked super-hot in a burgundy two-piece, and she had us gaping at the ease with which she did the hand-stand and under-water flips. She was a mermaid! I was, totally, utterly, mesmerised. As was Rock, unfortunately. I needed to come up with a way to keep Rock away from her. I knew I didn't stand a chance against him, chatty and outgoing that he is, but my heart wasn't ready to give her up, just yet. And, every now and then, Charmaine would flash the cutest smile in my direction, getting my hopes soaring high.

St. Maarten, rightly named the Sun-Soaked Island, was full of crystal-clear water beaches; every beach a kaleidoscope of what lay beneath. The Flying Dutchman zip-line we took at the Sky Explorer was out of the world. The euphoria of the experience lasted us through lunch, only to be outdone by another surprise Victor had in store for us.

Something even better than this? Wowsie! We couldn't wait.

True to his word, it was a *wowsie* moment. Victor took us to Maho beach where we would experience jets take off just fifty metres away from us.

There was no way that Samara and Robin could hold their own, in face of the blowing air and sand that gushed in all directions when the jets roared off, so the two and Mira, stayed behind. While the rest of us, Victor and Samar, and Rock and Snippy and me, found a good spot just beyond the fence, fifty metres away from a jet that was about to take-off. Victor told Samar a tip he had picked-up on the way there: *Turn your back to the fence and when the jet takes off, hold on to the fence real tight from behind. Do not let go, no matter what.*

We did the same, and we were both blown away, metaphorically and literally. Our hands were being peeled off with such force I feared I would be blown away far into the sea. The sea would've taken flimsy-me down and swallowed me immediately. Snippy, our wise one, wound her legs around the fence and held on for dear life. We dared not scream for fear the sand would go into our mouths. Eyes shut, mouths shut, we held on against the wild wind till the jet had covered a bit of a distance. When I opened my eyes, Snippy's mouth was gaping as wide as the sea in front of us, but Rock was nowhere to be found. Snippy and I headed towards the shore and found Rock wafting over the waves; the waves were bringing him back in. He's lucky he didn't go down under with his weight.

Next was Baby beach, where Robin did what little kids do when they see sand—make a sand-castle! Victor and Samar went off kayaking while Mira helped Samara collect pretty seashells for their potted plants back home. At a distance, Mira could see tiny versions of her men riding the ocean; she waved at them.

She seemed content. The devil is in the details. Up close, you'd see she was pissed off. Victor hadn't once made a move to come close or try to hold her hand. *Such beautiful beaches would get anyone walking hand-in-hand!* Adding to that vexation, her doctor hadn't mailed her the test results, as yet.

Back at the ship, after dinner, we came across Charmaine. We hadn't seen her since we had disembarked. She and Zaydan had lazed at a café in St Maarten, all day. Charmaine had taken charge over Zaydan's mind right after he had left Olivia, and has been with him ever since.

"We had the most amazing time at Maho beach. The take-off and landing were just mind-blowing," I was boasting to Charmaine.

"Have you done it, Charmaine? Stood right at the fence while the jets took-off, almost blasting your face away?" Snippy was certain Charmaine, fragile and dainty that she was, hadn't ever done such a thing.

"Course! A dozen times. Maybe more," she replied.

Whoa, Iron babe! Or did Charmaine say it to antagonize Snippy's green-eyed monster even more?

We heard something sizzle. Rock and I turned to look in Snippy's direction, but it was only an insect that had burnt itself on a light-bulb.

"Is that so?" Snippy's Brit accent, accentuated; a catalyst for war.

Rock and I jumped up instantly, almost banging into each other in the mad rush to get Snippy out of there. It was time we called it a night.

SOME THINGS YOU CAN'T TAKE BACK
SOME, YOU CAN'T GET BACK

Right after breakfast, Mira's feet began to wiggle. They shuffled for a bit, and then took her exactly where she wanted to be, but on getting there, she halted. *Is this even right?* She turned to head in the opposite direction. After a few steps, she stopped, turned, and headed back towards Zaydan.

Moments later, she was gazing at the ocean; Zaydan's words flowing into her with the same measured smoothness as in the lazy crests and troughs they were watching. It was becoming a habit of hers to seek him out. She was smiling more. She had even stopped carrying her book around with her; her passion left abandoned somewhere on one of the pool loungers, too wounded, too miffed to find its way back to her.

There was much she wanted to ask Zaydan but wasn't sure if she should. Or could. One thing slipped out despite her reluctance. "We all make mistakes in life, and sometimes, we wish we could go back in time and change course, not do those mistakes at all. Do you ...?"

"No," he replied, almost immediately. "I don't. There *are* things that I'm certainly not proud about. It may sound clichéd, but the situations I got myself into have shaped me into the person I am today. My flaws taught me lessons the hard way, so hard that I can never go back to my old ways again. Because of the person that I was, I would've ruined things for myself and for those around me again, eventually. But today, I'm wiser." He looked at Mira then, his eyes boring into hers. "All those years together, I had thought I was in love with Zeenat, and then, with Olivia. But I came to realize later, that I was in love with the *feeling* of being loved. I was sweet on the attention, and the extra adoration. The person from whom I was getting it did not matter. Where I was getting the most from, was what mattered—a selfish need to boost my egotism. Now, it's not about me, anymore. I miss my family, but I've stopped wondering what life would've been like with them by my side. I've stopped troubling myself. Some things you can't *take* back, and some you can't *get* back. Honestly, that was my tipping point, the game changer for me. I've understood that things happen for a reason. It was life's way of telling me to change; to grow, to evolve. Because back then, I wasn't ready to acknowledge the person I was. If I wasn't ready to acknowledge my flaws, how was I going to work on them? It was a much-needed reality check. I'm okay with wherever life takes me now because I know I will be able to handle it. Today, I'm quite … as they say … sorted."

Isn't it sad, Mr Umana, that Zaydan needed such a hard-hitting smack in the head to understand where he was going wrong? He said he did not want to go back in time to rectify or undo all that he did, because he had grown from his mistakes. He had evolved. He says he's learned to live with what life has to offer. But he missed out one crucial thing. He didn't say anything about Sorrow—the unsavoury mistress that lives with him, all the time now.

Seeing him all alone, Sorrow had started stalking him. At first, she seemed to be his solace, but then, she got into the habit of repeating his sob stories to him, over and over. He had thought he was done with her once his tears dried up, but that was not so. Despite not being welcome, she barged her way into his everyday life; an escort to his loneliness. And now, this *Fatal-attraction* mistress refuses to leave. She has nestled into a quiet corner and springs on him, every now and then, when he's least expecting it. The last time was at his friend's son's wedding. Watching his friend and his son take to the dance floor, Zaydan knew she was creeping upon him. He left the party early, rushed to his car as fast as he could, putting his favourite music on at full blast in the hope to blow her out of the windows. On reaching home, he latched his door behind him. Click. Click. Click. Three latches. But he knew he'd find her cozied up in bed next to him, going over his sob stories again. He had cried himself to sleep again. Some mornings she lets him be. On others, she is waiting for him, perched prettily in her corner, deep inside his chest, right on top of his heart; fat and weighty that she is now, making his breathing labored; wretched, broken.

Wrong choice of a life partner, wouldn't you say, Mr Umana! You think things would've worked for him had he given a thought to the repercussions of his actions *before* taking the steps that he did? Had he thought them through?

The waters were processing the newly acquired knowledge for Mira, layering it; archiving it for her. She felt calmed. It felt like Zaydan was slowly oozing his calmness into her, assuredly. Definitively. She had even started smiling like him.

She watched as a young guy, probably in his late twenties, made his way towards them and move to touch Zaydan's feet.

Zaydan is Indian? How come he didn't bring it up? Not a hint!

"Sabhya, please," Zaydan's arms stretched out to the guy, inviting him closer for a hug instead. "My blessings come from my heart. Why are you seeking them from my feet? I'm no god."

"Mira, this is my nephew, my sister's son, Sabhya. And yes, I'm part Indian." The query in her eyes was not lost on him. "My Kashmiri mom fell for my Greek dad, and eloped. I do have a few traces of Indianness. My sister married a very handsome Bengali, hence this handsome dusky hunk, here. He's held on to his roots well, as you can see." Zaydan was patting Sabhya on his back with pride. "He's on training here and he's doing very well for himself, I must say. Of what I've seen for the past three days, he could soon be the next Assistant Cruise Director. Proud of you, my boy."

Sabya moved to touch Mira's feet, too, but she shooed him off. *I'm a mother of a four-year-old, for crying out loud!* She blessed him with folded hands.

They had docked at St. Thomas as early as 8 a.m., but the kids had wanted to sleep in. 8 a.m. was too early to begin a *vacay*-day. It was now past 10 a.m. She needed to check on her kids; she excused herself.

Charlotte Amalie, located in the island of St Thomas, was as brilliantly coloured a city as could be. On this island, everyone was in their skimpiest, getting me feeling overdressed in my thigh-high shorts. *Is the hotness of this place always like this, or am I the reason for the sizzle?*

Fabulous food, excellent ambience, perfect weather; with beer in hand, Victor and Mira were already merry. *Now we have two more to watch over!* Mira gets silly when she gets tipsy. Smiling gaily, she was now insisting on climbing a tree. We were thrilled to see her sprightly, but Samar was like, *Seriously, mom!*

"What? I used to climb trees all the time when I was a kid. I'd buy chocolates, climb up a tree right outside my house and come down only after I'd polished off every single one. Learn to live a little, kiddo. Do what *you* like to do. Not what others want you to do. Or be!"

That statement was enough to validate her drunkenness; she was hammered. *I'm going to climb this damn tree.* Her giggles and fumbling were telling Samar and the rest that she wouldn't make it up the tree. But she climbed it, and perched herself prettily on a branch, for them to take pictures of her. Which they did hastily, before she fell off; they couldn't risk her doing a retake of the whole climbing and fumbling thing. It was way too embarrassing.

On her way down, Victor helped her. She let her eyes travel to his flexed muscles as he held her by the waist. His hands felt strong. His face let the twitches on it curve themselves and conjoin into a smile.

A little shopping here, a lot of window-shopping there, and we headed back to our dreamboat. It was just past 5 p.m. Mira suggested asking Zaydan to show the kids around the control room, the heart and head of the ship from where the captain and his crew did all the navigation.

***

"Mom, when we get back, tell dad to ask the lawyer for the adoption papers he got the other day."

"Are you still thinking about all that? We told you it has nothing to do with us."

"I just want to see them once. I know what I saw and if you're telling me the truth then what's the effing harm in seeing them?"

"Watch your language, young man! If your dad gets to hear you cussing …"

"Oh, really! Your only concern is that Samara and Robin don't pick up on these words. You obviously don't give a hoot about me or what I'm going through. You don't have the time to, you're too busy with that guy!"

"What did you just say? Are you suggesting something? 'Coz if you are, you better stop right there. There's nothing happening. And don't you *dare* suggest anything of the sorts!"

It was just that morning that she had corrected herself. *What the hell is happening? You need to distract yourself. There's so much to do on this ship and you keep finding reasons to go to him. Is that too bad, though? I'm probably going to die soon, so what the heck! There's no physical attraction, but he does get me thinking about him all the time.* The attraction she felt, what was the reason? Her smile that came on, at just the thought of him? She analysed two major reasons coming into play: a) the attention she was getting from him was so palliative, and b) the inadvertent guidance she was getting from his misshapen life. The fact that he was now polished and fashioned into the perfect man any woman would give an arm and a leg for, could also be a major reason, of course, but it couldn't figure its way into her analysis. She labeled her desire to seek his company every day as a search for emotional comfort, and nothing beyond that.

In fact, Zaydan too, with great discretion, had voiced his

disinterest for anything venereal when he noticed Mira being hesitant and reserved as she had made her way towards him that morning. They must have been brought together for some other reason. *Blame it on Kayla,* he had told himself, and left it at that.

Samar's outburst had made Mira realize it was not just she who had sensed the shift in her behaviour. It made us realize we needed to up our game. A nice clandestine evening, just Victor and Mira, would be ideal to bring back the romance between the two. *But where do we start? Charmaine, of course!* We went in search of her.

"Wassup guys?" Charmaine was lazing by the pool, next to Zaydan.

We told her our plan. She was kind enough to slip our directives into Zaydan's mind.

ALWAYS HAVE A PLAN B

A candle dinner invite for two was waiting on their bed as Mira and Victor entered their cabin. Laying there, it looked too irresistible to say no to. Mira had already said 'yes' before handing the card to Victor. As for him, he *had* to say 'yes'. The sight of Mira in tears in Zaydan's company had upset him more than he cared. And then, there was her sudden carefree attitude. So, a clandestine dinner it was.

With the kids in tow, we went out in search of Charmaine again.

We found her patting two Klein poodles, fluff in curly white Bolero hairstyles, gratifying the spot next to a handsome sixty-something couple. Our kids rushed over. They wanted to caress and cuddle and snuggle and coddle the poodles. The poodles seemed friendly enough, as did the sixty-something couple. We couldn't get our hands off the poodles; our fingers were getting lost in their fluff.

After a while, Samar decided to head off; something better had caught his eye. He searched the deck for his mom and dad, and spotted them at a distance. He wiggled his fingers the dumb-charade way: *Here's the little lot. Get here quick, if you want. I'm off.*

Rock wiggled his fingers at us: *I'm going with him.* Seizing the opportunity, he asked Charmaine, "What say we try out the Jacuzzi there while Papier and Snippy are watching over the kiddies?"

"Uh … yeah sure!"

Rock grabbed Charmaine by the hand and pulled her away.

She did turn to look in my direction, once. *I know she likes me.* My gut said so. But then why couldn't she come up with an excuse to not go with him?

They moved beyond the pool, walked past the last of the loungers, and were soon out of my line of vision. I was in extreme torture. Snippy, sensing my agony, *tsk-tsked,* smiling her wide-toothed smile while, mindlessly, cuddling the poodles.

"Watch it, Snipps! You might clip them with your sharpness," Ix said, turning my attention to the poodles. *Didn't their puff have more volume earlier?*

Victor and Mira had joined us and were thanking the French sixty-something couple for letting the kids play with their objects of pride. They had set out together in search of Zaydan to thank him; they were certain the dinner invite had been sent on his behest. Also, a game of Bingo was starting in half an hour, right after which there was a Russian dance skit. Victor wanted to round up his family and take them along.

Getting the younger lot to part with the poodles was proving to be as easy a task as taking candy from a child. *And where do we go in search of Samar?* But it was Rock and Charmaine who had me running amok, looking like a sprinting squirrel with binoculars glued to its eyes.

It was close to fifteen minutes when we were all assembled together.

Just as we were entering the hall where Bingo was to be played, Mira nudged Victor to switch his phone to silent mode. *Not right to disturb other guests.*

His eyes gave her the of-course-I-know-what-to-do look, which, within a second, flitted to the don't-try-to-be-too-smart-with-me look. Then, he slid his thumb to the side of his phone to put it on mute before he'd forget to do so.

Gawd! Will these people never let up a chance to be one up on the other?

They didn't win anything in Bingo, although Victor had been feeling very lucky. He did, though, manage to get a few solo snaps clicked with the Russian dancers. Afterwards, the kids were escorted to the Ocean View Café. There was, indeed, a round-the-clock escort on the house, courtesy Zaydan, to watch over them and assist them whenever necessary, so that Victor and Mira could dine alone, uninterrupted, at the Roof-top Terrace.

Hypnotic raunchy shadows, cast by candle-flames, were swaying to the seductive tunes of the guitar serenading them. But their magic was not working on Victor and Mira. Victor was behaving as though his wife was extra body-weight that he had been trying hard to shed. Mira was poised as though she'd been accosted by a stranger who was trying to chat her up while waiting for coffee at her regular Starbucks: *Yeah, he's serenading so well. I know, what an expansive ship. Oh, yeah, lovely weather, just loving it! ... Oh, there's my coffee. Nice chatting!*

With the kids not around, nor any of their friends, they felt strange; being alone, just the two of them.

"Samar still has his doubts," Mira thawed the ice that had formed dull, unloving shapes in the space between them.

"Yeah, I feel so, too. He's being a bit reserved and distant, still. In the family pic, after the Russian show, his look is so frosty. Almost harsh."

Both fell silent again.

"You think it's time we told them?" Victor, finally, mustered up the courage to ask.

Mira looked up at him, then; right into his eyes. Her fear, fearless, shameless, was sitting naked at the rim of her eyes. Fear that had been, for ever so long, not allowed to even be conceived. Not yet. But now, it had been conceived, and it had taken birth, prematurely. It had let out its first cry. Mira didn't want to nurse it. She didn't want it to latch on, feed off on her. She wanted to give it away, she wasn't ready for it. "I don't …" she said, letting the rest of her words trail and feed on her doubts. "You think he would …? She paused, again. "It would ruin the trip … for all of us, don't you think?" Having put it off for so many years, waiting for the right moment, now, when it was time, it was only natural that she would be apprehensive. "What's happening to us? Where did we go wrong? We couldn't have taken the wrong decision. And now our family's falling apart."

"Why do you say that? We knew we would have to face this, someday. All will be fine." Victor reached out to her, resting his hand on hers.

Mira didn't push it away.

"This has to be dealt with, with care and delicacy. It has to be planned well. And we have to do it together, you and me. I guess we could let it sit till we get back. Let's make the most of this time together." He extended his other hand on the table, leaving it facing upwards, for her hand to find its way into it. "Mira, look up at me. I'm tired of fighting with you all the time. And I'm tired of finding ways to reduce this distance we've put between us."

"You never once tried," Mira cut in.

"I do try. But, yes, I give up easily. And, yes, I … I wait for you to make the first move."

"Precisely!"

"Let's not do this to each other. Let's make a new start. I'll make an extra effort. You'll see a new me, I promise. It's taking a toll on the kids, too." He watched as her chin tipped; her shoulders, like the wings of a retired eagle. He got off his seat, walked over to her side and pulled her up, into his arms.

Defenses down (don't no one blame it on the wine; this took hard work from our end), she let him take charge of her; of her, of her senses, of her frail disposition. He had made the first move, she owed it to him. And that was the cue for all of her tears to come rolling down. Victor pulled her even closer, molding her into him, like clay; shaping her into him, limb by limb. Mira warmed up, taking deep breaths of the rugged scent of his skin. Rustic musk deer mingled with his man smells reminded her of better times. He whispered honeyed words into her ear, making her mush.

Rock didn't catch the words; Snippy was too embarrassed to tell; I could only figure.

But then, Mira started pounding his chest with her fisted hands; she began pushing him away. *Not happening. I'm not going to give in today. He makes a fool of me and gets his way with me, every time.*

"Stop it, Mira. What's gotten into …?"

"I don't wanna be made a …" Mira started to say.

"Shush, my Mira. Don't spoil the moment." Victor placed his finger on her lips. She still made to resist. That left him with no choice but to place his lips over hers.

Back in their room after a quick peek into the kids' room, gratified that they had retired for the day, Victor and Mira rushed to reboot their long-lost passion. They were behaving like teenagers at it for the very first time. Clothes were being strewn all over the room, shoes being kicked-off in every direction. Totally hands-on.

But then, Mira started pulling away again.

The alcohol had had its effect, but apparently, not enough to let her guard down. "You ain't getting your way with me till you tell me what you were doing in the hotel room, that day." She had her arms crossed over her naked breasts, but rendering enough view to tantalize him and vex the truth out of him. *Talk about grabbing him by the balls! Women really have their ways.*

"I had a meeting there."

"That late in the night? Does your line of work even *require* late night meetings?"

"You do know I am planning on expanding in other cities."

"Seriously? You expect me to believe you were meeting someone late at night in a hotel room regarding expansion of your bookstore? Really? Was it a woman you had the meeting with?"

"It wasn't anything of the sort. Trust me."

She didn't. Her breasts remained behind their casing.

He tried every which way to disabuse her thoughts, but in the end, he had to come clean. Sitting in front of him the way she was, he couldn't fight her anymore. "It wasn't me. It was uncle Kamaal. He got caught with his client and was kicked out of the house. So, he was staying the night there and wanted me to help him out."

"What bull!"

"I swear!"

"Really? Is it anyone I know?"

"No, you don't know her."

"Christ! Men!"

Victor glared at her.

She glared right back. "And how do I know you're telling me the truth?"

He was gaping. "You think I would shame my uncle with such stuff just to cover my ass?"

"So then why didn't you tell me all of this that day itself?"

"You think it's easy letting out stuff like this? I was effing ashamed. I didn't want you to know any of it."

"And that justifies hitting me and shoving our relationship down the drain?"

"I knew you would mock me with every chance you got. And FYI, I didn't hit you, okay?"

"You would've, had I not stopped you. Do you realize how hurtful it is for me to know that even after all these years, you still can't confide in me? I'm actually offended that you would think so lowly of me." The outbursts had her coughing. Soon she began choking. Victor grabbed some water for her and rubbed her back; soothing her, warming her. Gradually caressing, fondling; his fingers gliding over her spinal peaks, one by one; sensuous; lustful. She relaxed, lulled. She took another sip to drown the last of her cough.

He turned her around to face him. He wanted his desire to make her dizzy; as dizzy as it was making him. He kissed her neck, tracing her tears, catching them midway, halting them in their path; ending their journey, there. His lips then moved on to her mouth, muffling her words, cajoling them to become moans of pleasure. They were melting into each other. Two candles aflame, their warm wax flowing into each other, their shades and shadows mingling. And then, there was a knock at the door.

Samar, with Robin in tow, had an *is-that-what-I-think-it-is-happening-in-there?* look on, when the door finally opened. "He's missing you, Mom." With a shrug and a sorry-I-didn't-know look, he left. Without Robin.

Oops! Rock looked at me. I looked at Snippy. Snippy looked from Rock to me.

Why had we not thought up a plan B?

'But I Didn't Promise to Let You Forget I'd Forgiven It'

Come morning, it was their day at sea. There was no rush to do anything, and Mira's conversations with Zaydan could wait. Everything could wait. She was with her man.

I peeped over at Robin. His face was snuggled cozily in his kangaroo's tummy; both were still snoring.

I looked over at the two pining hearts. Victor was eyeing Mira from over Robin's head. *How noiseless can you be?*

You've gotta be kindin'!

"But I thought you'd forgiven me for that, and promised to forget it." He whispered, quoting a saying by a pleading man.

"Yes—but I didn't promise to let you forget I'd forgiven it." Mira knew the woman's reply in the saying and quoted it verbatim.

Cheeky! Victor wasn't going to give in so easy. *Just a quickie.*

No! He's such a light sleeper.

I was so enjoying their banter.

Not wanting to disturb Robin, they moved to their balcony for bed-tea, and a cuddle.

"You seem to be spending a lot of time with Zaydan. Should I be worried?"

Mira smiled to herself. She knew he was down-playing his

jealousy; she revelled in that little declaration. Her long kiss cleared his doubts. They were warming up to each other in slow degrees, taking baby steps. It looked like a good time to let him in on her fears. "I went to our GP before the trip, 'coz of my cough. He had some tests done."

"And you're telling me now? And?"

Mira looked up to give him the well-obviously-we-were-not-talking look but she let it go, on seeing his expression; it had lost the hungry flush of a few seconds before. "He seemed a bit concerned. I was hoping to receive the results by now. I messaged him yesterday; still waiting for his reply."

"All will be fine." Pushing the sinking feeling away, pulling her closer to him, snuggling her, Victor said a silent prayer. And a promise to himself to quit smoking, completely.

No matter what the situation between them was, or had been over the years, he couldn't think of life without Mira. He did love her, even if he hadn't let her onto it. He did love her even if it took just the hint of a terminal illness for him to realize it.

Her GP had actually dropped in a mail early that morning. Mira's test result was negative; there was nothing major to worry about, just a nagging cough due to some allergies, which, had they been treated on time, would not have flared-up. I kept them busy so she wouldn't check her mail, just yet. Sometimes a little worry is good. It stimulates emotions that have been conscientiously, *egotistically,* concealed and buried. For the moment, I was gloriously watching those emotions flow freely from one to the other, although with limited gestures.

They had to watch themselves; Robin was already tossing and turning in their bed.

***

It was their sixth day of the cruise. At night, they were to attend the captain's dinner. It was to be a grand one.

The day called for lazing and relaxing, spoiling themselves. For Victor and Mira, it meant starting the day with a nice long dip in the Jacuzzi on the pool deck and then pampering themselves at the Spa with massages, facials, steam and sauna. They booked Robin and Samara for the Afternoon Party, where they would be looked after by an escort for two hours, and then be escorted to the Fun Factory. Samar had planned his day the previous night itself. He would go in search of the girl he had been watching, on the sly, since he had sighted her while playing with the poodles. *Isn't she the same girl I'd seen at the Easter Fun Fest in our park back home?*

Snippy figured she'd hang around the little tots, although she was not interested in having Rock and me and Charmaine around. She knew our foolishness would be done with once the cruise ended; watching us make fools of ourselves, and feeling jealous in the meantime was not particularly entertaining.

As luck would have it, Rock chose not to hang around Charmaine and me; said he wanted to be with Samar, to give him guidance on how to woo a girl; to teach him the tricks of the trade. He was lying. He'd probably lost interest in Charmaine. That's the thing about Rock. He chases girls, plays them, and then loses interest fast enough. *How can anyone be so conceited? He's such a … such a … I could cuss on his name, all day long! Good for me, though!*

But it was only later in the day that Charmaine let me in onto the reality of his actions, and onto her feelings for me. I got to learn about the entire conversation Rock and she had had last evening. As we sat, side by side, by the bow of the ship, just a few inches away from where *Jack* and *Rose* had done the Titanic pose; just a few moments away from the beginning of another love story, our love story, Charmaine replayed her conversation with Rock for me to hear (we're archangels; we can record things in our minds, and replay them as and when we wish):

So, about Papier, don't you think he's such a …? I heard Rock saying. *Is there something I'm missing here?*

What're you talkin' about?

It's the smile that comes on at the mention of his name. It's a big give-away. And the look in your eyes as you turned to look back at him.

I, uh … Nothing of the sort!

Uh, huh! So, as I was saying, he's such a dud-head, don't you think?

I could hear the ghost of a tease in his voice.

I would have to know him better for that, I heard Charmaine say.

Ah, ha! You're smiling that smile again. Something's cooking for sure. Come out ... come out with it. There was silence, then. He was waiting for her reply.

As was I. Had I been there, with them, I could've seen her expression.

But hey, on a serious note, he's a fab guy and I can tell he's really into you. Oh, yeah! It's all over his face … and that's why I pulled you away to let you know that, with just two days to go, you *will have to make the first move. In case you are wondering why things aren't moving forward with you guys, he's a bit on the shy side. So … all the best to you. I'm with you guys a hundred percent … there, whenever you need me. Muah!* His voice muffled at that point, letting me know Rock was hugging her.

Then, I heard Rock say, *Let's hang around for a little bit longer. Let him think you and I are a thing. I'd love to see that gob-smacked look on his face. What say, huh?*

Now that's wicked! But … you're a darling! Charmaine's cute voice said.

Ain't I just! And I heard him do his wicked belly-laugh.

So Charmaine was mine. All mine. I was a million fireworks ready to go off all together, spiraling into the sky, displaying my joy, far and beyond, for the world to know that she was mine. I didn't even have to face the anxiety of proposing. Rock is *such* a darling! A softie with a hard crust; that's the cutest thing about him. I do love him so! That thing I said earlier, about him being conceited and stuff, I guess I was just …

Rock was out of the way; it was Snippy who was being the ass now. Ever since she got to know about me and Charmaine, she seemed to have flipped. Her accent got more accentuated. She was saying things like: *I'm doing smashing!* And *I'm a cool dude!* And *I ain't goin' there, there is boring!* She was trying to look cool, and all. To make matters worse, every time she'd get the chance, she'd snip off a tuft of hair from the poodles, solely because they were dear to Charmaine. She started by clipping off hair from the not-so-visible places; she got so addicted to venting out her envious flush on the poodles that every few hours they would be sashaying down the decks with a new hairdo. She had become Ms. Scissor-*legs*, snipping away till they looked like over-pruned dog-shaped shrubs. I can tell you one thing for sure, the sixty-something French couple were no longer friendly.

Every time they'd come across each other, Snippy and Charmaine would be having a silent wrangle match. The poodles weren't really the reason. That Charmaine was ready to put up a fight for me thrilled me to know; it felt good. Two women; not one, but two women fighting over me. *What a feeling!* And to think I was going to commit suicide. *Mein Gott! What a fool!*

Come evening, Mira and Victor were looking radiant; the pampering had done them good. They picked the kids from their room, rescuing them from the remaining fifteen minutes of baby-sitting, and headed towards the Sunset Bar. Victor dropped a message to let Samar know of their plans, but Samar was good on his own. He had found the girl he was looking for, had chatted her up, and had her by his side, smiling. He was smiling too, after a long hiatus.

GET ON WITH IT BEFORE ROBIN COMES

On the way to their room, Victor and Mira came across Zaydan and Sabhya. Both Zaydan and Sabhya, were laughing their wits out; loud laughter, to the point of being obnoxious. The tiny blue anchors on Zaydan's shirt were getting bumped up and down, trying desperately to stay on-board. Sabhya was standing close by; if you could call that standing, that is. He was doubled into two, trying to contain the hysterical stitches of laughter. Bent over, with a buckled jiggle in his legs, he looked nothing short of an ostrich with its head in the ground.

Victor and Mira turned to leave; they still hadn't thanked Zaydan for the private dinner, but that could wait. They didn't want to kill the euphoria.

On entering the room, Victor kicked off his slippers and jumped into bed for a siesta, flat on his stomach. Mira grabbed her mini humans and dragged them to their room for a shut-eye, but they were too abuzz, flitting back and forth like two dragon-flies. It was a while before Mira headed back to her room. She found Victor snoring. She lay on her bed, her form making indents in the mattress; craters, like dunes in the sand. She looked at her man as he snored.

A little over an hour later, heads started bobbing up; moons rising, eight of them, one by one. I got up with the taste of love in my mouth; I didn't have coffee that evening, I let the taste linger.

Magnifique! That's what every murmur sounded like, as Victor and Mira stepped down the spiral stairway. Victor looked regal and lordly in his vanilla-white silk *Achkan.* Its golden buttons bespoke richness; the ancestral emeralds adorning his neck, gave the perfect touch of colour and handsomeness to his attire. Mira's blanche satin sari graced every curve and contour of her slender form, delicately. There's something about a sari. Six whole yards of it, draped, concealing very-nearly the entire body frame, yet, oozing with a savagery burst of sex-appeal and *oomph.*

Mira had wanted to go Indian, as had Victor. Their three gems walking just a step behind them, although not in Indian attires, complemented their stature—two tuxes in pearl-white and an emerald gown.

Samar had taken ages to get ready; he was out to impress. Mira had sent Victor to the kids' room three times to get Samar going. She didn't want to arrive late at the captain's table.

"What's taking you so long? Your mom keeps sending me over," Victor confided in Samar.

"I was just helping Robin look for his chocolate that I ate last night," Samar said closer to his dad's ear.

"WTH man! Stop fecking with him, will you. He's not gonna let us sleep tonight, again!" He didn't want Robin to come knocking at their door again. "You better get him lots of stuff from the candy counter after dinner."

Dinner time was fun. Everyone was at their best; dressed their best, elegant and crisp. The kids got to shake hands with the captain of the ship. All of a sudden, Victor did a wheezy intake of breath through his teeth. Sure enough, lamb biryani was being served at their table. He feasted on more than he needed to. All three kids turned to look at their mom. *Dad's a goner tonight. For sure!* But they found her smiling.

Hot babes in little black dresses and super sexy stuff where everywhere but, that night, Victor had eyes only for his wife. He couldn't wait to see the entire length of her sari crumbled on their bedroom floor, abandoned. Shapeless. Soulless.

Back in their room, their kisses were passionate, and hurried. They dived into bed; both were thinking the exact same thing: *Get on with it before Robin comes.*

But Snippy wanted them to go slow; sensual and unrushed. She wanted the reason to be love. She dimmed the lights in the room to naught. Only a sliver of the silver-grey sky could slither in; giving prominence to the bodies lying on their sides. Two bodies, next to each other; bathed in carnal hunger. Touching, yet not enough; built-up tempo being put to test.

Victor kissed his wife, gentle and hungry; sensual and savage. The entirety of her lips within his; his hardness yearning her softness. Their passion, deepening.

All of a sudden, he began to wriggle. He shuffled, shifting his haunches.

Vic, don't stop. I'm sorry. I lov …

And, then, he stiffened.

And then, she got it, the whiff of a notoriously foul smell. *Eww!*

Mira, instantly, rolled off to the other side of the bed, pulling the edge of the quilt to mask her nose. By the time she dared to remove the quilt from her face, the mood had died.

He sure ain't getting any tonight either. We, definitely, didn't have a plan B. How could we have anticipated that kind of an episode?

Not much could be done for Victor and Mira that night so I thought I'd make things happen for myself instead. I let Rock and Snippy know I was stepping out to be with Charmaine. I guess they were okay with that, they seemed to be smiling. I wouldn't call Snippy's smile a smile though. A smile is supposed to be happy.

I lowered my lips onto Charmaine's. We did, eventually, pull apart. If we didn't, we would have kissed days away. And my thoughts had things to say. "Tomorrow is our last day together. The morning of the day after, we shall be docking at Fort Lauderdale."

"So, we'll spend the whole of 'morrow together. I'll come along to Nassau with you and the rest."

"Yeah … sounds like a plan." *She didn't mention anything about us. Is this all there is to it? Why isn't she into me? Is this only a fling for her?* "So, see ya tomorrow." *Is this it?* I got up in gradual movements. *Should I have kept sitting? Did I break the momentum? Do I now, pull her into my arms? Will it be our last kiss? Our parting kiss?*

She gave me a peck on my lips and put an abrupt end to my dilemma.

A peck! A tiny peck. One tiny peck!

"Yep! Looking forward," she said. "And … uh …" She looked at me then, but all she finally said was, "Goodnight!"

I couldn't let her part that way. Leaving the night that way felt incomplete. I felt incomplete. "You were going to say something. Please, say it."

She smiled, shifted her gaze to my hand on the railing. "You … haven't … uh, kinda fallen in love, have you?"

Blow! Right where it hurt most. I shut my gaping mouth and turned to look away, towards the ocean. There was a black-and-blue patch running along the wide measure of the ocean. The ocean was as bruised as I was.

I've already …! Haven't you …? Don't you want to fall in love with me? Why doesn't she want to fall in love with me? Is she scared I'll not keep in touch? Not want to continue what we have? What just happened here? "Uh … of course not! But I have fallen in like."

"Ha ha… cute! Love you to bits."

Love you?! The colour of the patch in the ocean was segueing into a pale purple tint; its wound healing.

"Me, too." The tone of my voice gave *me* goose-bumps.

"You're sure?"

"What?"

"That you're not … in love?"

"Yeah," I said immediately, louder than intended. I didn't look at her when I said that. I could play around with my voice, with its varied pitches; hide, pretend, sound something I'm not—unhurt for instance. But my eyes are like the clearest form of glass, transparent, honest, naked; showcasing every arduous sentiment to the outside world. I didn't look back into the ocean either. I didn't trust it to colour my mood anymore. And, I asked, "You?"

FINDING CONTENTMENT IN WHAT YOU HAVE AND NOT LOSE OUT IN THE WAIT FOR WHAT YOU WANT

The next morning, I got up with the taste of bitterness in my mouth. A yearning. Bittersweet love, it is called. I didn't brush my teeth immediately. I let the rawness linger.

We were to dock at Nassau at 12:30 p.m. Which meant Mira had about a good two hours. She dropped, very-nearly dumped, her younger lot in the kids lounge and made a dash for her favourite spot. Rock and Snippy took charge of Robin. I was, obviously, too distracted. It was my last day with Charmaine.

I found her with Zaydan and Mira at our spot—the Lover's Spot. *Why would Mira want to be with Zaydan here?* I was flustered, and edgy. *I thought she had it all figured out. What is this, now?*

Charmaine, on seeing me, jumped off the railing and pulled me into a warm hug. "It's cool! Look at her," she said.

Mira was seated with her back to us at the far-edge of the bow, at the tip of the ship from where she could see nothing but the boundless measure of the blue waters all around her. Hoisted up there, with her back upright, it was just her, there. Just her—her inner being, her consciousness—receptive only to everything the vast wide world in front of her had to offer. Head tilted back, eyes closed, she was taking deep breaths; replenishing, letting peace fill itself in all the spaces inside her where it had lost ground. As I watched her, I understood her need to be where she was. To be like a bird that reaches a measured height in the sky, and then lets its wings go still; soaring free, with the sky as her guide.

Zaydan heard her breathing take on a sedated rhythm. "Can I ask you a personal question? You don't need to reply if you don't want to. Just assess the answer for yourself. Let your inner voice give the answer, for only you, if you please."

Mira was conscious of what he might ask. She dreaded the question. But not as much as she dreaded the weariness in her reply.

Have you ever seen an Elephant plant, Mr Umana? The one with the really big leaves that look like the ears of an elephant? Any given moment before that day, Mira would've wanted to lie on its big leaf, cosy up foetus-like and hide, away from disturbances, and queries.

But at that moment, there, all she could do was nod.

"Are you happy in your marriage? I know it's a very lame question but I want you to get off the beaten track of answers and assess what your expectations are from this marriage after all these years."

Mira's gaze remained adrift; not too far out, where the sea looked placid and at peace, yet, not close enough to be rattled by the jumpy waters under. Just adrift, somewhere in-between the peace and the unrest. "It's uncanny that you ask this of me, today, 'coz just last night, I had a dream that kind of cleared a few things in my head. I think spending so much time with you may have triggered the dream. And watching you with Sabhya yesterday, laughing away, so carefree, enjoying yourself ..."

"Oops." Zaydan cupped his mouth with his hand. "I did see you guys as you were leaving, but I was caught up in the moment … Sorry. My bad!"

"No, no. It's absolutely fine," Mira said, in a light tone. She marveled at how the lack of pretentiousness in his eyes shaved off near about five years from his face. "Rather, we were enjoying watching you have a great time. Enviously! I think seeing you so content, I had, somewhere at the back of my mind, started envisioning Vic to be somewhat like that. So, in my dream, Vic was this super perfect husband, doing everything I ever wished. He was not leaving his socks strewn around, was coming home on time; we were going out so much more, enjoying drinks together. Laughing over silly stuff! He even got me flowers without any reason. In the dream, of course! He was perfect, simply perfect. He was doing everything right, every single day. But soon he started pointing out flaws in me. Imagine that! And somehow … you know how dreams are, the mysterious mechanisms they work by … days pass, and I begin to get a bit agitated and nervy over his behaviour. His perfection was driving me to the point of paranoia. I was beginning to get suffocated. I got up from my dream hyper-ventilating! It got me thinking *I'm actually okay with the way he is. So what if he isn't perfect! He's, definitely, less suffocating than the perfect Vic.* I guess, what my dream was conveying to me is … all these years I wanted a better version of him. I kept trying to change him for the better, and when I saw the better version of him in my dream, I wasn't happy with that one either. The dream was a reality-check. Am I sounding ridiculous?"

Zaydan only smiled. "You were wise; you thought you would

make him wise, too. You are wiser in acknowledging that you should stop trying. In the search for more, we ruin the life we have. *Why can't Victor be like the other husbands?* Greener pastures! Not realizing we already have a great, if not the best, version of a person there is for us at the time. And what if the *other husband* isn't so great from up close? Has baggage with him that you are not familiar with? My own life is a case in point," Zaydan pointed out to her. "It takes a reality-check to yank us out from our fantasy world and toss us into the real world. To show us what we are made for and what we are not. I bet you must've thought, a million times at the least, of getting out of your relationship. And, yet, you are still here. Just this fact is enough for you to acknowledge that you are still hoping to find a way to live a good life with him. And since you have taken this decision, consciously or sub-consciously, then go the extra mile to make it work. It's either out or in. Don't hang in-between with the 'what if' all your life."

Mira turned her gaze back to the waters, the perfect place to dump her issues. She held her breath at the '*what if*'. Looking out as far as she could, at the imperceptible line that segregated the two blues—the deep blue of the ocean with its impenetrable secrets, and the blue of the sky that waits with anticipation every single day to dive into the ocean to decipher the secrets—she lets out all her 'what ifs' with a resounding sigh, willing them to find a home within that realm. *I've been looking in all the wrong places. The peace of mind, the harmony was right here, all this while. The potential to hold on to our relationship and make it work was within me, all this time. I can't change people, and I can't change what's coming my way. What I can do is find a way to navigate the path in front of me, rather than wasting time in perfecting the only path I'm familiar with. It's about finding the right balance, between what I have and what I want. Finding contentment in what I have, and not losing out in the wait for what I want.* She breathed in, filling her lungs with a new joy and all things wonderful. "I feel good." She turned slowly, looking at Zaydan she said, "I could listen to your words of wisdom all day."

"I'm glad! But this is so embarrassing; I'm not so full of wisdom. Had I been, I wouldn't have gone through what I did. Sometimes, when we lose track of the right vision, life steps in; it walks us down a hard path. The path may not be long, but it seems to be long 'coz of the added load we carry. Sometimes … *that* path is the only way to really learn, the only way to change. We don't pay heed to the lessons of life when someone tells us about them. It's only when we experience them ourselves, when we're smacked in the face, that we get a real taste of them. I told you about my experiences, the lessons I learned from my worst mistakes, 'coz you are perceptive, and you are open to learn. If you value your relationships, those relationships become blessings. If you don't, they become lessons. Walk your journey with those lessons. And you'll never again fail in life. To be content in life, you have to have gone through many a discontented time."

To be content in life, you have to have gone through many a discontented time.

Oxymoronic, isn't it Mr Umana? Discontentment shows you the value of contentment.

It is through your journey of life that God is giving you a chance to gain experiences. You are the protagonist of your story. You are facing those experiences. You are enacting those experiences. And you are the spectator, getting enlightened by those experiences. It is you, the protagonist, at the giving end. It is you, the spectator, at the receiving end. It is all you. And it is your choice whether you wish to be wise, or otherwise.

"That thing you said about finding a way around people you can't change … we, sometimes, come across people who piss us off at every juncture they can, they get on our nerves. Those people are tough nuts, I tell you. Every time we come across such people, their negativity and shrewdness hit us smack on the face. In moments such as those, I find myself just standing there, watching the moment slip by, berating myself for not giving it right back to them. How do I find a way around such people?"

"Each gives what he has. You must've heard the story of the Berlin wall."

Mira began to nod, but then, she stopped herself. She wanted to hear his take on it.

"This huge wall divided East and West Germany back in the days of their animosity. One day, some people on the East Berlin side dumped a truck-load of garbage on the West side. The people on the West side could've done the same but they chose not to. Instead, they stacked a truck-load of canned food, milk, breads and other provisions on the East side and put a sign on the stack saying: *Each gives what he has*."

"That's beautiful. But sometimes we … just can't even if we wish to."

"In reality, the negative attitude of people is a sign of their insecurities. They have things troubling them. They're full of anger and hatred, but don't know how to deal with that and neither do they want to step down from their mighty pedestal … the height to which their alter ego has taken them. Don't let their negativity rub off on you. Learn to ignore. That'll be the tour de force of triumph for you. 'Coz that negative attitude thrives on attention, and attention you're not gonna give it, anymore. Soon, it will die its own death. There's one more thing I would like to mention here. Stop having expectations from anyone, from any relationship; an expectation to change, or to do as you would wish them to. I imprinted this rule, nice and bold, in my mind. And believe you me, things really began to change for me then on."

Mira went silent. *This is exactly what Kayla has been harping about, for ever so long: Have zero expectations from anyone. When you do not get what you are expecting from someone, you get disturbed. You go all out to brandish the person. But, when you have zero expectations, even the little good that they do, thrills you, because you didn't see it coming. You weren't expecting anything at all. It elates you, makes you joyous.*

OMG! Mira picked up her phone and typed '*You're such a bitch!!*'

'*Wat d hell, babes? What hapnd?*' Kayla was quick to reply.

'*U put me up to this, didn't you? U got me on this cruise 'coz of Zaydan. You knew he would work his magic on me. No wonder he was everywhere I went the first few days. Like an idiot I had thought he was hitting on me. Idiot! You shud've told me. Although, I feel like a whole new person. P.S. I love you.*'

'*Love u too, babe … I was expecting your msg days back. Now go have a ball of a time. XOXO.*'

We had known all about Kayla's plan. Snippy had read the messages she had sent Zaydan the morning after her anniversary dinner; the morning Mira confided in her about Victor.

"How did you know it was me?" Phone still in her hand, Mira asked Zaydan.

"Sorry, what? I didn't get you."

"Kayla. Did you, like, go through the system to find what room I was in, or what?"

Zaydan crimsoned like he used to back in his school days, when he would get caught for innocent mischievousness. "She forwarded me a snap of yours from a recent dinner at her place. Don't look at me! She had me practically throw myself at you, every day."

"That's so her!" Mira warmed up with love for her friend back home.

"Can I ask you a personal question?" Mira blurted out. *What the heck! It's not just laundry we've washed together; we've washed our unmentionables together, too, now. So, yeah! What the heck!*

Zaydan couldn't say no.

"Are you happy? Have you found your peace? I mean, I can see that you are sorted. But … are you in your happy place?"

Zaydan let the question sink in. It was a loaded one. Some concerns are like Thanksgiving turkeys; the heavier they are, the longer the time they need to roast. "I feel the terminology 'Being happy' does not have a definitive definition. Every person describes happiness in their own way. It cannot be confined into any one conclusive form. It has no boundaries. It follows no rules. And for all we know, it may just be a myth we're running after. The first time around, when I got married,

I was really happy; extremely happy. And because I was so happy, so content, I felt I had it all, had it made. But I started taking things for granted … and the relationship started getting stale for me. I didn't seem to feel as happy, anymore. Second time around, same thing. So, if you look at it that way, running after 'Happiness' all the time, is not really that great a thing. It's the happiness *within* you that matters. Finding happiness within you by understanding what is inside you. Finding happiness in moments, in big and small moments. Even, in doing-nothing-at-all moments. *Carpe diem* doesn't mean finally going for the dance class you had been postponing for ever so long, or doing the shark cage diving you weren't taking time out for. The true essence of *carpe diem* is to grab every moment of your every day and make it *yours*. Simple moments, like the time you spend with your child in the park; don't let it be a moment you want to get over with. Grab it and make it a moment for your child; for yourself, make it a moment that takes you back into your childhood days. Moments you spend stuck in traffic, use them to listen to music of your choice to help you get over the daily grind; de-stress you. I lost some very precious moments in my life—precious moments I could've had with my loved ones—in the race for bigger ones. Moments that I thought, back then, mattered. But it's memories you make with your loved ones that stay with you. I don't have many, to pull me up in my down moments. So, to answer your question, am I in a happy place, after all I went through? Well, I am, definitely, in my element. I have evolved. But most importantly, I now, *live* my moments. I don't pass them by in the hope for better ones. So, yes, I am happy where I'm at now. I'm sorted. You get what I'm saying?"

Mira nodded.

"You know who really helped me, and got me out of the muck?"

She thought it was a rhetorical question but when a few seconds ticked by, she realized he was waiting for a response. "Umm … parents? A Guru? A sibling?" Mira kept giving options and Zaydan kept shaking his head. "A best friend? Oh, was it Zeenat?" Had to be her, but his look told her she was wrong again; that she had overlooked the most obvious.

"You know the biggest secret to evolving truly? To finding that inner peace?" He was building up the tempo, was teasing her; watching and waiting for her to break into a bit of a sweat. "My inner voice!"

"Oh!" she smacked her forehead with the base of her right palm. "Duh!"

"Sit alone and talk to yourself. Open up to your inner self. Let it talk to you. Usually, we don't listen to our inner voice because it is the one energy that knows us, through and through. It knows our most genial and our most devious thoughts and moves. It is us, who else could know us better? It shows us our reality, our authentic self. It makes us reflect. But we don't want to see the ugly side of us that comes along with our authentic self. We prefer passing the buck, we prefer cribbing to family and friends about the situation we have been placed in, pointing out the flaws of others. It is so much better when we have someone else to blame, isn't it? We tell them our biased version of the story, so we can revel in their sympathy. Then why in hell would we let our inner voice burst our bubble? But, in effect, it is our only true guide. When you say you're having second thoughts, what does that mean? It's your inner self telling you to rethink your action. Zeenat's rejection after my second marriage failed, was a big smack. It made me reflect and introspect, to listen to my inner self. And my inner self let me know I was not so coveted, after all. Then on, I was a whole new person. And … I love this new person. Believe you me, the day you learn to listen to your inner voice there will be a shift in you, a humungous shift. You will feel good. You will be *there*."

Mira turned to look out at sea again. It was good at doing the dirty work for her, carefully layering the newly acquired knowledge for her, processing it, archiving it into distinctive folders segregated by distinctive blue hues; the deeper the hue, the deeper the life's experience.

One folder was still empty. "One last question," she said.

"I feel like I'm being interrogated, so I can be convicted justly. Haven't I served time, already?" Zaydan had his hands joined together, pleading mercy; laughing his laugh. "Go ahead, your honour!"

"OMG, is that what I sound like?" She made a modest attempt to cover her mouth with both her hands. "Just this last one, I swear." Now it had to be her last. "Did you have any children with Olivia?"

"A son, Brad. But he wants nothing to do with me."

Mira could see the curtailed movement of his lips, could see his eyes requesting his tears: *it's been too many years. Let us be.*

"I could've had a good life with him. But, I guess it's understandable, given the circumstances. He hasn't forgiven me, yet. Someday … someday!" A quiet moment stole its way in. "He thinks I am immature and impulsive, that I don't think things through; don't see the upshots before I take a call to do something. He finds me odd, weird. It's just that I do things differently. He would use those as an excuse to argue with me. Even tiny matters, like … he would pick on me for not taking my car for my daily commute. I take it out only when I have to go for a meeting or a formal do."

That is odd. Mira just nodded; she was trying to understand the schematics behind it.

"He said it makes me look like a penny pincher … a down-slide to my stature." Zaydan had his shoulders raised and neck tilted to the right, for the *how-ridiculou*s gesture. "I have a bicycle, a top-notch one. The weather is usually pretty good to bike around. I've also been learning to use the Segway, in fact. Why not!" He saw Mira's eyes widen with expressions bordering on horror. He chose not to pause for her comment. "It is, of course, taking me much longer to get a grasp of it. Bones are not too sturdy now. Know what I mean?"

"Hmm, wow! You know to live it up. I admire your chutzpah. And you're a never-ending Wikipedia of experiences." *He's so comfortable in his skin. Will I ever be like him? At what age should I begin?*

"Funny you say that. Brad would tell me to act my age. For ever so long, I've wanted to tell him I'm the one who's actually acting his age. In fact, he … he's what? Twenty-one I think, and he's already acting like a fifty-year old. Don't know how old he'll be when he gets to *my* age." Zaydan did a short version of his belly-laugh. "You know, when you get to my age, you stop worrying about what others think. We can't control their thoughts; we can only have a control over ours. We need to stop being people-pleasers. We've done our bit, been there for them. It's about time we start living for ourselves. We have to stop listening to the voices outside our head and listen to the ones inside. We make our inner voices so redundant, that with time, those voices stop guiding us. They probably throw their hands up in the air and give up on us."

Hey, we do not give up. It's you guys who pretend not to hear us. I was fuming. "Charmaine, you need to set the record straight. Tell him. Tell him it's not us that move away." *No, no, no … don't move away, Charmaine. You can keep resting your head on my shoulder.* The entire time Zaydan and Mira were talking, Charmaine and I were cosied up, arm in arm, making the most of our together time.

I stole a glance at the ocean. It was beaming a bright blue hue, its waves curved up into a thousand million smiles. *Hope she doesn't turn turtle again. I won't be able to live with that. Will I ever be able to forget her? Don't! Don't think crazy stuff. Don't spoil the moment. No negative thoughts.*

"I do talk to myself." Mira saw one of Zaydan's eyebrows arch. "But … yeah, I need to listen more." She didn't go deeper. She was good with getting things out of others but for herself, she wanted things that were unstirred and unshaken, to remain unstirred and unshaken. "Whoa! It's been over two hours. I better get going." She pulled herself up and made her way towards Zaydan; thought she'd give him a hug for all that he had been through, for all that she had put him through all over again the past few days, and most of all, for all that he had walked her through.

He had already jumped off his seat; too chivalrous to keep sitting when a lady gets up to leave. She stood there for a wild second, doing nothing; the odd smile on her face telling him she's correcting herself. And then she hugged him anyway.

There are some moments in life when words fall short. A hug, at that moment, can justify warmth and gratitude in the right magnitude.

WE HAVE A PLAN B

Nassau. Simply beautiful. Super fun.

We were granted a seemingly generous seven hours to explore the place; to scale the many adventurous drops and slides at The Atlantis, and comb the pristine white-sand beaches of Paradise Island. But, it appeared, time in Nassau had a sly sense of humour. Like whispers in the wind, the seven hours passed us by, leaving us with a touch of wistfulness. The sun had turned a dusky orange by the time we headed back.

The last night of the cruise-liner tip-toed out of the kids' room; it had hummed the younger lot to sleep. Samar's mind was free from slumber's grasp, but he was relaxed. Mellowed. It wasn't easy getting him to that tranquil state, but that's what we're all about. Why do you think the girl by his side, the girl whom he was charmed by at a fest, months back, would be at the very same cruise at the very same time as him? Coincidence? Seriously? Give us some credit!

The kids were sorted; we could channel all our energies into Victor and Mira. *These two need to make love! Tonight!*

Victor and Mira had grabbed a couple of beers in Nassau, but once back on their boat they opted for red wine. They were relaxed, and in love once again. Their trip had proven remarkably smooth. In fact, better than either of them had expected. It was their last night on the cruise, and we intended making it a night that would make up for all the lost nights gone past.

Victor was relaxing on the lounger in the balcony. Mira sat close, one leg a few inches away from his; seductive, suggestive. Tonight, was theirs; we would make sure of it. We even had a Plan B, in case of an unprecedented interruption.

Watching Victor and Mira getting cosy was making me miss my love. With everything seeming to be in place, unfolding according to the plan, I saw no reason for all three of us to keep a watchful eye over the lovers. I excused myself. It was my last night, too.

Our spot was already taken. A twenty-something guy, and a girl near-about his age, were lip-locked for the four odd minutes we waited on them. They seemed to be in no rush to leave. Charmaine and I were forced to move on and look for another spot. *We'll make our own lovers' spot on this cruise-liner!*

It was way past midnight when I re-entered the parents' room. Rock and Snippy flashed their teeth at me with end-to-end smiles. *Nice!* Victor and Mira had finally gotten their act going.

Hang on! Aren't those sheepish smiles? Apparently, Rock fell asleep while Victor and Mira were still warming up. Watching Mira now—half flat on her stomach, half on her side; one of her heels still on—painted a clear picture that she must have fallen asleep before any action could take place. Victor must have eventually, at some point, given up and crashed into the only available corner of the bed; assuming a spooning position with Mira as best he could.

I glared at Rock, "What the hell, man!"

"Hey, you know how crazy my day was. I was beat with all those rides. I must've dozed off for like five minutes ..."

"Seriously, you guys?!"

"Don't look at me! I was with the kids, making sure they stayed asleep." Snippy had her hands up in defense. "*You* could've stayed behind and not gone at all. Or was *that* more important?" She tipped her head in the direction of the door, as though, the entire span of space outside the room, beyond the door, represented Charmaine.

"Hey, cool it guys! I'll work something out before the trip is done, I promise. Just leave it to me." Rock jumped in to save my neck. Or was it to save his? 'So, what's the deal with Charmaine? You guys gonna keep in touch?"

I looked at him. I felt anger at him, and at Snippy, but there was another gnawing restlessness tugging at my soul. Like a persistent itch I couldn't scratch. It was making my breathing noticeable, with a crackling sound; every cell in me had dried up. Parched, brittle; I was in pain. Extreme pain.

There is a kind of pain, Mr Umana, that can't be expressed really well; there's no one word that can describe it in its entirety. It's beyond the pain one feels when a toenail comes off, with a tiny part of the it hanging there; and anytime something touches that toe, you wince. It's not the *I'm in pain* pain; it's a pain like no other. A pain more excruciating than that of sandpaper scraping your bared skin. Scraping, at the same place, over and over. At that moment, I was feeling that pain; the pain that cannot be described in its entirety.

The next morning wasn't good for any one of us.

Samara wanted to understand why they couldn't extend their trip on the cruise. She couldn't comprehend: *you need to get back to your homework before school restarts.*

Robin wanted an explanation why they couldn't stay on the cruise forever. *What kind of an explanation does one give to that?*

Samar had the comfort of knowing that the girl he met on the cruise lived not too far from him, back home. Although, of course, it wouldn't be the same as spending that many hours with her, as he had on the cruise.

Mira was, clearly, going to miss her daily discourse. It had been nice, all that talk. Victor was a bit agitated, too, as he walked down the gangplank: *There goes my chance to get any. I could have just as well stayed back home and partied in our backyard for ten nights. I thought the change of scene would have helped in getting the mood going. I suppose I'll just have to get used to living with dusty balls.*

Rock and Snippy were the only ones not too troubled. They were leaving dangerous waters behind. Rock didn't need to hold on to things while moving about, in fear of rolling off the edge of the railing. Snippy didn't need to be stressed about fitting into skimpy bikinis anymore.

As for me, I wanted to tell my heart: *And now that you are not wanted, you can stop!*

It was comforting, though, to see Charmaine composed. It would've killed me to see her cry. *Or was it more painful that she didn't?*

The flight back was a quiet and restful journey. Our solace lay in the cherished memories we had woven throughout the trip. We clung to those precious memories, preserving them in our hearts, for future perusal. Memories are good at remaining ingrained within us forever, ensuring that the absence of good times is never truly felt.

One by one, we dozed off. But Victor and Mira couldn't sleep. It was their last chance. Rock, Snippy and I made sure we kept the kids fast asleep while their parents sneaked into one of the washrooms together.

Do Not Let This Happen To You

Back home, the sun was up and about; smiling brightly. But wakefulness eluded us; we were groggy; half-asleep. Jet-lagged. And dreamy; reluctant to let go of visions of the breathtaking places we visited during the cruise, and of art-deco-style Miami where we partied two whole nights and two whole days, on our way back from the cruise.

Except Snippy. She was up and about like the sun; giving the tread-mill a run for its money. She wanted back her bikini-ready physique.

I thought I'd give Snippy some company. It's not easy working out alone. You need incentive, someone to look at, to feel the adrenaline rush. I dragged my groggy body out of bed and plopped it on the handrail of the treadmill. *Me?* No, I don't need to work-out. I'm predisposed to be thin. I'm paper-thin, remember? Although, yes, I should work-out to be fit but I guess, I'm just plain lazy.

"What? Out of sight, out of mind? Now that Charmaine's gone, I'm back on the radar?" Snippy sniped at me, and turned to look away. I saw her hand reach for the safety key. I pushed it away. *Chill! Will ya!* She hit the emergency button and jumped off. *Why is she getting so worked up?* But it seemed to be something else.

Samara was calling out to her mom; she was flaming like a sizzling hot plate. Mira rushed to her side; she went into panic mode. But a mom can't let panic hold her back from covering her baby with a warm quilt; it can't stop her from putting socks on her little one's feet, or from administering Tylenol with a warm tea-like concoction. Not even from placing a washcloth dipped in warm water on her stomach and under her arms and at the back of her neck. If there was more, Mira would have done that too, before calling the doctor for any further instructions.

By late afternoon, Samara's skin had gone red in patches; the colour of the sand on Mars. She was getting breathless. Her condition required more than a mother's care.

When the clinician got out the naso-pharyngeal swab, everything in the emergency room started swirling for Mira. She reached out to the table at the side of the bed for support. *Why are they wearing helmets and gloves and face-masks and face shields and respirators? She's already been screened for the virus at the drive-through site outside a few hours ago. They had poked the swab into her nose for the longest time ever. She had almost gagged, my poor baby. She has tested negative. Then why are they doing it, all over again?*

The doctor on duty, Dr Bennett, ushered Mira and Victor into his cabin. As soon as they shut the door, he began a barrage of questions: *Did you travel recently? Which places did you go to? Who all did you come in contact with? You were on flights and on a cruise; contact tracing has to be done on your entire travel history.* Dr Bennett seemed extremely strung out. "All countries have been totally virus free for more than two years. We were sure we had beaten it. But …" Dr Bennett was saying. *God! Tell me this is not happening.*

What? No! Please! Please? The doctor was mistaken. He had to be. *Didn't it end? How did it ….*

Your guess is as good as mine.

And the vaccines? The booster shots?

"Please co-operate. We've started following protocol. We didn't want to wait it out. Couldn't risk it. I need you to understand the grave situation we are in. Your daughter, uh …"

"Samara. But I'm sure there's some mistake. Samara has asthma, and she must have developed some infection. The infection must have caused the fever … and the breathlessness."

"Yes, Samara. She is nine?"

Yes, just nine! Mira wanted to scream back at him.

"We've started treatment on her, already. Please understand, you need to go into immediate self-quarantine. You know the isolation algorithm; I would request you to not come to the hospital unless we call you. If you do wish to visit, if any of you feel unwell in any way, please inform us beforehand so we can take the necessary precautions." Dr Bennett felt the need to repeat the protocol but he could tell that most of what he was saying was simply passing through their bodies, like sand through a sieve. There were no takers for his words in that room.

Mira wasn't nodding; all she could hear was that she couldn't take Samara back home with her. Not that day, not for some time.

Victor heard himself speak. Although it didn't sound like him, he knew it was him because he had the same queries, in the exact same words, running in his head: "Is she okay? Is she in any kind of pain?"

"She is rested. We are watching her round the clock. You, too, should get some rest. We will, definitely, let you know of her progress."

Upon returning home, they found Robin snuggled into his kangaroo, fast asleep. Samar was slouched on Samara's bed; he had dozed off while gaming on his phone. Victor and Mira were unsure of how to break the news to them.

Mira looked around the house. *Where do I start?*—with everything they had touched since they came back the previous night. All night Mira was wiping down; every door handle, their rooms, the toilets. And she had to prepare concoctions to boost their immunity, everyone's—Robin's and Samar's and Victor's and hers. Everyone's but Samara's. *Please God, save my baby. Save my Samara. You can't do this to us. This can't be happening. Not to my little baby!*

The three of us, Rock, Snippy and I, were mute bystanders, as we watched a world fall apart. But we weren't going to let this happen. We weren't going to let the Rais' world fall apart. We weren't going to let anyone's world fall apart, anymore. As much as we hated to do so, we turned to Azraella. *Is she … on your list?*

"Don't look at me. I have nothing to do with this." In all the years we'd known Azraella, we knew she never went beyond her call of duty.

Then who? And who do we turn to? A miracle was needed!

By the time Victor and Mira reached the hospital the next morning, Samara had left us.

Mira insisted on taking her baby in her arms. *Just one last time! Please!* She was given protective clothing and headgear and a mask and gloves. She prepped herself; her eyes, all the while on the door between her and her daughter. *Baby, Mommy's coming. I know you're there still … I know you are waiting for me. I'm here now.* But the door refused to open, refused to let her go through, to where Samara lay; refused to let her take her in her arms. *But there's so much love I have to give her still. There's so much I have to teach her, so much I have to learn from her.* All it allowed her to do was catch a glimpse of Samara, one last time, from behind a see-through partition, faraway-*ly*. She couldn't look at her baby's closed eyes and fool herself, *she's only sleeping.* She couldn't lift her wrist and check for a pulse, *when it feels the touch of her mother's hand, it'll start again, I know it will.* She couldn't straighten her hair; *the string of the ventilator has made such a mess of it.*

When they came to pull Mira away, they found her rocking back and forth. Cradled in her arms was emptiness. *I'm sorry I couldn't keep my promise. I'm sorry … I love you with all my heart. I will always love you.* There were tears flowing down her face. She hadn't heard herself cry, she wasn't howling. Her pain, the pain that cannot be described in its entirety, had taken away her crying sounds.

It was when they carried away a small frame in a small white overall, that her wails made their presence known. Her wails made the walls of the hospital shake. The tears that came with those wails rattled the floor they fell on, causing shudders, causing quakes. Quakes forming large cracks that were spreading far and wide, reaching out to every human on earth: *Do not do this to yourself. Do not let this happen to you.*

GOD MAY HAVE NEEDED HER MORE

Mira had cried then too, the day the warden at the NGO where she worked, had handed Samara over to her. She had rocked Samara, all of three months, in her arms then, too.

Samara's birth father had been insistent he didn't want a girl, so her birth mother, who worked in the same NGO, had given Samara up for adoption there. Mira hadn't eaten for two whole days till Victor agreed to adopt Samara. Her request had come as a shock to him; adopting a child was something they had never considered. He needed time to think it over. But when she said, *giving life all parents do, but saving a life only the greater ones get a chance to do,* he let go of his inhibitions; not wanting to miss out on the opportunity to do a noble deed.

They had never looked back, never regretted their decision. All the more so, when they learned of the accident in which Samara's birth parents had been crushed under rocks in a landslide in Tamil Nadu, a few months after the adoption. Victor and Mira had been rattled for days on end, with the thought that Samara, too, could've been there, under the rocks, with her parents, had they not adopted her.

***

"Had I known she was not going to be with us, I would've loved her every waking minute." Samar paused for a few seconds; the eulogy he had written for Samara was trembling in his hands.

He needed to gather himself. His nerves had things to say. They had to come clean. "After seeing my name on the adoption certificate—actually, I had read just the letters S.A.M. and assumed that I was the adopted one—I was really nasty to Samara. I was jealous because I thought that my parents loved her and Robin more, and not me. I found reasons to pick on Samara and take my anger out on her. Robin was too small to feel my scorn, so I took it all out on her. When she would call out to me, I would pretend not to hear her." He let the tears roll. "I had a lot of 'whys' in my head. Why did my real parents give me up for adoption? Why did my present parents adopt me if they didn't want to love me enough? Why were they denying the fact that I am adopted when the facts were right in front of me? I was angry with them, and I was angry with Samara and Robin. But now I realize parents don't love their adopted child any less. Their love for Samara is proof enough." He paused again. "I wish I could take it all back … but I can't. And I can't get her back. Just for once, I wish I could tell her how truly I love her. And how sorry I am. I … I'm sorry."

Samar was aware of the hush in the hall. Of those present, some were crying silent tears, some were stunned. He had more to say, he wanted to let them know that Samara was right …that the Universe *is* listening to our every thought, all the time. She did vanish from his life, from everyone's lives, because the Universe had listened to him. *She was right! She was … right!* He wanted to tell everyone that the Universe could do things you wished it to, but once done, it couldn't undo them. But he didn't say it; he couldn't get the words out. When Victor got up to help him step down, Samar hung his head, and quietly stepped down.

Everyone watched as Beverly walked up to the dais. Kayla stood by, as Beverly expressed her love for Samara:

"Samara, from the moment you came into my life, you and I became 'we'.

We laughed crazily at the slightest of things and we cried at the silliest.

We held each other's hand; we had each other's back.

We promised to be there for each other, we promised to grow up together.

You broke the promise, you broke every promise.

And here I am, unable to break the 'we', and go back to being just 'me'.

Tremors could be felt in the hall. When children speak of their pain, the air around them cannot help but shudder. Victor and Mira stepped forward to hug Beverly. Forced smiles were all they could muster for her; their voices couldn't get past their choked throats.

Only a modest number of mourners attended the funeral—immediate family members, close relatives and a few friends. Social distancing was observed, although the Rais had been informed by Samara's doctors that Samara did not have the virus. They hadn't said much beyond that, except that investigations were still underway. But people were still wary. Since recent times, deaths were happening for unfathomable reasons; people were abruptly dropping dead; cardiac arrests.

Delayed repercussions of the virus? Or was there something more into play?

What is it you go through after someone dear to you passes, Mr Umana?

Mourning. Ah yes! One word: mourning. I find it unjust to assign it only one word. *He's in mourning. She's in mourning.* That's it?

Don't you think it's a lot more? A whole process. An extremely long one, a lifelong one. It's not just a feeling you feel for a few moments, it's a whole big emotional uproar. A whole disarrayed world on its own. Of crying, mostly. You're still not done with the crying, and in comes the excruciating pain that pierces through you, making you wonder: *Has my time come too*? After about half a zillion of those crushing seizures which feel like heart failure each time, it transcends into agonizing pangs that come and go. Once you've learned to get used to the agonizing pangs, in comes the dull ache; continuous, and unhurried, as though it's out on a leisurely walk. Once you've let the dull ache swarm around you, and settle in all your crevices, grief barges its way in. You've just about disciplined yourself to live with the grief—only after you fought and fought with all your might and tried to send it away, but to no avail—that a voluminous void comes knocking at your door. Soundless, speechless, the vast emptiness sneaks up from under your bed, slips under the covers and snuggles in. Lying on its side, head propped on one hand, pityingly, it makes the promise to watch over you, even as you sleep.

Yeah, I think it deserves more than just one word.

He's in subservience to mourning. She's in subservience to mourning. There, that's a tad better!

Mira was in s*ubservience to mourning.* Endlessly.

Victor kept himself busy with work. He needed to get out of the house; go anywhere that would not evoke the sense of emptiness in him. Schools reopened, so both Samar and Robin had something to keep them busy for most of the day. But for Mira, every day crawled by. Like happenings in a waiting room. Like a snail on a journey.

Like a tiny raindrop on the edge of a tin roof. And like a movie in reverse, every day was a resurrection of Samara's memories. Of the Fruit Loops colours she used to pick out and eat, purple being saved for last. Of the Fruit Loops colours she picked out and didn't eat at all. Of the books piled in front of her every time she sat down to read. And then there were the constant reminders everywhere: photographs, an empty chair at the dining table, her preferred bean bag in the family lounge, and her favourite ad that always had to come on whenever they'd sit down to watch TV. Samara was everywhere. Where could Mira hide?

She hadn't stepped into Samara's (and Robin's) room since it had happened. Robin had been sleeping with his parents ever since; he was too small to sleep next to a bed that had suddenly gone empty. Mira was afraid to step into that room. She was afraid if she did, she would rummage through Samara's dresses and seam her grief into their hems. She was afraid she would open every one of Samara's story books and alter the happy endings. She was afraid she would, totally out of habit, remove the ruffles and creases of her bed-sheet, and in the process, take away Samara's last night in it.

Kayla had been coming over almost every day. She usually came alone; it hadn't gone unnoticed by her how Mira would refrain from looking at Beverly while addressing her. She also caught a hint of a jump in her, when Beverly would say something. Most girls that age sound alike.

"I never got around to asking Zaydan if they did, eventually, donate his son's eyes and heart." Mira asked Kayla one day, out of the blue.

"Yes, he did. It wasn't easy, was like walking on thin ice but he knew if he didn't, he would hold it in his heart all his life, that he could have helped someone and didn't try hard enough. Zeenat realized her littleness of heart only later, years later. Only after she got to feel her son's heart still beating in another's body. I cried when Zaydan told me her reaction. When she came face to face, she felt as though an unknown force made her reach out to touch the guy's heart. She then, hugged him to feel the heartbeat, the rhythm of which she knew only too well."

Hearing Kayla's words, Mira felt unsteady. An overwhelming feeling was questioning the strength of the bones in her legs. "The dying of a body, the ending of a life, doesn't need to be the end of everything. It can be kept alive; it can be a beginning, too. Donating organs is such a noble cause. But you need a really big heart to actually do it."

Kayla didn't interrupt. She let her friend talk.

"Everyone keeps consoling me: *God meant Samara to be with you for only this much time. He may have needed her more.* I wonder …" Mira looked up at Kayla, her eyes cradling a tiny tear; a half-bubble, prisming the story of her plight, "had she gone any other way, would I have had the nerve to donate her organs? Whatever it was that took my baby away from me … I guess, it inadvertently … in its own way, it … it spared me from that dilemma." Mira tried to control the quiver in her voice. She was looking at the positive side of things. She needed to sound it too.

Ever since they lost Samara, Samar had been hanging close, *being there* for his mom; helping her around the house, doing things without being told. Even looking after Robin on some days. Anything to take his mom's ache away, anything to ward off the guilt and regret that had been surfacing from under his bed.

The day of Samara's birthday, exactly sixty-eight days after she had passed, was the day Mira steeled her heart and marched into Samara's room. It was time to run her fingertips over the skin of every object in the room; awaken them, just as she used to awaken Samara every morning. It was time talk to them, and let them talk to her; tell her the stories they used to tell Samara.

Hours went by, the hours she would have spent washing dishes, doing the laundry, vacuum-cleaning, lunching. She did none of that; all she did was breathe in Samara, and breathe out the pain. It was time she packed away Samara's things; her clothes, her stationery and books. *Could Robin use these? Oh, my! So many highlighters. And what is this? A journal? Samara kept a journal?*

Samara hadn't told her anything about a journal, but thinking back, Mira did recall her mentioning what Ms Atwood had said about keeping one: *A journal is the one friend you can open up to, without keeping a check on your thoughts. A timeless legacy of your inner most musings.*

Mira grabbed the journal and held it close to her chest. Samara was in the journal. She was there, once again, for Mira to hold and to hug. Lovingly, longingly. To kiss hungrily. She was anxious to read her daughter's unchecked thoughts, but before she did, she ran her hand over the pages; one page, then the next, and the next. She wanted to feel the texture of every page her daughter's hand had touched. She wanted to catch a whiff of her daughter's breath as she may have whispered the words while penning them down. She wanted to experience every emotion her daughter may have felt; she wanted to miss nothing.

She then turned to the first page:

12th of September, 2025

Time - 6:30 p.m.

Dear diary,

I'm Samara Rai.

Age - 8 years

Ht - 133 cm.

…

…

I love you. And I love my Mommy. And my Daddy and Robin. So, so very much. I don't love Samar, but he is ok. And I love Beverly to pieces.

Mira flipped the pages to midway:

8th of February, 2026 - 9 p.m.

I want to study and become a scientist. Is that too boring? I want to be a rock-star too. How will I do both? What if I don't rock it like a rock-star? Beverly and I could start a band together. Then, we'll definitely rock!!

12th of February, 2026 - 8:12 p.m.

Mommy and Daddy fought again. They're always screaming at each other. I want it to end. I love Mommy but I love Daddy too. I fight with Samar all the time, but then we forget and we're back to being friends again. Till we fight again. Which is after just a few minutes. But that's ok because Samar is an ass. Even Beverly thinks so. But Mommy and Daddy are grown-ups. I thought grown-ups were sensible.

She flipped a few more pages.

5th of August, 2026 - 10:35 a.m.

I'm super excited! We're going for a trip. We are going on a cruise. Yeah!

So, so excited.

Samar is being the ass he is. Hopefully he doesn't ruin it for all of us. I'm so excited. I wish Beverly could come with me. That would be fun!! Super fun!! I'm going to take my two-piece swim-suit which she and I bought together. If she goes, we could both wear ours together. We would look like twins. Yes!!

Signing off for today.

Mira flipped right to the end.

14th of August, 2026 - 9:45 a.m.

We're finally leaving today. I'm not gonna let anything spoil my mood. I will have a great time and I'll make notes. And when I'm back, I'll put everything down here. Lots of pix too. Muah!!

Suuuppeerrrr excited!!!

Mira went back a couple of pages.

8th of August, 2026 - 5:18 p.m.

Samar was proved wrong. I knew it all along. We showed him pix of his birth at the hospital. Idiot! What a scene he has been creating all these days. For nothing! *We* should have given him away for adoption. At least now, after seeing his pix, he won't ruin our trip.

Until later!! Xoxo!

9th of August, 2026 - 11:22 a.m.

Samar told me he was sure it was him but after seeing his pix he is kinda cool now. What did he mean by saying: Now you should be worried, *Sam*-ara?

Where are my birth pix? Should I ask Mommy? She looks too preoccupied with the packing and stuff. Is Samar doing this only to trouble me? But Mommy and Daddy love me sooo much. Ughhh, he can be such a pain!!!

I'll ask Mommy to get my pix out once we are back.

Just five days to leave. Samar knows just how to ruin it for me! Ughhh!!!

Did she know? Did she figure it out? I wish I hadn't come in here. I wish I hadn't read all this. What do I do with this now? Mira felt her world—the old world that had shattered to bits, mingle with the new world she was not ready to accept yet—swing around her like a whirling dervish. Round and round, it went.

TO THE ONE WHO SOUGHT TO OWN THE WORLD AND THEREBY LOST A HOME

Doesn't it pain you to see Mira in so much grief, Mr Umana? Doesn't it do things to you? Aren't the nerves within your body twisting and coiling themselves around your heart? Constricting it? A python, coiling its length around you, suffocating you, squeezing the life out of you. Do you feel it?

Doesn't it pain you to see how, every day, mourning shoves its hands down Mira's throat, and with monstrous force pulls out her heart? Because it dared to beat while her baby's heart is ash-ed into the ground. That's what I want to do to you, Mr Umana. That's exactly what I want to do to you. I want to shove my hands all the way down your throat and yank out your heart. Yank out everything that dares to give you life. Pull them out and leave them to shrivel and wither. And then, watch your breath gets shallower, and weaker; hissing out of you till it is only a whisper.

Why?—you may ask.

Because you deserve every bit of it.

Why?—you may ask, again.

Because you killed Samara. Yes, you, Mr Umana. You are responsible for her death.

How?

By letting another contagion in. A deadlier one. A red one. From Mars.

Do you have any idea what you've done, Mr Umana? You may have made it to Mars; you're out to own the world, but in the process, you keep moving further away from 'Home'. For ever so long now, you've been contaminating your own home; you've contaminated Nature.

You still haven't gotten a tight grasp on Covid-19; it slips out of your hands every time you try to grab it by its neck. Since the day that tiny virus showed you its might, it's had *you* by the throat; threatened to knock the friggin' living daylights out of you. It's had you scared witless.

Then why, *sir*? When will you put an end to all of this? To your hunger for more?

Why couldn't you let the doorway be? The doorway that the Curiosity rover discovered on Mars. Why did you have to walk through it? Why can you not let some things just be?

You didn't know it then, and don't know even now, that when you entered that door, your intrusion disrupted the peaceful equilibrium that prevailed there. As a retaliatory measure, a Martian pathogen infiltrated your environment which targets individuals' minds that experience profound anxiety or distress. Research analysts are calling it MSS, the Martian Serenity Syndrome. Without warning, the syndrome swiftly immobilizes the thoughts of those individuals who habitually, aggressively, experience intense worry or pervasive unease, and brings an instantaneous cessation to their heartbeats. This is why people have been dropping, left, right and centre, without any warning signs. All this time, you've been passing it off as cardiac arrests; repercussions of the virus, or the vaccinations. You haven't been able to figure out the real cause. Well, now you know.

Samara was not a habitual worrier. Her worry was about what Samar had said to her, about conspiring with the Universe. *That* was her real worry, just a flipping worry. In cases as hers, it is not instant; the pathogen is slower in infiltrating the human body through an elusive energy manipulation, causing a cascade of physiological decline that inevitably results in mortality within a brief period of one or two days. And to think we were dreading Azraella's crafty vocation. In the face of this pathogen, Azraella seems trivial by comparison.

We tried so hard to save Samara. An earnest appeal was sent out. It was forwarded by our higher powers to the heavens above. Samara could have been saved. But … our prayers went unheard. Because there was too much noise everywhere. Dark noise; of fear, of disbelief. Or maybe the gods just didn't care anymore. They were dispirited and probably felt it to be a lost cause—our efforts to enrich lives, when just living had become so formidable. So challenging. Or, maybe, they just left everything in the hands of the *gods* below?

Whatever their reasoning may have been, our baby is gone. Because of you.

She was just a child. Just a child, sir! Why couldn't you do something? Why couldn't you play God now?

There has been chaos and upheaval everywhere and there would have been so much more if it wasn't for us. That is why you and your loved ones are still here. But there's only so much that we can do.

I am so done with you. I shall not address you as 'sir' from this moment on. You do not deserve any honorific status. Not anymore!

And I shall not ask to be excused for the same. It's not your prerogative to excuse me, any more. You're on your own, from now on.

You do know the *you* here, right? *You* … the Human race. The entire Human Race. I'm sure you figured it out by now. I'll be bummed if you haven't. You did look up your name, didn't you? 'Razza Umana' … means The Human Race in Italian. You must have looked up the meaning of Mondano Terreno, too. This is why I'm writing to *you* about all of this. To the CEO of the earthly world: the self-proclaimed CEO. To the one who sought to own the world, and thereby, lost a home.

So, Mr / Mrs / Ms Umana/ The Human Race, it's time you admit that you screwed up. Big time!!

When Covid-19 had taken its first step on *our* Earth, I wanted to walk out on you. Just drop everything and be up and gone. But I stayed. There was a method to my madness. I thought, even in the face of adversity, we could turn things around, make the virus a blessing in disguise. We gave you time to spend with your family, gave you time to rejuvenate. Gave you a chance to see nature in its true form, admire it, appreciate it; value it. We thought it would be a chance for you to start afresh with a smarter mind, be level-headed, far sighted, and more astute. We felt for you, gave you a second chance; thought you were worth the effort. But, no!

Covid-19 was Nature's own way of giving back to you for what you had been giving it since the beginning of time—an infected, diseased environment. It wanted you to slow down. Slow. Down. Your. Pace. Slow down the pace to your premature death.

Do you realize, your tomorrow is entirely dependent on how you pass your today? Your thoughts, your actions, your visions of today account for how your tomorrow will be, how your life ahead will be. It was for that reason that I was with you always, to perfect your today. But, as I said, it's too late now; I've given up on you. Remember me telling you, *the finale of my story is conditional on you?* Well today, I'm at the threshold of self-death. Because of you. Because that is the only way I will ever stop caring for you. And this time, there's no turning back. This time, you really hit my kill-switch.

Just so you know, when I go, Rock and Snippy go with me. Forever. All for one and one for all. You will be on your own, ruining things for yourself, without either one of us watching over you. No signs. No life-saving pleas. No *Magic.*

THE PRESENT DAY

THE END OF MANY THINGS UNWANTED

That's why here I am today, on my balcony, in the exact same spot once again; standing alone, with deadly weapons fisted in my hand. Giving the why and wherefore to my death.

I open my hand and look at the now un-rounded pills. How they have disintegrated! Shapeless white ghosts. Undefined, like my life. I look at their tousled form. Like mine, disheveled, dispirited. But the anatomy of their workability still holds. They can work their magic, can take a life even in this disintegrated form. My anatomy is like Cinderella's at the stroke of midnight—when it is time, *poof I'll go!*

I feel it is, finally, time. I close my eyes and lift my fisted hand to my mouth.

It is time!

Out of nowhere, something that feels like a soft, yet firm, hand slips into my un-fisted hand. I sense a figure coming up from behind me. The sun's glow, just beginning to glimmer from somewhere behind the figure, creates a halo of gold over its head. *An angel!*

Charmaine! *My* angel!

I open my mouth; I have questions. She puts my curious cat to rest with a kiss. With her kiss, I taste mornings spent together. I taste the pleasantness of endless evenings, and the warmth of endless nights. I taste gathered moments, for an enthralling tale to be told.

Yet I ask, "The way things were left off after the cruise, I'm surprised to see you here. I'm surprised you still remember me."

"I'd have to forget you first, to remember you." Her encrypted eyes are now unraveling in folds, eager to be read. "It was when we parted that I realised the depth of my feelings for you."

I open my fisted hand and let the pills drop. I push them to the corner of the balcony with my foot. I wipe my hand on my nightshirt, on my *saved-for-a-better-day* nightshirt.

So, here's the deal, Mr Umana, a.k.a, The Human Race.

Standing here, I have come to the realisation that I do not want to give up my life. This may sound paradoxical, but when you are faced with death, is when you begin to truly value every single moment of your life. Besides, why should I end my life if you don't know how to live yours? Why I should give up *my life* because *you* goofed up. And keep on goofing up. You should be the one going. What am I doing instead? Taking my own life. Silly me!

You're certainly not worth my life. And in any case, I owe my life to my Charmaine, now.

Azraella was so damn right about you. She very often said, and I quote: "Now you keep away from those nasty human beings. They're nothing but trouble, I tell you. Mutations of nature! Look what they did to the home God blessed them with. A friggin' mess! I wish I could eradicate every single one of 'em"—unquote. We should have paid heed to her warnings a long time ago. But it's never too late, is it?

And oh! I forgot to tell you the best part: Azraella has given in her resignation. She doesn't want to do her job, anymore. She loved it till some time ago. She loved being the detective, fishing out the sorry-ass souls who weren't enjoying themselves here; taking them to heaven, where there was no dearth of happiness and love. For the ones that screwed things up, she was gladly making trips to hell. But recently, she's been getting too overwhelmed: *Hell's overflowing with crap, so overbooked. It's a friggin' wrestle fitting 'em all in. A friggin' mess, it is! And the way these guys are now, I don't wanna touch them with a ten-foot pole. So, I'm calling it quits, guys. If you can figure a way to work it out, cool! But I'm definitely out!*

No! That's not how it is. I know what you're thinking, I can see you've already begun to get the party going, *No one's going to die from now on, now that Azraella has left the job! Yay!!*

Nope, doesn't work that way! With her gone, you're just going to get more depressed, more frustrated and will most probably land up killing each other, eventually. Oh, but you're already doing that; lynching, slaughtering, massacring, and whatnots!

So, here's the thing. Rock, Snippy and I, and Charmaine too, now that she's with me ... we're thinking of stepping into Azraella's shoes, all four of us. Which means, there are going to be *four* replacements for Azraella from the time we take office. Which means, now give me a vigilant listen ... the speed at which we're going to fish out people is going to be four times faster than it has been so far.

And that ... will be *the end of many things unwanted.*

Do I hear you shitting bricks?

No! We're not being 'inhuman'! You are better at that. Yes, we have had a change of heart but there are defensible reasons for that.

First, you guys pay heed to what we say only when you are grabbed by the throat; are in a near-death situation. Secondly, there are too many of you, sad and bad souls out there, multiplying in hordes, and thus, addressing the problem single-handedly, as was the case with Azraella, is totally out of the question now. The third reason for our change of heart, just to let you know, is that Azraella was one of us. She was, like us, dedicated to bettering your lives. But over time, she realized it was easier to eradicate the tough nuts than fix them. Which, has got us thinking: *Why don't we go the easy way too?* Since you've made our current job difficult for us, we're quite tempted to proceed with this plan of ours, with immediate effect.

What? Do I hear a whimper? A whisper of a request? For a last warning?

But you have had too many last warnings, already, what with all the viruses and stuff!

Moving on …

About Charmaine, how she dropped from the sky at the absolute perfect time to stop me from giving up my life for *a lost cause* … well, Charmaine had it all planned before we parted on the cruise.

That's why she was so composed on the last day of the cruise!

She hadn't let me in on her plans because she didn't want to get me excited until she was certain about herself. She had fallen in love with me too fast, too uncontrollably.

As for the Rais, things for them gather at a snail's pace. They are still picking up the pieces; it's been only a year or so. Not long enough to stop feeling the void, but long enough to accept it as a significant part of their lives. Not long enough to stop the tears, but long enough to hold them back. Not long enough to foresee a tomorrow without Samara, but long enough to persevere the continuance of 'tomorrows'.

We have a plan; we've already begun to throw hints at Samar. He is the right person for the job, and it's a great chance for redemption for him.

He's been resisting Rock's suggestion so far, feels his parents will not be able to register the suggestion; they'll rebuff it. That it's too early for the pain to be shoved to the back of the cloak closet; Samara's overcoat is still hanging there. It's too early for memories of her to be dusted off the mantle. Hands have not let dust settle on her photographs still. But one fine day, a day in the very near future, he will get tired of resisting Rock's suggestion, he will give in. He has learned not to resist the voice in his head, the hard way.

After eight months of cajoling and coaxing, the Rais will adopt an eight-year-old girl, Munni. The Rais will give her a new name ... Samsaara.

I can already visualize Rock flipping his lid on hearing the new name. *Are you kiddin' me? Are you friggin' kiddin' me? Why are Indians so fixated on deriving names for new additions in the family from their previous kids' names? Samar, Samara and now Samsaara. Seriously!*

I think it's just so apt, Snippy will say, in her hoity-toity, Brit accent. *Do you even know what Samsaara means? It means the rebirth of a person. The continuing cycle in which the same soul is repeatedly reborn. Samara has been reborn for them in this little soul. I think the name is just phurrfect!*

Samsaara won't come alone. She'll bring with her the sunny side of mountains. And rain from the summer woods. She'll bring with her the cheery chirping of birds. With her will come stacked Christmas stockings. Cinnamon-ed muffins and cupcakes and pies that had been forgotten will find their way into lunch-boxes. There will be the caramelized bite of the sun on a snug picnic day.

Won't that be a sweet ending to my story?

I feel so proud of us, of Rock, Snippy, me and Charmaine. We did well for them, didn't we?

But you, my dear humans, I'm really worried about you. Cracking you is taking the breath out of me.

Do I dare give you another chance? Do I dare anticipate humaneness from you? It is, after all, a mere 'e' away … from human to humane.

I do, though, wish you to acknowledge that every decision you take, and every move you make, can be assessed, and measured in your mind before the act is done *if* you listen to your inner voice.

You know that buzzing sound you sometimes hear in your ears? You keep trying to shake it off. Well, that's us. It's when we're making good things happen for you. If you listen really hard, you will hear the word, *Rochambeau,* ringing in your ears. When you do, know that your angels are watching over you.

And finally, in memory of Samara, I would like to say to you, more often than it is ethical to say: *Nurture with love, and love will thrive in return.*

I have said all I had to say. It's time to sign off.

Thank you for your time,

Yours most sincerely,

Papier

EPILOGUE

A Confession:

I never had any intentions of committing suicide. Never crossed my mind. Uh-huh!

Why in hell's name would I want to give up my life for you? Not happening. The entire story was fabricated, right from the beginning. The cock-eyed narrative of my attempt to commit suicide the first time around … that too!

Another Confession:

Samara did not die. She is still here. The entire sob-ass story, excuse my French, was concocted because I wanted you to feel terrible about yourself. I wanted you to despise yourself for the mess you have made of your life and your home. I was playing you. I needed to give you a jolt to make your heart feel again; a sting that would pull at your heart. Emotional blackmail, you can call it, if you wish. But I needed to do this before it got too late for you. This was the only way I could get your attention. You have everything so messed up in your head, all because you haven't been listening to us. So, I thought what the heck, let me mess with your mind some, too.

(Not A Confession, but …) ***An Important Information:***

There's one thing I should let you know. It's about Azraella's job: *that* bit is not fabricated. She did leave her job; the vacancy still stands. And we're still tempted …

This part of the story is the only bit that is true. As true as the viruses that scared the living daylights out of you.

ACKNOWLEDGEMENTS

In my endeavor to craft this book, my first, I was blessed with an unquenchable determination to not give up, and not hesitate from stealing moments from time, to write. And then, there were the huge inspirations that pushed me on. For the determination and the time, I have my Waheguru to thank.

For the inspirations, I have many to thank along with my Waheguru.

So, to all those inspirational souls who played a significant role in shaping the writer in me, be it with a nudge (gentle or unwavering), or by inadvertently seeping thoughts into me: I wish to say a generous *Thank you.*

A huge cheer to my early readers: Suman Kohli, Kamna Taneja, Neelam Chopra, Biba Kohli and Shabbir Katabji for reading a very raw and unpolished first draft, only because I couldn't contain myself. Their responses were most helpful. There were some, I must admit, who did not respond after reading the initial, unpolished version. Ironically, it was their lack of response that was most helpful, for it clearly stated my piece needed working on.

Hermit Pen among many others, thank you for asking how further I have gotten; thank you for pushing me to get even further. Thank you for believing.

A big thank you to all my friends for putting up with my absences.

My deepest love to Pansy Sabarwal, for being my pillar. Always.

And above all, my deepest love and gratitude for my family for their grace in giving me the space, and for dealing with me snuggled up in my writing corner, day in and day out. A special acknowledgment for my husband, Rolly Chadha, who had to put up with a there-but-not-really-there wifey. My children, Manav, Gaurav, Tara and Sonal, and my grandkids, Veer, Kyna and Jahan, you all are, undoubtedly, my bigger accomplishment. You all make me proud. But I wish to give a special shout out to Manav and Sonal for dealing with all my nitty-gritty queries and worries, and mostly, for pushing the boundaries of my imagination. I am forever grateful for your constant presence on this journey … I simply love you.

My heartfelt appreciation to my exceptional editor—who is now, not just my editor, but a dearer than dear friend—Shobha Sengupta, for her exceptional dedication and diligent editing in shaping and enhancing my dream. I would also like to thank Charu Rekha and Rashmi for the insightful editing of this book.

Sincere gratitude and great appreciation for my esteemed publisher, Mr. Harpreet, and the entire team of Petals Publishing, for their tireless efforts to bring my dream to fruition. Thank you for taking the chance on my work, giving it a home, and providing it the platform it deserves.

But foremost, my immense gratitude to my readers for giving my writing the chance to make its place in the universe. I hope my world of words takes you to the world you imagined when you picked this book.

Printed in Great Britain
by Amazon

38179641R00169